(M) MORLEY
Morley, Des.
A whisper of evil

12·17

A WHISPER OF EVIL

D1605719

Dodge City Public Library
Dodge City, Kansas

Dodge City Public Library
Dodge City, Kansas

A WHISPER OF EVIL

Des Morley

This Large Print edition is published by BBC Audiobooks Ltd, Bath, England and by Thorndike Press®, Waterville, Maine, USA.

Published in 2004 in the U.K. by arrangement with Robert Hale Limited.

Published in 2004 in the U.S. by arrangement with Dorian Literary Agency.

U.K. Hardcover   ISBN 0–7540–7698–9 (Chivers Large Print)
U.K. Softcover   ISBN 0–7540–7699–7 (Camden Large Print)
U.S. Softcover   ISBN 0–7862–5944–2 (Nightingale)

Copyright © Des Morley 2002

The right of Des Morley to be identified as the author of this work has been asserted by him in accordance with the Copyright, Designs and Patents Act, 1988.

All rights reserved.

The text of this Large Print edition is unabridged.
Other aspects of the book may vary from the original edition.

Set in 16 pt. New Times Roman.

Printed in Great Britain on acid-free paper.

British Library Cataloguing in Publication Data available

Library of Congress Cataloging-in-Publication Data

Morley, Des.
    A whisper of evil / Des Morley.
        p.   cm.
    ISBN 0–7862–5944–2 (lg. print : sc : alk. paper)
    1. Undercover operations—Fiction. 2. Missing persons—Fiction.
    3. Large type books. I. Title.
PR6063.O7443W48 2004
823'.914—dc22   2003061638

CHAPTER ONE

The girl in the yellow summer dress left the Piazza Pitti, turned right into Via Maggio, and then began to walk more quickly as she approached the Arno. The shadows of the high buildings were lengthening, drawing clerks from their offices and sending them into the streets to fill the trams that clattered across the city. The girl crossed at the Ponte Vecchio and in a few minutes, found a taxi. As she sank into the back of the ancient cab, she decided that going walk-about in Florence was as exhausting as she had been told.

'Where do you wish to go, *signora*?'

'The Hotel Biancospino. It's on Viale Machiavelli.'

'*Sí signora.* I know it.' He put the car into gear, slid away from the kerb and joined the busy traffic flowing along Via della Scala. 'Have you seen the Santa Maria Del Fiore, *signora*?'

The girl smiled inwardly. 'Of course.' She recognized the approach. If her reply had been different, he would have offered his taxi for the day at a vastly inflated fee. 'The cathedral, *and* the eighty-four metre campanile. I do believe I have seen everything of interest to me.'

He subsided into a morose silence, glancing

1

at her intermittently in the rear-view mirror. Pretty, he thought; not a great beauty, but with a good figure. Her auburn hair was short and well groomed. Her age? At a guess, about twenty-four. He saw her staring back at him and smiled.

'The cab is free if you will have dinner with me tonight. I finish at six.'

She laughed out loud. 'Whatever will my husband say?'

He grinned impudently. 'He will ask you if you lost your wedding ring in the Arno.'

Flustered, she covered her left hand.

'You're out of line.' She softened. 'Unfortunately, I have engagements tonight and tomorrow. I am leaving Florence the day after.'

She watched the buildings sliding past the window, recalling with regret that when the arrests were made in the morning, her task would be over; so too would her stay in Florence. It had been a wonderful week. In her spare time she had visited museums and galleries, cathedrals and statues, and stared covertly at *David*.

At the Hotel Biancospino, she handed the driver some Italian banknotes.

'Is that enough?'

'More than enough, *signora*. Thank you.'

He watched her as she walked towards the hotel entrance. He shook his head sadly and drew away from the kerb. She turned as the back of the cab disappeared into Via Cora. He wasn't bad looking, she conceded, and if things were different—well, who knows? She smiled. Just turned thirty and I've still got what it takes, she thought smugly. She looked up at the neo-classic hotel façade. Romance everywhere except where I am, she told herself.

The reception was busy, but in spite of the crush at the counter the voices were muted in the affluent ambience of the red carpeted lobby. Porters and pages moved with avaricious adroitness amongst the guests, while four desk-clerks were being harassed by queues of newcomers waiting to register. She went up to the suite on the seventh floor, an apartment furnished in the same style as the façade. She decided that neo-classicism was not her favourite style, although the Adam fireplace and the statuette in the niche above it were a little less austere than the framed prints on the walls. The bathroom was large, with towels she could wrap around herself twice. The opulence was in stark contrast to the frugality of her style of living at home.

Her thoughts shied away from a contemplation of her real self. For several months she had been someone else, a woman who lived on the edges of criminal society without obvious connections with the world of hoodlums and racketeers. She had played her part well, combining sophistication and

3

elegance with the dissolute characteristics of those who lived on the threshold of corruption. Slowly, the quarry at which her mentors had directed her began to circle. Finally, she had infiltrated the organization they were seeking to destroy. She had been constantly aware of the dangers of her assignment, but she had never held any illusions about her chosen career. She was good at what she did and was skilled in every discipline.

She stood now on the balcony looking down at the boulevard, wondering when Gaffney would return.

* * *

It had begun on a cold, wet day at her home in Pretoria. She owned a small simplex in Lynwood and when she had arrived home after a short holiday in the Cape she had found a letter amongst her mail. The envelope was blank with no address or return address. It had obviously been hand-delivered. The half-sheet of paper contained a simple message. *Uncle John is in town. Call him.* She threw an involuntary glance around the room for any signs of entry, but there was none. She realized at once that her holiday had not removed all the tensions of her last assignment. The furnishings in her home were plain and uncluttered. Sofa and chairs from bargain

4

sales, upholstered in spotless cretonne, and curtains of plain grey bull-denim. The whole was designed to prevent undetected entry. Her instinctive reaction was, she thought sadly, the indelible strawberry mark of her trade. Oh hell, she thought, with unaccustomed melancholy, I'd better see Uncle John.

Two hours later she was five miles from the city, jogging on the footpath alongside a stand of gum-trees. The rain had stopped and drifting clouds intermittently shadowed a weak sunlight. Her hair was tucked under an oversized baseball cap, and her baggy black tracksuit hid the trim lines of her figure. While she had not attempted to conceal her sex, she knew that no male in his right mind would give her a second glance.

This was the fourth time she had kept this rendezvous, and each time she wondered why the hell she had been instructed to jog. Why could she not, just once, ride in a nice comfortable car. Uncle John was a bloody sadist, she thought irritably.

Where the path crossed the road a man in the green-and-white suit of a local athletic club overtook her. He saluted as he strode away with the effortless action of a seasoned runner. She envied him. She was out of condition, and began to regret her recent inactivity. She saw two couples picnicking in a clearing just off the path. They paid her no attention, but she saw the red tablecloth hanging on a low branch. A white cloth would have told her that the meeting had been aborted. Then with some relief she saw a white Toyota approaching. As it passed, she saw the passenger raise his hand. She continued for ten paces and entered the clearing on her left. She followed a narrow path to a smallholding surrounded by a razor-wire fence. All the wildwood had been cut back for fifty feet from the perimeter. A man stood on the porch of a Victorian house. He was dressed in faded denim slacks and shirt, a picture of the quintessential countryman. A sign on the gate read:

DANGER
RAFTERS CANINE BREEDERS.
DOBERMAN AND GERMAN
SHEPHERD.
STRICTLY NO ENTRY
Ring the Bell and Wait.

Four somnolent Dobermans lay on the lawn below the front steps. As she thumbed the bellpush, the dogs stood up, pointed their noses in her direction, and watched her in ominous silence. It was unnerving, but she knew they would not attack unless they heard a command from the man on the porch. She stood back as the gates swung towards her. The dogs remained silent and watchful as she walked up the drive. She was aware of their attention, and imagined their salivating tongues waiting for the command to attack.

The house had five rooms, only one of which was a bedroom. It resembled a dormitory with four beds for the security staff who worked six-hour shifts. Uncle John was never in residence and his sporadic visits were usually for the purpose of briefing operatives.

She followed him into the office at the back of the house. He threw her a towel.

'Would you like to shower?'

'Do I have to jog home?'

'Only about a mile. In half an hour, a car will deliver you to Danville Drive.'

'I'll shower at home.'

He motioned her to the chair opposite a coffee table laden with coffee pot, teapot, crockery, and a plate of scones. He sat on the big comfortable settee opposite her. She noticed a new Jaques-Louis David print over the fireplace. She commented on it and he looked pleased. He had insisted that, in addition to their other skills, his people should have a short course in the arts. It was her introduction to a lifetime passion, culminating in her visits to galleries in Florence.

As was his custom, his briefing was mercifully quick. He was of average height with a short, salt-and-pepper haircut. His brown eyes made her feel that he saw into her very soul. It was not a comfortable experience.

He stared out of the window. Then he made himself comfortable.

'Our quarry is a man named Pierre Gaffney. He is deeply involved in the IDB trade.'

She frowned, puzzled. 'Isn't illicit diamond-buying the province of the De Beers people?'

He nodded. 'We don't want to put him away for buying illicit diamonds. We want him for importing drugs.' He picked up the teapot and raised his eyebrows questioningly.

She nodded. 'Yes please. Milk and no sugar.' She refused the scone he offered her. He took one himself and bit into it.

He began to pour. 'Gaffney faces two very simple problems.' He paused as he handed her the tea. 'To get the diamonds out and the drugs in. We will help him solve both problems.' He made himself comfortable. 'The drugs squad has been hitting him hard for several months.' He sipped his tea. 'But that doesn't help us. We want Gaffney, not the hirelings. The drug squad is quite satisfied with its success in stopping the drugs.' He added with emphasis: 'We want Gaffney.'

She put her cup on the small table beside her chair.

'Where do I come in?'

'We are going to build you a reputation as the best smuggler in the country. It will take months, and it will be dangerous, but you have all the qualities I need for this operation.'

'And they are?'

He paused and smiled. 'The most important is your fluent Italian.' He put his cup on the

8

coffee table. 'You will smuggle Gaffney's diamonds into Italy.' He stood up and walked to the window. 'At present, all we know is that he has the diamonds. We don't know where they are. In any case we want him on the drugs charge, and the Italian police, with whom we are co-operating, want the source of the drugs.' He turned and nodded to her teacup. 'Finished? Good. Come through to the briefing-room. Captain Roberts is waiting for us there. He will be working with you.' He paused and smiled. 'If you pull this off, Mr Mandela will probably pin medals on both of you himself.'

Sam Roberts was a lightly built coloured man with grey hair and humour wrinkles at the corner of his eyes. He was a taciturn individual who had a profound knowledge of the ways of criminals and was a master of the Cape Malay patois. She had never worked with him, but she knew he had a formidable reputation as an investigator. He was a university-educated officer whose promotion had been long overdue. He had never appeared in court, always remaining in the shadows, unseen and unheard. Uncle John's choice was the best he could have made.

*   *   *

She looked down from her balcony at the sunlit street. Florence was beautiful in

9

summer. She thought of Pretoria, where it was still winter and temperatures were at freezing point. In the street below her, girls in colourful summer dresses gave the street a festive air.

She recalled the months spent in creating a new identity, the days of study, repeating details of her recreated identity to Captain Roberts until she could answer his every question without thinking first. It began with her new name, Janet La Barre. Then came the names and backgrounds of every person whom she would meet in her new life. Roberts was kind—and brutal. He continued to push her until he was satisfied that she was totally immersed in her new identity.

When she complained of fatigue, he castigated her.

'You can't afford to be tired. A single slip will kill you. The people you are going against are like mad dogs.'

And so she went on, until he was satisfied she could enter the next stage. She was put into a helicopter and flown along the country's borders, until Roberts was satisfied that she could mark every illegal crossing on the map.

Finally he taught her when to mix Cape Coloured slang into her speech, and taught her how to do it without sounding artificial. At first, he would stop her by declaring: 'You're hamming again.' Then at last he nodded unsmilingly. 'Now, I think we can let you loose on the mad dogs.'

Her decisive moment came when she was abandoned by Uncle John and his unit, and left in the care of the enigmatic Roberts. Slowly, through the weeks, she built up a reputation for being able to acquire anything that could not be bought or stolen. She moved confidently through the sub-cultures of three cities, and when Roberts detected that she was under surveillance, he sprang the trap. He set up a trip to the Swaziland border, where they lost their followers. From there she was picked up in the bush and taken to Maputo in Mozambique. Two days later she appeared in Harare, where Roberts contrived to have her seen by one of Gaffney's accomplices. She stayed there for a day and then disappeared, reappearing in Johannesburg with a supply of mandrax.

Two days later a man dressed in a neat pinstripe suit appeared on the doorstep of her Sandton home. When she opened the door, he said: 'My employer would like to meet you.'

She looked at him without interest as she drew the belt of her négligé more tightly around her waist.

'Who is your employer?'

'Pierre Gaffney.' He smiled. 'I'm sure you know who he is.'

She studied him coldly.

'Piss off, little man.' She stepped back and shut the door.

Next came the threatening phone calls. She

ignored them. Roberts predicted that it would take three weeks to hook Gaffney. In fact, it was only two weeks before his Mercedes drew up in front of her house. Three men alighted. Roberts's comment was laconic: 'My, isn't he the eager one.'

He watched Gaffney through the net curtain on the window as he approached the house alone. The two minders stayed in the car. Roberts was surprised that the man had accorded Janet that much respect. The bell chimed. Roberts opened the door with the chain still in place.

'Yes?' His voice was soft.

'I want to see Mrs La Barre,' Gaffney said impatiently. He was a thin grey-haired man with dark expressionless eyes. Roberts opened the door and nodded towards the living-room.

It was the first of several meetings, which always culminated in her refusing to do business on his terms. She knew he was checking her identity, but it was flawless. He was cautious, but finally, after the drugs squad had frustrated two of his deals, he agreed to give her an assignment to deliver a small parcel of diamonds to Rome if she could give him suitable guarantees. Uncle John came up with a solution. He produced four impressive-looking title deeds, which proved she owned property in three cities, and that it would not be to her advantage to disappear.

As she looked down at the Viale

12

Machiavelli, she felt a small glow of pleasure as she recalled his unwitting capitulation.

She heard a key in the door. It was Gaffney. His customary expressionless features were creased in a wolfish smile. His coat hung over his arm, his tie was loose, and his shirt was damp with perspiration.

'It's all set. The swap will be made in the morning. The Italian is coming in an hour to fix the details, then it's all up to you.' He pulled off his tie. 'Hell, I'm frazzled. I'll just have time for a shower.' He turned at the bathroom door and grinned. 'Get this lot into Jo'burg, and you'll have the biggest payday of your life.'

She yawned. 'I want to eat now, Gaff. If I want to get out before breakfast tomorrow, I'll need an early night.'

'Go ahead. I'll celebrate afterwards.' He paused. 'Have the waiter take your tray to your room. The man doesn't want any witnesses.'

'That's cool.' She pressed the bell for room service.

It was past nine o'clock before their visitor arrived. She sat in the darkened room waiting for the two men to settle down. Unexpectedly, Gaffney moved their meeting to his bedroom. She opened her door a few inches and waited. The muted sounds of traffic drowned the voices across the sitting-room, but occasion ally the visitor raised his voice in anger. They talked quietly for a while, and then as the

13

discussion became heated, she heard him clearly.

'It's not good enough. Some you sent me were in poor shape.' His voice dropped, but she still heard every word. 'Of the last consignment, two girls died. How did that happen?' She heard Gaffney's placating voice. But the visitor interrupted him. 'The merchandise from Hong Kong is much better quality.' The voices dropped and the conversation became inaudible.

She shut her door quietly. The glow she had felt from the golden day was gone. She felt unnaturally cold and her heart was hammering in her chest. Her hands were damp from shock. She knew now the extent of the Gaffney empire and was glad it was almost at an end.

The arrests the next morning were a formality. The three Italians arrived with their attaché cases and were sent up to the suite where the arrests were made. By prearrangement with the police, and ironically at Gaffney's insistence, she had left the suite and gone downstairs. She waited in the manager's office. Half an hour later she saw the four men being hustled through the foyer and into the waiting cars.

When she reported to Uncle John, she included details of Gaffney's conversation with his visitor. She caught the noon plane home.

From the Boeing, the mine dumps gave no indication of their size. Nor of the tons of rock and years of toil it had taken to raise them to their present height. Janet stared down at the sprawl of Johannesburg and wished she were back in Europe. As the aircraft circled, she recognized the houses of suburban Kempton Park, and to the north, the cramped township of Tembisa. Beyond that lay the purple haze of Pretoria and Centurian, the town built to honour the late unlamented Verwoerd.

From the green queue she carried her small suitcase to the slot where she had left her car. She was relieved to find it had been returned intact by those who had whisked it away for safekeeping on her departure. As she thrust the key into the lock, she felt a presence at her shoulder. She tensed and turned swiftly. The man who stood behind her was young, well dressed, and carried an A4 manila envelope. She looked at him questioningly.

He smiled. 'Greetings from Uncle John.' He walked over to a white BMW and drove away.

She got into her car before tearing impatiently at the envelope. It contained three smaller envelopes. She opened and read the contents of each in turn, returned them to the manila envelope and pushed them into her handbag. She sat and stared at the dashboard, seeing nothing of the instruments or the dials on the tape deck.

So, it wasn't finished yet. There was much more to be done before she could be restored to her world, the world of sanity where

15

nightmares faded into a faint disquiet. Her scalp was beginning to perspire, and she lifted the auburn tresses from her neck, sensing the slight breeze that touched her neck in an almost sensual caress. She pushed the key into the ignition, started the car, and drove out of the car park. Captain Roberts was seated in her armchair as she walked into her flat.

He greeted her surprise with a glum nod.

'I don't like this job any more than you do,' he said. 'The man insists that we're elected.'

CHAPTER TWO

Chaing Mai in north-eastern Thailand is the centre of the world's wholesale opium trade. A hundred kilometres to the north-west is Mae Hong Sun, a border village on the River Pai.

It was here, on a steamy summer night, that the head of the Black Silk triad met with the head of the Sun Ki Son. The Black Silk controlled the import of the banned substances used in the manufacture of heroin and the Sun Ki Son were desperate to find a new supplier. The meeting was held in the village whorehouse, known by its clients as the Hen Coop. The prostitutes were cleared out of the main room, guards were posted at the doors, and an elaborately decorated tea set was placed on the centre table for ceremonial purposes.

A woman dressed in the drab grey robes of a house sweeper went into the big room before the meeting to dust the table and chairs and to sweep the floor. Her name was Su Yung, and she was not a woman of the village. When she arrived, she had made it known that she had come to visit her brother Tse Chung who, unhappily, had died a month before she got there. The villagers treated her with great sympathy, and after the ceremonial grief period she was allowed to stay with the village chief until she could return to her home in Chaing Mai. To earn her fare home, she asked for and was granted permission to take employment as a sweeper in the Hen Coop.

Su Yung hummed as she worked in the opium-thick stink of the house of pleasure, where girls of all ages from eleven to fifty flitted about the bamboo-roofed house they called home. Out in the streets dust rose from the primitive carts carrying produce to the open markets. Dogs lazed in the sun, while from the water furrows rose the fetid stench of the swamps.

Su Yung finished sweeping and began to dust the furniture. As soon as she was certain she was unobserved, she moved to the head of the table, and having taken a small spherical object from her robes, slipped it under the overhang where it adhered to the smooth wood by means of a tacky pad. She went out and retired to her house, a rough bamboo lean-to over the road from the Hen Coop. It was a convenient place from which to record the signals from her bug on a small tape recorder.

The day following the meeting Su Yung bade farewell to her kind hosts and returned to her Chaing Mai, from where she took the first train to Bangkok. There she met the head of the American Drug Enforcement Agency. He was a short man with a barrel chest and thick forearms, grey hair, and the appearance of a benign gnome. His name was Hyde Bodill, and she knew him as a shrewd, ruthless hunter.

Their meeting was on the fourth floor of the Royal Orchid Hotel, in a room overlooking the river. The woman who sat with him on the balcony bore no resemblance to the aging crone who had swept out the whorehouse in Mae Hong Sun. Small and neat, her black hair pulled back from her beautiful almond eyes, she wore a dress of simple design which nevertheless accentuated and flattered her figure.

Bodill placed his small teacup on the table beside him.

'Did you have any trouble?'

She shook her head. 'Not as much as I would have had in the city. It did not occur to them that a lowly sweeper would possess sophisticated electronic equipment.'

He looked thoughtful. 'I must confess, I had

no faith in the chemical embargo.' He shrugged. 'Acetic anhydride seems to be available all over the world.'

She frowned. 'It is, as long as the Black Silk triad does not control it. They have come to an amicable agreement with Sun Ki Son to supply all the derivative drugs in exchange for the heroin franchise in Hong Kong.' Su Yung had no discernible accent, but she spoke with a mere trace of a lisp.

Bodill stood up and walked slowly to the end of the terrace where a view of the river reflected the city's myriad lights. The sight gave him no pleasure.

The girl stood up and joined him.

'What is your estimate?'

He looked at her. 'At least fifteen hundred tons within three months.' He looked down at the river. 'And the legitimate medical requirement for the whole world is no more than twenty tons.' He shrugged. 'Well, no one said it was going to be easy. You did well. I was worried about you.'

She was silent for a moment. Then suddenly her expression reflected a deep distress.

'There is more. Much more.' She appeared to find it difficult to speak. 'When the meeting ended, the Sun Ki Son leader complained about a lack of girls for his Hen Coops. The Black Silk man told him it was no problem. He could get girls from all over the world, including Europe and Africa.'

19

Bodill stared at her with growing consternation. Then he sighed.

'I'll pass it along to the proper authorities, but we will lose some tourists. Especially the young ones travelling alone. Not only in Asia, but also in any unsafe place on earth.'

*   *   *

Ramona Gomez paused at the crossing outside the school gates until the crossing monitor waved her over. She walked along Stamford Hill Road and stopped for a moment, uncertain whether to walk through Sutton Park, or take the long way around the Crescent. Although the park would be quicker, she always felt nervous walking across shadowed lawns and past trees and shrubs, imagining sinister shapes behind every tree. Reluctantly she crossed Adrian Road and walked towards the Crescent, reminding herself that although she was twelve and able to take care of herself, she was not old enough to avoid all the dangers of being a pretty young girl in a big city.

The man sitting on the park bench several metres inside the entrance watched the girl pause and walk on. He wasn't too disappointed. Perhaps tomorrow she would cross through the park close to his van. If it was not her, perhaps another just as slim and pretty.

Ramona did not know how lucky she had been. This time.

CHAPTER THREE

On the South African east coast, Durban was wilting in the hottest summer for twenty-five years, with a humidity reading that was almost off the scale. At three o'clock in the morning in Rydal Avenue it was darkest where a giant fig-tree spread a dark green canopy over the street. The avenue was gloomy at any time of day or night, but in the early hours of the morning the oppressive heat clothed the darkness with a shroud of menace. Rydal Avenue was one of those streets where houses had ceased to be homes and had become places for people to sleep three families to a floor. Occasionally deadbeats were found sleeping off a binge on the front steps. It was a place where the woodwork had rotted away and walls were collapsing because the plaster was porous and water seeped into aging foundations. The whole neighbourhood was destined for what polite folk called urban renewal, and in places the demolition had left voids in the street like gaps in an old man's teeth.

Mrs Eripides was not a deadbeat. She had lived on Rydal Avenue all her life. Her wealthy

21

father had bought into the upper-class development in a street of elegant double-storey homes. She still owned the property she had inherited, but now number 16 was only marginally better than its neighbours. Now her home was the top floor, while the ground floor was let mostly to transients who stayed for about three months. They usually left ahead of the police or their creditors. She always asked for rent in advance, so she was not perturbed when she heard the familiar sounds of departure coming from downstairs.

It was a sweltering night, and she got up from her damp bed, took a six-pack from the refrigerator, settled herself on the upstairs balcony, and prepared to sit out the night, cooled by the light sea breeze and her six-pack.

She knew her tenants would leave soon. The signs were there. When they began to shout and throw things at one another it was time to look for new tenants, especially if those in occupation were not married; she knew the two below were not.

They had arrived over two months ago. She had wondered about them. He always wore a neat grey suit, and a fedora, which he always lifted in greeting. She hadn't seen a fedora since she had seen Humphrey Bogart wearing one in *Casablanca*. The woman, a pretty redhead, dressed well and carried herself like someone who mattered. There were obvious signs that they were not married. Moreover, she discovered that they did not even sleep in the same room. Of course, she would never have called it snooping; she merely went in when they were out to see if the furniture had been properly cared for.

She had heard them quarrelling earlier. Then she heard a man's angry voice and a loud bang. Half an hour later she had heard the garage door open, and when she had gone into the kitchen she had looked down at a foreshortened view of a figure in a suit and a fedora hitching up the trailer they had brought with them. He moved the car and trailer to the front before returning into the house. She went out to the veranda, uncapped the last of the six-pack, and settled down to enjoy the breeze. She heard a door slam and the car and trailer drew away from the kerb. She saw the brake lights flare as the car turned into the main street. To hell with them all, she declared.

She waited for the other tenant to leave. She waited for two days, but there was no sign of her. She took her master key, opened the front door, and called out. She was met by a wall of silence. She went through the bedrooms, looked in the bathroom and tiny kitchen, and looked about her with puzzlement. The rooms were empty, cleaned out of any evidence of her previous tenants; no papers, boxes, cartons or any of the detritus of their occupation. The silence was absolute,

23

like the oppressive stillness of a crypt. She started as a stray drip from a faucet plopped into a basin. Suddenly the warm dampness of the night became a cold frisson between her shoulder blades.

Then she saw the dark stain on the floor.

* * *

Arbroath Road was a lot older than Harry Collins had remembered it. The houses sagged like tired old women. Peeling paint and rotting gutters marked the corrosive hand of time. Number 6 was at the far end, where a railway line curved gently past a dilapidated sports stadium that had once been the proud home of a Durban football club. Harry had once played for that club. At thirty-five he still had the strong shoulders and athletic build of fifteen years ago, but the light toffee-coloured hair above the good-looking features was touched with grey. Time had marked him with the same hand that had aged his old home.

He pulled in to the kerb and sat for a moment feeling the sad mantle of nostalgia descending as he looked towards the corner where the postbox had stood. He used to meet her there every morning before work. She would appear from the next street and find him there, waiting. She would give him a quick smile and they would talk for a few minutes before a bus took her away.

They were young and in love. In retrospect, he wondered if she truly loved him. Love is forgiving, but she had never forgiven him his one lapse into infidelity. Perhaps when you are eighteen pride becomes impenetrable armour against forgiveness. He did not see her again for twelve years. They had both married, but his marriage bore the brunt of what might have been.

Her call had come in the middle of a conference with a client. His secretary had taken her number and he had called back as soon as he was free. When she answered, her voice was exactly as he remembered it.

'Betty Rolands.'

'It's Harry. Harry Collins.'

She had been silent for a moment. 'Hullo Harry. Thanks for ringing back.' For a director of her own publishing company, her voice was strangely hesitant. 'I hear you're on your own now.'

'Right.' He wondered if this was social or business. His tone was bantering. 'Do you want some big money moved?'

She laughed and her tone became relaxed.

'Nothing so melodramatic. Harry, I understand you have some sort of security business.'

'No.' His tone was blunt. 'We move money. That's what my logo says. That's all I do.' He paused. 'I can put you in touch with some good people in the security business.' He took a

25

deep breath. He knew at once why he was feeling defensive. She wanted a favour, but did not even bother to find out what business he was in.

She sensed his disapproval.

'I'm sorry Harry. I should have checked.' She paused. 'This is personal.'

He heard the words and they were like a bugle sounding retreat. The years had provided a respite from the aches of the past, and he wanted to keep it that way.

'Personal. In what way?'

She read the caution in his words.

'Well not exactly personal. Do you remember old man Kelsey?'

'Of course. He was our neighbour in Arbroath Road.' His tone was quizzical. 'How can I forget. His son, Andrew, was killed in a motorbike accident. He had a daughter, Kay.'

There was a long pause.

'He needs help, Harry.'

For a moment, he wondered if this was something that he needed right now.

'Harry.' Her voice was quietly apologetic. 'Do you think you can help?'

He was irritated. 'I don't know. I don't even know what the problem is yet.'

'Of course.' She sighed. 'It's Kay. She's disappeared and he's crazy with worry.'

'Kay?' His tone expressed his concern. 'How long has she been gone?'

'About three years.'

26

His voice rose. 'Three years?' He realized he was almost shouting. His voice dropped. 'Three years? For heaven's sake, Betty.'

'I know, Harry. I'm not being very coherent. I keep in touch with the old man.'

He wasn't surprised. It was the kind of thing she did.

'For a couple of years, he received mail from her regularly; from Mauritius, Australia, places like that. Then all at once it stopped. He's had nothing for nearly a year.'

'Why doesn't he talk to the police?'

'He did. They made a token inquiry and dropped it. Nothing to go on.'

He pondered for a moment.

'I don't know.'

'Please, Harry.'

He heard the entreaty in her voice and began to feel hemmed in. He recalled tilting his chair and looking around his plush office. He did not want to leave it to visit an old man. From his window he could see the waves curling on the beach, while on the Parade, ten floors down, cars and pedestrians flowed in both directions. The heat was melting the tar, but inside the air-conditioning hummed efficiently. He wondered why he was beginning to perspire. He felt trapped.

'Look,' he said, 'I don't know how much time I can devote to this, but I'll talk to him.'

'Thanks, Harry. I'm grateful.'

He remained silent, staring out at the

27

windsurfers beyond the breakers.

'Harry?'

'I'm still here.'

'Come out for dinner one evening. Do you know where we are?'

'No, but I'll look it up.' He paused. 'How's your husband?' He managed to say it as though he cared.

'He's well. He's in Paris this week.'

'I'll call you.'

*　　*　　*

It was getting hot in the car. He got out and locked the door, looking surreptitiously at number 6. It looked deserted, somehow, its emptiness a reflection of the hollow years of its owner. He supposed Kelsey must have been happy at some time in the distant past.

All at once, like a lap-dissolve from an early film, Harry remembered the street as he used to know it; the trim on every house freshly painted, the gardens newly mown and the occupants happy in their suburban contentment. Now, except for Kelsey, they were all gone.

A train hooted, startling him out of his reverie. He walked slowly to the gate of number 6. The man who opened the door was stooped and grey, dressed in a pair of worn, baggy trousers and a brown cardigan over a soiled shirt. Harry thought self-consciously of his designer slacks and expensive sports shirt. Kelsey peered at him for a moment. Then he brightened.

'Harry. Harry Collins. Come in. Come in.' He led the way into a living-room that reflected the decay which the years had wrought on the street. Frayed carpets, sagging armchairs with worn plush and armrests greasy with age, all testified to the old man's loneliness.

When they were seated, Kelsey talked slowly of things out of the past. Dry fragments of memory fell from him the way a tree sheds its leaves, and Harry realized for a brief moment that he was bound to the old man by shared years. Their lives had merged and for a brief moment they had been elements of a single entity: the street and its people.

Harry looked surreptitiously at his watch.

'Betty said you wanted me to help you.'

'Kay is all I have left.'

Harry saw the slow forming of a tear before the tattered remnants of dignity came to Kelsey's support. The old man blinked and raised his head.

'I haven't heard from her since last February. She sent me a card.'

'Did it have a return address?'

Kelsey nodded.

'I'll need all her letters. And a clear photograph. Where did she work?'

'At Columbus Mining. I rang them and they

said she had left three years ago. She said she was travelling with a trade mission to Asia. I thought it was with the mining company.' He frowned. 'When I heard she had left her job I wondered if she was into something illegal.'

'Oh, why?'

'Some time last year a fella came here and asked if I knew where she was. He asked a lot of questions; where she had been, who her friends were and had I seen her lately. Stuff like that.' He smiled slyly. 'I told him I hadn't heard from her in three years.' He shrugged. 'I asked him if he was from the police, but he wouldn't answer any of my questions.'

'Did he give a name?'

'Yes. Lindquist. Tall thin man with fair hair. It was obvious he didn't know her. He asked what she looked like. He asked for photographs, but I told him I didn't have any.'

Harry smiled. 'But of course you have.'

Kelsey nodded cheerfully. 'Of course. Several. But he didn't believe me.'

'Oh. How do you know?'

The sly smile returned. 'Three nights later, when I went over to Jackson's for bridge, someone broke in. Nothing was taken and I suspected it was for the photos.'

'Did he get them?'

'I had hidden them under the carpet. I was afraid he would come back with a search warrant or something.'

Harry shook his head. 'The police would

30

not have burgled your house.'

'The NIS would have. I've read about them in the papers.'

Harry smiled. 'Why would the National Intelligence Service want a picture of Kay?' He grew serious. 'It's really strange.' He stood up. 'Let me have the letters and a couple of good photos, and I'll see what I can do.'

'Thank Betty for me.'

'I'll do that.'

Harry went out to the car. The heat pressing down on him drew the sweat from his pores; it trickled between his shoulder blades and stained his shirt. His clothes enveloped him like clingfilm. Inside the car, it was hotter than a steelworks, but by the time he had turned eastwards towards Argyle Road and the beachfront, the air-conditioning had lowered the temperature to a bearable level.

He did not see the blue Chevrolet that followed him home.

Harry's offices were on the tenth floor of a high-rise which overlooked the Golden Mile, that street of five-star hotels fronting the Indian Ocean. His apartment was on the other end of the same floor. James McGrath, a dour, gruff Scot, carried most of the administrative work in his business.

He took a long shower, selected a clean shirt and dark-blue slacks, black socks and a pair of black beefroll loafers. He went to a cabinet and poured himself a beer. He went to his office carrying the tankard and a packet of crisps, and worked through the correspondence his secretary had left for him. He finished the beer and the crisps, and then stared at Kay Kelsey's letters which he had left at the edge of his desk. He sighed and pulled them towards him. Whatever he felt now, there was no turning back.

There were two cards and three letters. The photograph was taken on a yacht. It was a photographic cliché: the subject, wearing a tiny bikini, leaned dreamily against the mast, staring at the horizon. He had forgotten how beautiful she was. He picked up the first card, written from Mauritius, describing the hotel and the beach and what a wonderful time she was having. It was the usual dull message, the formal duty card. He dropped it on the desk, and looked at the card written eight months ago. On one side she had written her own address, 16 Rydal Avenue, and a short message.

He frowned. Rydal Avenue? He remembered that it was south of the city. Bellair or Seaview. He read the message.

Dear Dad, I have decided to stay this side of town for a while to be near the office. I will give you a call soon.
Love. Kay.

That was all. Nothing to indicate that this

was the last message she would send to her father. He picked up a letter dated a month after the first card. He read it through to the end: another duty message, dull and uninspiring. He put it aside and picked up a letter postmarked Umdhloti, a village on the north coast. In it, Kay had described her flat opposite the seafront. The last paragraph intrigued him.

I am excited about my next trip. I can't tell you about it now, but I will be away for about three months. Don't worry about me.

Harry stared at the words. Why the mystery? Why couldn't she reveal her destination? Who was she working for?

He examined the remaining letters, but they provided no more information than those that he had read. He stood up, stretched, and walked to the window. He was surprised to see the lights on in the darkening street. He considered his options. He wondered if a delay of twelve hours would make any difference. He was tired and a trip to the southern suburbs at night was an uninviting prospect, but finally he was compelled by his curiosity to act at once.

*   *   *

Harry parked his car across the road from

number 16. He turned off the lights, opened the door, and stood on the kerb. There was no moon, and no streetlights. He looked critically at the double-storey Victorian house, which resembled not so much an impoverished dowager as an aging whore in her last good ensemble. The whole street was in the throes of evanescence, hiding behind a massive fig-tree as though in fear of the wreckers' ball. Most of the houses were in darkness, but in number 16 a downstairs window glowed behind deep-maroon drapes. His preoccupation with the house drew his attention away from the darkness beyond the fig-tree, where a blue Chevrolet without lights glided to a stop 200 metres down the street.

Harry walked up the steps to the stoep, rang a bell that operated by turning an ancient key, and listened to the footsteps approaching the hallway. The steps paused and Harry sensed movement behind the spyhole lens.

'Who are you? What do you want?'

'My name is Harry Collins. I want to talk to you about one of your tenants.'

'Which tenant? What's his name?'

'A woman. She stayed here in February last year.'

'What's her name?'

'Kay Kelsey.'

'Never heard of her.'

'She could have been using another name. If you open the door, I can show you a photograph of the girl I'm looking for.'

There was a slight hesitation, and then the door opened to the end of the chain. A sharp-featured, grey-haired woman peered out with one eye. Harry held up the photograph.

'Kelsey wasn't her name when she stayed here.' The woman spoke with sharp belligerence, daring him to contradict her. 'She called herself Mrs Lindquist.'

'May I come in? I am acting for her father. He hasn't heard from her in a long time.'

She studied him for about ten seconds. 'I don't know. I don't let people in after dark.'

Harry shrugged resignedly. 'May I come back in the morning?'

She studied him for a few more seconds. Suddenly she shut the door and Harry heard the chain rattle in its slot. The door was opened.

'Come in. I'm too old to care if I'm murdered, and you look respectable.' As she led him into the living-room, she added: 'It's probably what those girls told Jack the Ripper.' She nodded to the sofa.

'I assure you, you're safe with me.'

She sat on the chair opposite a flickering television set. The sound was off, a glossy magazine was on a low table beside her, and a glass of amber liquid and a bowl of chilli-bites were beside it. The furniture was old but clean and the wooden arms of the suite had a patina that came from regular polishing. The wallpaper was faded, but unmarked.

'Can I get you a beer?'

He shook his head and smiled. 'I have to drive home.'

She looked at him quizzically. 'What did you say your name was?'

'Harry Collins.' Suddenly Harry realized that this woman was brighter than she looked. He remembered the first rule of interrogation. *Always ask a suspect his name twice. If he is lying the first time, he is likely to stumble over it the second time.* 'But you knew that, didn't you?'

She smiled and nodded. Then she recalled the conventions of polite society. 'I am Mrs Eripides.'

Harry nodded his acknowledgement of the courtesy.

'You say the woman was calling herself Mrs Lindquist?'

'Yes. They stayed for about six weeks, and then they left. Suddenly. At three in the morning.' She looked away from him and sipped her beer.

Harry was aware of an awakening tension, as though she had meant to tell him more, but had remembered the consequences to her.

'I would appreciate anything you can tell me about them. This is not a police matter, and it will go no further.' He thought for a moment. 'Her father is desperate. He is offering a large reward for any pertinent information.' The lie came easily. He was certain that this woman knew something significant.

Mrs Eripides looked at him speculatively.

'I don't know. It's been months. She could be dead by now.'

Harry felt a thrill of apprehension. The tension now was palpable; it was evident in the way her hands fluttered unceasingly in her lap. This woman knew of a death. Harry was sure of it. He leaned back casually.

'Of course, I certainly don't want to get involved with the police. Anything I discover will go only to Mr Kelsey.'

The woman leaned forward eagerly. 'You mean anything I say will go no further?'

Harry nodded. 'That's it. Any reward will come to you as soon as we have established the facts.' Harry hoped she would miss the ambiguity of his words.

Mrs Eripides stood up quickly, as though the knowledge she possessed would burst from her. She took her empty glass through to the kitchen, and when she returned with it replenished she appeared to have regained the control she had so nearly lost. She sat on the edge of the sofa, looking at him over the rim of the glass. Harry knew he was about to hear what had happened in this house those many months ago.

Mrs Eripides was silent for a full minute. When she spoke, her voice was quiet and controlled.

'They lived down here. In this part of the house. When I have tenants, I stay upstairs, and use the outside stairs.' She set her beer down on the small table. 'They had only been here a few weeks, when they began to quarrel.'

'What about?'

Mrs Eripides shrugged impatiently. 'Almost everything. He kept accusing her of lying about something. I never did find out what that was about.' She looked into her glass and sipped. 'One night—it was very late—I heard her cry out. He said something and there was a loud bang. It was quiet for a long time after that. Later, in the early hours, I saw the car leave with their trailer.' Two shrewd eyes watched him expectantly, waiting for him to ask the right question.

Harry knew that from now on she would only answer questions he put to her, volunteering nothing that he could not elicit from her by guile.

'Did they leave together?'

A twitch at the corner of her mouth told Harry that this was the question she had been waiting for.

'No. Only one of them left in the car. I saw the driver in a hat and coat hitching up the trailer. I went downstairs later but the flat was empty.' She paused, watching him with bright, shrewd eyes. 'Only one person was in the car, but I don't know what was in the trailer.'

Harry was suddenly aware of the changed

38

.

atmosphere in that room; it was a change in temperature, as though the warm, humid night had been chilled by the cold breath of something evil. Impatiently he shook off the feeling.

'Are you certain only one person left this house?'

'I'm positive.' She stood up. 'Come, I want to show you something.'

She led the way to one of the darkened rooms off the hall. She switched on the light. A bare forty-watt bulb burned in the ceiling fixture, but even in the dim light, Harry could see where she was pointing. The carpet alongside the bed was stained, fading at the edges, as though it had been scrubbed.

Harry stared down at this evidence of tragedy. He looked at her as he said carefully: 'May I snip a piece of the carpet to identify the stain?'

He expected her to protest, but to his surprise, she shrugged.

'Please yourself. I'll get a pair of scissors.' She brought him scissors and a small freezer-bag. As he was tucking the snippet of carpet into the bag, she led him back to the living-room. He was about to take his leave when he remembered he had not asked a vital question.

'Do you know where they lived before they arrived here?'

Her expression told him he had asked another significant question.

'A card came just after they left. It was forwarded from an address in Durban North.' She went out and returned immediately with a postcard. The address on a computer sticker read: 3 Garnet Avenue, Durban North. Harry turned it over. The message was a reminder of a sale at a local furniture store.

He looked up to see her regarding him expectantly.

'Did they ever have visitors? Friends? Business acquaintances? Anyone?'

It was another hit. Her expression changed to one of satisfaction.

'Only once. Two men. They came at night.'

'Do you remember what they looked like?'

'I remember them clearly,' she said eagerly. 'They came up the back stairs by mistake. They were surprised when I answered the door.' She was still for a moment as though pondering how much she should tell him. Harry remained silent. 'One was dark with black wavy hair. He was short, with a flatfish nose. The other man was a short oriental with long straight hair.' She smiled. 'I watch people. That's all I do these days. The older I get, the more interested I become.' She gave a self-satisfied nod, and Harry realized she was near the end of her supply of useful information.

Harry glanced at the postcard. 'This man Lindquist. Can you describe him?'

'He was tall, very thin, with fair hair.'

Harry nodded with satisfaction. That was

40

how Kelsey had described his caller.

'Thank you, Mrs Eripides. May I telephone you if I have any more questions?'

'I don't have a telephone.'

'Oh.' Harry recovered from his surprise. 'Then may I call again?'

She nodded without interest. 'If you wish.'

Harry heard the faint sound of a rising wind. It was coming from the south-east, and he felt the slight drop in the humidity level. He heard the whisper of an errant breeze curling through the eaves and the soft creak of the rafters. It was as though this dark, musty house was shedding its final secrets through the words of the wily old woman.

'Don't forget the reward.' Mrs Eripides was no fool. She was sharp, and he was certain that her words held a certain quality of irony that caused him to wonder if she had ever believed in a reward. 'Just send me a cheque.'

He was feeling slightly shamefaced as he drove away. He had seriously underestimated the woman's intelligence.

He thought about the blood. He needed advice. Joe Davidson was the man to talk to. He was too preoccupied to notice the blue Chevrolet that followed him on to the freeway. The driver left him at the beachfront and drove out to Durban North, and then into an avenue of expensive homes with large grounds. He turned into a driveway at the northern end. He opened the front door, which came with an expensive lock. He went to the telephone in the study at the back of the house, dialled an overseas number, and waited for the satellite connection to be established. He heard a woman answer.

The man spoke quickly. 'Put me through to Victor.'

'I'm sorry, there is no Victor here.'

Impatiently the man went through the recognition procedure.

'Isn't that the home of Victor Bartlett?'

'Victor who?'

He gave his own code name. 'This is Rabbit.'

'Hold on, please.'

There was a short pause, then a new voice spoke.

'This is Victor.'

'A man named Harry Collins has been poking around. First at Kelsey's and then, tonight, at Rydal Avenue.'

'He could be trouble.'

'The old woman may know more than we think.'

There was a long silence. The caller heard the faint sounds of transmission across space. Then Victor spoke.

'Get rid of her. Immediately.' A pause. 'We can't afford any more difficulties now. We have the bank job at Kloof coming up. We need that money.' His voice rasped. 'Get rid of her.'

'It may be difficult.'

'If you can't do it, give the job to Li, but I won't be happy about that.' There was silence for a moment. 'I will have to remember that you weren't capable—or willing.'

The man called Rabbit was no coward, but his fear of Victor was greater than his aversion to violence.

'No sweat,' he said with more confidence than he felt. 'Li and I can do it together.'

'As long as it gets done.' There was a slight pause. 'Have Collins watched. If he gets too close, deal with him.'

'I'll do that first thing in the morning.'

'Have you found Lindquist?'

'Not yet, but we're working on it.'

'You seem to be having trouble getting anything done.' Victor's tone hardened. 'I want you to tell me you'll find him in forty-eight hours.' His voice became soft. 'You will, won't you.'

The man called Rabbit heard the menace in the words.

'Of course, Victor. I'll find him.'

'Good.' There was a click and the man heard the empty silence. He felt perspiration on his neck which was not entirely due to the heat of the night.

The man called Victor sat back in his chair and swivelled it to face the view of the downs stretching away to the channel. He picked up the phone.

43

'Get me Pearson.'

The woman at the reception desk dialled rapidly. A voice answered on the second ring.

'Pearson.'

Her voice was deep and curt. 'Hold.'

Pearson waited while he was transferred. Victor was equally abrupt.

'I want you to watch Grundling's people at Garnet Road.'

'Anything in particular?'

'They have an elimination job.'

'Right.' The connection was closed.

CHAPTER FOUR

Joe Davidson pulled one last time on the weights, and then released them slowly, his powerful muscles shining with perspiration.

I'm too old for this, he thought. *Half an hour and I feel like an old man.* He paused. 'Come to think of it,' he said aloud. 'I *am* a bloody old man.'

The gym was crowded. Echoing sounds of exercise machines pounded the walls, and the air was thick with the odours of sweat, liniment, and deodorant. Davidson walked through to the locker room, showered, and donned grey slacks, a golf shirt, and brown loafers.

He wasn't a tall man, but his physique

reflected the hours he spent in the gym. His hair was grey, but he carried his fifty-five years well. His face was unlined and his brown eyes were clear. His high cheekbones and prominent chin gave him the appearance of droll good humour. Though he dressed well, he was not ostentatious. On the contrary, he strove for anonymity. He had an almost miraculous ability to merge into any group, a talent that was invaluable in his profession.

When people asked him what he did, his invariable reply was: 'Anything for a penny.' In fact, he ran a lucrative recovery business. When, in the rare moments he was pressed to say what he did, he found it easier to say what he did not do. He was not a private detective; he was not in the security business; he did not recover stolen goods for clients. In truth, what he did was a combination of all three.

His methods were unorthodox and he was rarely punctilious about the bounds of legality. Those who retained him rarely quibbled about his methods, mainly because they never knew and did not care about how they were served.

He always went armed. He was a fine shot, scoring high on the range, and even higher against live targets, but he was no wanton killer; he never pulled the trigger unless his life or those of innocent people were threatened. He was never preoccupied with the dead, and if he recalled them at all, they sat deep in his memory, unlamented bundles lying in the dark corridors of time. He did not remember any of those who were not criminals, and to those who censured him, his reply was laconic. 'Where were you when he was pulling the trigger?'

He left the locker room, and walked to the double doors that led to the stairs.

'Finished already, Joe?'

Davidson paused in mid-stride. The owner of the gym was relaxing in his cubicle, sipping fruit juice. He was young, fair, and well built. His tan was the product of hours in the surf.

Davidson glanced at his watch. 'Hell, Riley, don't you think an hour is enough for an old man.'

Tom Riley grinned. 'An hour! Bullshit! I watched you con your way through thirty minutes of light exercise.'

Davidson smiled. 'Forty-five minutes,' he lied cheerfully. 'And it was a work-out you would have had trouble with.' He looked at his watch again. 'No messages? I was expecting a call here.'

Riley shook his head. 'She must have gone off with a younger man. Probably peeped in and saw you at the weights.'

Davidson smiled. 'I'm irresistible to women. Anyway, it wasn't that kind of call.' He lifted his arm in salute, walked through the double doors to the stairs, and went down the short flight into West Street. The post-office clock was chiming the half-hour.

46

The city centre was thronged with office-bound clerks, scurrying to beat the clock. The traffic, six lanes on a one-way street, roared eastwards as the lights changed, and the heavy smell of exhaust fumes smothered the odours from the restaurants and breakfast joints.

Davidson stood at the kerb, conscious of the movement around him. He loved every moment of it. This was his town, the place where he grew up, and he could chart every change of the city in the last forty years.

His offices consisted of two small rooms with a view over the Victoria Embankment. His entrance was devoid of any identification, and his only concession to security was a steel-lined teak door and the latest electronic locking system. The furnishings were plain and functional, a pine desk in each room, some filing cabinets and a coffee percolator in the outer office. Visitors were accommodated in a worn easy-chair opposite his desk.

The telephone was ringing as he unlocked the door. He heard the answering machine trip the ringing. After his own message, his caller began speaking.

'Joe, this is Harry Collins. I have a blood specimen I want analysed. Give me a call.'

Davidson ran the tape back to the beginning. The first caller that morning had an accent that identified him as a black man. The voice was deep and harsh.

'Kloof branch of East Coast Banking at

47

closing time today. The second car is already parked in the trees off Assegai Road. Call me at nine sharp, and every half-hour until ten-thirty.' Davidson erased the tape and looked at his watch. It was right on the button. Nine sharp.

He dialled the Pietermaritzburg code, followed by a seven-digit number. The call was answered on the first ring.

'This is Shotgun. I'm alone.'

'Is the escape car clear?'

'Yes. I'm the only one knows where it is.'

'How many?'

'Four, including me.'

'Good.' He paused. 'Go through the route with me.'

'From the bank, I cut across to the entrance to the N3, leave the freeway at the Summerfeld flyover and turn right into Assegai. The car is just off the road in a small plantation. There is a sharp bend warning sign fifty metres before the plantation. It's a blue Opel.' There was a pause. 'We drive past it on the way to the bank. About three o'clock. We leave one man there as a look-out.'

'Will he be in addition to the other three?'

'I figured you'd take him out before we get there.'

'Right.' He paused for a moment. 'You remember the drill. When you stop the car, delay opening your door. The others will hurry. They always do.' He went through the

48

drill in his mind. It all seemed satisfactory. 'What are you wearing?'

'An Ingram eleven.'

Davidson's voice rose. 'Where the hell did they get that?'

'Makes you wonder, doesn't it?'

'And the others?'

'An AK 47, a Browning nine-millimetre. The third man has a realistic P thirty-eight. A toy, but it looks real.'

'That's it then. Good luck.'

'Thanks. I'll need it. I'm shit-scared.'

'Aren't we all.' He replaced the receiver.

The office was warm. The airless humidity made the city centre an uncomfortable place in the summer. He picked up the receiver and replaced it. He decided to ring Harry Collins from his air-conditioned flat.

*   *   *

Davidson lived in one of a block of six simplexes standing on two acres of trim lawns and neat gardens. His flat faced east, giving him a view of Durban Bay, the Bluff and the Indian Ocean. Three bedrooms and two bathrooms would have been too big for him had he lived alone. The woman who opened the door to him was about a hundred and sixty-five centimetres. Joe always thought of it as five feet, five inches. She had dark, shoulder-length hair and eyes a colour that Joe

49

often said was emerald-blue. She wore a blue gown and her hair was damp from the shower. As he kissed her, he caught the fragrance of the soap she used.

She turned his wrist and looked at his watch. 'You're early.'

'I wanted to see what he looked like.'

'Fat chance. I let him out the back door when I saw your car.'

'Oh. Is that who it was? I thought it was the garbage collector.'

She laughed. She always laughed, and he was grateful that he loved a woman with a sense of humour. She appeared to possess a vulnerable naïveté, but it hid a quality of strong-minded independence that denied others access to her space. There were few personal situations she did not control if she decided it was worth the effort. One of these was the question of her name. She was born Margaret Ryan, and when friends thought that Maggie or Peggy would be friendlier, she became coldly polite until it was understood that she answered to Margaret and to no other name.

He went through to the study where the central air-conditioning had lowered the temperature to a comfortable seventy-two degrees. This room was distinctly his. Margaret had seen to that. One wall was panelled in light meranti. On the opposite wall were shelves of books. Behind a solid mahogany desk was a window extending along the entire length of the wall. Above the desk he had hung an original by Eleni. It was a painting of a deserted cottage in the woods. In it, she had captured all the solitude and loneliness of an abandoned cabin.

He picked up the telephone handset and tapped out the number for Harry Collins. He was answered by the shrill sound of the busy tone. He looked at his watch. He would give Collins ten minutes. He needed plenty of time to check the escape car, and to time the route. And he had to eliminate the look-out.

In the last five years, South Africa had become a violent country, with bank robberies and cash-in-transit heists commonplace. Banking security was big business, and Davidson took over when the usual precautions had failed.

Margaret appeared at the door.

'Coffee?'

'No, thank you. I have to go out again.'

'Take care. You're not much, but you're all I've got.' She smiled as she came around the desk and put her arms over his shoulders.

'Where is it?'

'Kloof.'

'I'll worry. You know that.'

'Of course. But I'd rather you knew.'

'Yes.' She straightened. 'When will you go?'

'In about ten minutes.'

She kissed him on the cheek and went out,

closing the door behind her. Davidson listened to the whisper of the air-conditioning, reflecting that she was the only person he knew who would not admonish him about his safety. It was indicative of their trust in one another that her concerns went unvoiced. She knew that he was aware of how she felt, and that the expression of it would be an affront to their relationship.

He realized that he had been staring at the telephone. Jolted out of his reverie, he dialled Collins once more. His line was still engaged. Collins would have to wait.

Davidson went to the painting, slid it to one side revealing a small safe. He dialled the combination and took out a revolver. The weapon he held was no ordinary revolver. It was from a radical design invented by Ghisoni of Pavia, which he had named the Mataba. Signor Ghisoni had placed the cylinder in front of the trigger instead of above it. The cylinder was of the swing-out type with a preloading facility for eight loads. The balance was perfect.

Davidson inserted a full load, checked the action, and put two more pre-load packs into his pocket. He closed and locked the safe and prepared to leave the house.

CHAPTER FIVE

Davidson glanced at the dashboard clock. Eleven o'clock. He turned slowly from the freeway exit into Assegai Road. There was still time to reconnoitre the area where the escape car was hidden. He drove towards the stand of eucalyptus gums on the right of the narrow road. The whole area was a patchwork of smallholdings about forty kilometres from Durban, and half-way to Pietermaritzburg. Its rural character made it an ideal place to leave the escape car. Pedestrians were scarce and motorists would not see anything unusual in a car turning into the grove of trees.

He saw the sharp-bend sign and the entrance to the grove. He passed it without turning his head, and slowed a hundred metres beyond it. He turned through an open gate before bumping on to the verge of a farm road. He switched off his engine and sat for a while, listening to the unceasing, muted sounds of the freeway half a mile away. He heard the call of a dove and the incessant lowing of a cow bereft of her calf. It was cooler in the shade of the tall gums, while the still air was redolent with the scent of eucalyptus and the odour of cattle. He leaned over and took a small bag from the back seat.

Davidson opened the door and stood beside

the car, paused there for a few minutes, and then, carrying the small bag, walked towards a thick screen of trees above the road. He followed a path that ran a few metres inside the property. Where the path continued to the right, he turned left and pushed his way through a thick barrier of shrubs. Then he saw the escape car. It was facing the almost invisible track leading to Assegai Road. It was an ideal hiding place. It could be driven to the road in a few seconds. He tried the doors. They were all locked.

So, he thought, it comes down to plan B.

He opened the bag and took out two spiked balls, similar to those at the end of the Swiss morning star mace. These were smaller and the spikes were longer. He tucked them firmly against the rear wheels, covered them with sand and leaves, and stood back to examine the effect. He was satisfied that they would remain undetected. He went to his car and drove back to the freeway.

*   *   *

Number 3 Garnet Road in Durban North was a large, double-storey, mock Tudor house set in an acre of well-tended gardens. Azaleas grew in profusion against the boundary wall and the lawn was trimmed to a green carpet. Harry took the photograph of Kay Kelsey from the cubby-hole, got out of the car, and walked up the drive. He looked for a bellpush, and then noticed a small speaker and a single button; he pressed it and heard the soft rendition of *Jingle Bells*. He waited with growing impatience. Then, as he began to feel the warm sun on his back, a harsh, tinny voice broke the silence.

'Yes? Who is it?'

'My name is Harry Collins. I'd like to talk to you about a couple who stayed here about a year ago.'

There was a long pause. The door remained closed.

'Would that be the Lindquists?'

'Yes it would, ma'am.'

'Have you any identification?'

He took his ID card from his wallet.

'Yes ma'am, I have.'

He heard the sound of a key turning and the door opened to the extent of a brass chain. He realized that the elderly woman at the door was in a wheelchair. She reached for the card, examined it briefly, and handed it back

'What do you want to know?'

Harry held up the photograph.

'Is this Mrs Lindquist?'

The woman examined the likeness for a few seconds, and then shook her head doubtfully.

'She is similar in some ways, but Mrs Lindquist wasn't a redhead. She was a blonde.'

'A wig?'

'Impossible. I saw her drying her hair in the

sun after a swim. They used our pool.'

Harry looked at the calm eyes under the grey hair. There was no doubt in her expression. Of course, she might be a consummate liar.

'What did Mr Lindquist look like?'

'He was a tall, thickset man with grey hair.'

Harry was startled. 'Are you sure, ma'am? The man I'm looking for has fair hair.'

'I see.' But it was obvious she did not.

'How long did they stay?'

'Not long. A few weeks.' She was silent for a moment. 'But it was most peculiar. They left at midnight. We both saw them leave. My son Lawrence and I.' She waved a hand impatiently. 'It was just as well. We were about to give them notice. They played loud music and towards the end they quarrelled a lot.' She looked at him speculatively. 'On the last night we heard loud voices and a scream. Then he left, towing that trailer of theirs.'

'Are you sure it was Mr Lindquist? Not his wife?'

'It was a dark, wet night but I distinctly saw him come from the cottage in his hat and coat.' She paused, one eye peering malevoently at him behind the door. He realized she was becoming impatient. 'I was looking out through the study window.'

Suddenly he felt a strange sense of doubt, and even more strongly, a growing incredulity, but he knew that behind that chain, her story was unassailable.

'I take it they took everything they owned? The cottage had been cleaned out?' He could not conceal the irony in his tone. If she detected it, she ignored it.

'Everything. Even the kitchen had been scrubbed out.'

Harry recalled the scrubbed carpet at Rydal Avenue and felt an odd sense of *déjà vu*.

'Did you forward any mail to them?'

'I don't know where they went from here, but they might have left forwarding instructions at the post office.'

'Did he have any visitors?'

'Only one. An oriental fellow.'

Harry thought about the forwarding address. Why would Lindquist want mail delivered to an address where the other Lindquist would be staying? And the oriental visitor? Was it the same man? Damned coincidence if it wasn't.

The woman moved the door slightly. 'I can't tell you any more. I must go.'

Suddenly he was looking at the closed door. As he went down the path, he thought she looked a little like his maternal grandmother. She had the same sweet smile, white hair, and gentle manner. But his intellect rejected the visual similarity. There was something missing.

As he unlocked the car and drove away, she watched him from behind a curtain. When the car was out of sight, she stood up and turned on the man who called himself Rabbit.

57

'You stupid, ignorant bastard. I told you to check the post office for a forwarding instruction.'

Rabbit followed her to the hall.

'Why the hell did you give him all that information?'

She looked at him pityingly.

'Don't be more stupid than you have to be. We don't know how much he knew. He may have been checking. I had to answer truthfully. What if he had called on the neighbours? He might even do that.' She picked up the phone. 'If I had given him one wrong answer and he knew it, it would have blown everything.'

'Why answer the door at all?'

She gave him a slow withering look.

'You dumb bastard. Because it could have been anybody. A meter reader, a tradesman, even the police. We can't afford the slightest suspicion.'

She sighed. Lawrence had been a trial from prep school. His inability to absorb the simplest lesson condemned him to a secondary role in any enterprise. Victor had offered her, as the madam in a high-class house, an opportunity to quit her business. He had installed her in this comfortable address, and shown her how she could make more in a month than she had made in five years at her old trade. Victor had agreed to employ her son as part of the deal. Lawrence, fat and bald, was one of the misfortunes of her old business, and

58

she could only guess at his father's identity.

She said patiently: 'He thinks I've told him everything about Lindquist and the girl. He won't be back.' She tapped out the numbers for her overseas call. Victor should be told about her visitor.

*   *   *

Davidson walked carefully along the sandy path, his tennis shoes silent in the soft earth. Through a screen of foliage, he could see the blue Opel. He waited only ten minutes before a man in a blue denim suit walked up the path, opened the car doors and boot, and checked the interior. After a cursory glance around the small clearing, he leaned against the car, took a pistol from a shoulder holster, checked the action, and replaced it under his arm. It was a Browning nine-millimetre.

Davidson moved cautiously to a point where the path cut across the track. The guard was directly in front of him, about five metres away. He was a small, slightly built, black man, wearing a bank-robber's characteristic woollen balaclava, which he could pull down over his face. Davidson took a few silent steps towards the unsuspecting guard. It was quiet in the woods. Even the birds were stilled by the thick afternoon heat. He moved another step, his body relaxed, the revolver slack in his hand.

He felt in complete control. He had been in

59

this situation many times before and, as so often in the past, he was completely confident of the outcome. Death awaited one of them. The certainty was there in his mind, mingled with the familiar feeling of regret.

When he spoke, his voice was harsh and deep.

'Stand completely still. Don't move unless you want to die.'

Davidson reflected later that the man had had some training in combat skills. He was the kind with the misplaced confidence of the unskilled. He fell to the ground, rolled over twice and came up to the firing position with the Browning levelled. He came up exactly where he was expected to be. Davidson shot him through the right eye. In a reflex action, the Browning flew high into the air, clattering on the roof of the car before falling into the sand.

Davidson returned the revolver to his hip holster, and picked up the Browning. He wiped it clean, checked the action, and saw that the safety-catch was still on. He stood for a moment, listening to the quiet. He moved quickly, dragging the body into a deep thicket, covering it with leaves. He went back to the path, pulled down a small branch, and dragged it over the blood and the marks of the dragged heels. The blood was still visible, so he took several double handfuls of sand and sprinkled it over the stain. He cleaned his hand with his handkerchief and settled down behind a thicket to wait.

After a while he heard a car approaching at high speed, and surmised that this was the robbery car. He hoped the police were not in close pursuit. He would like to have everything wrapped up before handing the case over to them; that way, Shotgun could get away without being involved. He was one of Davidson's best informers, leading him to vast amounts of stolen property. He was a skilful driver and when he had been invited to participate in the robbery, Davidson knew that the man could not refuse. If he had, his body would have been found at the edge of the township. He did not want Shotgun exposed to township retribution.

His surmise was confirmed when he heard the engine slow as the driver dropped down through the gears. As soon as he heard the car stop, he moved quickly into the open. Simultaneously, three men raced up the track towards him. All three were burdened with heavy black plastic bags. As they saw him, they stopped, surprise throwing them into a moment of confusion.

'Drop your weapons. Get down on the floor.' Davidson's voice was loud and harsh. He kept his eyes on the man with the AK47, knowing it was futile to expect him to surrender. Bank robbers believed that the possession of a machine pistol made them invin cible. Moreover, it was inconceivable that anyone would face them with a revolver and survive. Davidson saw the muzzle of the AK47 swing towards him at the same moment that the Browning was lifted. The two shots from his revolver were almost simultaneous, but they had hit targets a metre apart. Both men fell and lay still.

Suddenly, a machine pistol chattered. Davidson swung towards the man he had thought was carrying a toy pistol. He was falling forward, almost cut in half by Shotgun's Ingram.

'Sorry man,' he panted. 'He got a real one from somewhere. I couldn't warn you.'

Davidson's neck was cold. 'I should have taken it for granted. I was careless.'

Both men looked around at the carnage in that small clearing. The black man's weapon hung at his side. He was shaking.

'We got troubles, Joe.' Davidson heard the tremor in his voice. 'This is an organization job.'

'I thought it was private.'

'That's what I thought.' The man's fear was palpable. 'They told me today it was for the Chinaman. A man called Li.'

'Who is he?' As he spoke, Davidson was aware of the desperate need for haste. There had been the rattle of machine pistols; there was the smell of fired weapons; there were four dead men in the woods. The place would soon be swarming with police.

Shotgun looked helplessly at the figures sprawled in the inelegant postures of death.

'I don't know who he is, but he knows who I am.' He placed the Ingram carefully on the roof of the car. 'If he finds me, I'm dead.'

Above the sounds of the freeway, they heard the wail of sirens.

'Don't worry,' said Davidson. 'I'll get you out of this. Hurry. Help me get the body out of the bush.'

Working swiftly, they brought the body out and laid it near the others but closer to the road. Davidson wiped the Ingram clean, pressed the hands of the guard on the metal casing, and then tossed it on to the sand near the guard. It was primitive and makeshift, but it would confuse the investigators, and might even satisfy them. Shotgun collected the shell casings from the Ingram, rubbed them briskly with a handkerchief and tossed them to the right of the dead man, where they would have been thrown from the fired weapon.

'Now get the hell out of here. No, not to the road. Through the bush. Meet me at my office tonight at nine o'clock. Now go.'

As the black man disappeared into the bush, the police cars slowed and stopped at the skid mark on the black surface.

*   *   *

Superintendent Strickland looked down at the dead guard.

'Strange that he could have been killed by one of his own gang.' He turned his cold perceptive eyes on Davidson. Then his eyes strayed to the police photographer, fingerprint-men and technicians, all busily collecting evidence. Strickland continued without looking back at Davidson. 'How did he manage to do that, do you think?'

Davidson shrugged. 'It wasn't difficult. He dived to the right just as that man fired.' He pointed to the man close to the Ingram.

Strickland stared back, unconvinced. He was a neat, middle-aged man who had impressed Davidson as soon as he entered the copse. He had picked on the one weakness in Davidson's story. How had the third man been killed?

'Hmm. He dives to the left, so his body must have been at an angle, but he gets five bullets in a row across his back.' In spite of his dark suit, Strickland seemed unaffected by the heat. His mouth twitched in a small movement that Davidson interpreted as disapproval. 'And I take it you don't want to make a statement without your lawyer present?'

'Why would you believe that?' He pointed in turn to each of the men he had killed. 'When your ballistics people examine the bullets that killed those men, they will report that they came from my revolver. The one I handed you. I explained how I came to be here and how I killed them. The fourth man was unlucky enough to get in the way of his comrade. I am prepared to give you a statement to that effect without my lawyer present.' He stared into the cold eyes regarding him with displeasure.

The Superintendent turned his back on Davidson and considered the activity around him. He knew that there was something wrong, but there was no evidence that Davidson had lied. He had never met Davidson, but he had heard of him; of his marksmanship, his professionalism, and the ruthless single-mindedness with which he pursued his objectives. He might not be on the side of the angels, but he was on the side of the law, yet Strickland contemplated him with the kind of displeasure policemen reserve for civilians who involve themselves in the pursuit of criminals.

Strickland pursed his mouth. 'You say you received information about a planned hold-up. Why didn't you notify Murder and Robbery?'

'Because my source was unreliable. He had been wrong twice before. I wanted to check it out, but they arrived while I was here.'

Davidson indicated the bodies. 'There was nothing else I could do.' He was aware of the fading light. He curbed his impatience.

'I will want the name of your informant.'

Davidson assumed a rueful expression.

'I'm sorry. I don't know who it was. He never gives his name.' He looked at his watch. 'You will have to excuse me, Superintendent. I have to attend to some important matters. I will call at your office in the morning.'

As he walked away, he was conscious of the superintendent's stare following him out of the copse. The superintendent was angry, not because he knew there was something about Davidson's story that did not add up, but because he knew the man would receive a substantial reward for recovering the money. The policeman grudgingly acknowledged that Davidson was entitled to it. After all, it was not likely that the man had risked his life because he was public-spirited.

*　　*　　*

At 3 Garnet Road, Durban North, the woman heard the buzz of her door speaker. She moved swiftly to the net-curtained window from where she could see the figure on the porch. The man had enquired about the Lindquists. She wanted to scream epithets at him. Somehow, she knew he would be bad news, but she took a moment to compose herself. She pressed the speaker button.

'Yes, who is it?'

'Harry Collins, ma'am. I called yesterday about the Lindquists.'

'What is it now?' She could not control the

66

slight impatience in her voice. She paused for a moment. 'I'm sorry. I can't come out now. I'm alone.'

'That's OK, ma'am. I have just one more question. What kind of car did the Lindquists drive?'

She was silent for a long time, wondering whether she should deceive him. Then she wondered if it mattered.

'Ma'am?'

'I was trying to remember.' She paused. 'Yes. It was one of those foreign cars. Italian, I think. An Alfa something.'

'An Alfa Romeo.' She heard the satisfaction in his voice. 'Thank you, ma'am. I won't trouble you again.'

She went swiftly to the window and watched him drive away. Back in the study, she dialled the overseas number.

'Victor please. It's urgent.' She went through the recognition procedure. When Victor came on the line, she heard the impatience in his voice.

'Yes. What is it?'

She told him about her caller.

There was silence for a moment. 'That settles it. I want them both dead. Him and the woman at Seaview.'

Her voice shook. 'Who shall I give it to?' She was terrified by Victor's ruthlessness.

'Damn it.' His voice was almost a shriek. 'I don't care who does it. Just get it done.' The line went dead.

Her hand shook as she gently replaced the handset. She had better get the Chinaman in at once.

* * *

Ramona Gomez stood with the group outside the school gate. As the crossing monitor signalled them, they surged forward, some heading for the bus stop on the corner, others turning left towards Venice Road. Ramona walked on alone towards Sutton Park, where she paused as she always did, tempted to go through the park. It was a choice she faced daily, and until now she had never taken the shorter way. That way was the stuff of bad dreams; it was the way of dark shadows and flitting shapes in the undergrowth, and of silence and fear. She recalled her mother's strictures: never take sweets from strangers; never get into a stranger's car; never walk in lonely places by yourself.

Ramona looked along the path through the park, took a deep breath, and made an important decision. She turned into the park and walked towards the public swimming pool at the far gate.

A classmate at the bus stop saw her disappear from view, and the police determined later that she was the only witness to the girl's disappearance.

*   *   *

It was after eleven when Davidson returned from his office, but although he had rung her to tell her he was safe, she was still waiting for him. She led him into the darkened living-room, where the only light came from a small lamp in the corner. Davidson sank into the recliner. While the study was his domain, this room was hers. She had impressed her personality on the whole room, from the tasteful fabrics to the choice of furniture.

She returned, setting the tray on the centre table. She placed his cup on the small table beside his chair, pulled her robe around her, and sat on the sofa, her legs tucked under her. She watched him sip his coffee.

He looked at her over his cup and growled accusingly:

'You waited up. You shouldn't have.'

'You know you'd have been disappointed if I hadn't. So don't give me a hard time.'

He grunted. 'You go off to bed. I have to wait for Harry Collins. He insisted on seeing me tonight.'

'I'll go if you want me to, but I'd rather wait with you.' She paused. 'If it's private . . .'

He waved a dismissive hand.

'It's not private. I'd like you to stay.' He closed his eyes and leant on the headrest. He had told her a little of the events of the day, and she had guessed the rest.

This was a part of him that always perplexed her. It saddened her too, that the man she loved was sometimes portrayed as a ruthless man without a shred of compassion. While she acknowledged that he had killed in self-defence, she knew him as he really was; he was sensitive and kind and she could understand the apparent contradiction, because she knew the complexities of his early years.

He was a product of those grey, post-war years when, to survive, a whole family had to find employment in a job market flooded with ex-servicemen. He had told her of a time when he had run wild with a pack of ten-year-olds led by Alf Collins, Harry's father. They slept amongst the sand dunes at the Country Club Beach and they lived by finding lost golf balls and selling them back to affluent golfers. He had told her of the fight to retain what was theirs against older predators, some of whom were armed with clubs and knives. As they grew older, they learnt that they needed one another, and as they honed their skills against formidable opponents, potential adversaries learnt to avoid them. It was a familiar pattern, a game played out in every big city in the world, but as he spoke of those times, Margaret began to discern, within the dark pattern of his life, the ray of light that Davidson could not conceal from himself. While both his parents worked long hours, they always gave him the devotion and guidance that diverted him from the path of delinquency.

She had never met Alf Collins, who had been killed in Angola during South Africa's ill-advised incursion into that country. Nonetheless, she felt that she knew him through Harry Collins.

She was always aware of how different her own life had been. She had spent the whole of her life in an environment regulated by the canons of polite society. She had been coddled when very young, and protected while growing up. Her father, a wealthy architect, had given her love, but blended it with a firm refusal to allow her the latitude enjoyed by her peers. Strangely enough, she did not resent this, but considered it sufficient if she could make her own decision when it really mattered. She surmised that it was this difference in their circumstances that had captivated her, and attracted him. They were drawn to one another by the knowledge that each had so much to contribute to the shared experience.

Harry Collins arrived on the stroke of midnight. He was carrying a manila envelope. He greeted Margaret with a hug and a kiss on the forehead.

'You're looking more beautiful every day.'

Davidson growled. 'You watch out for him. He's as bad as his father. Flattered every girl in sight, even those over sixty.'

Harry laughed. 'And with good reason. Dad could get anything he wanted, whether it was a date or get his shirts ironed.'

She laughed. 'I'll get you some coffee.'

Davidson held up his hand in mock resignation. 'You see. He's done it again.'

She smiled, touched his hand, and went out to the kitchen. By the time Harry had described the call from Betty Rolands, Margaret returned with the coffee.

Davidson looked thoughtful. 'Betty Rolands. I remember her. Quiet girl. A caring type.'

'The same. She asked me to see old man Kelsey. It seems he hasn't heard from his daughter for nearly a year.' He took the photograph and letters from the envelope. 'I called on him two days ago. He gave me some of her correspondence and this.' He handed the photograph to Davidson. He related how he had visited the first address on the postcard, and what he had found. He described the house and what Mrs Eripides had told him about the departure of the tenants. 'There was a fresh bloodstain on a bedroom carpet.' He took the small plastic bag from his pocket. 'I took this sample.' He placed it on the letters. 'They had two visitors. One of them was Chinese.'

Davidson's scalp prickled. 'Do you think the girl was murdered?'

Harry shrugged. 'I don't know. I can't even

72

say whether it is her blood. I would like to get it analysed.'

'I'll arrange it in the morning.'

Harry nodded. 'Right.' He picked up the redirected postcard. 'I went out to this address today.' He described the old lady who had answered the door, and what she had told him about the midnight disappearance. 'Now according to the old lady, it wasn't the same girl and it wasn't the same Lindquist.' His brow furrowed with exasperation. 'Otherwise all the circumstances were identical.'

'And their car?'

Harry nodded with satisfaction. 'I had forgotten to ask. I went back to Garnet Road.' He smiled. 'Same car, and probably the same trailer.'

'But different girl and different Lindquist.'

'The old woman didn't think it was the same girl, but there must have been a common human factor, if the car was common to both couples.'

There was a long silence in the shadowy room. There was no sound of traffic on the highway, and Harry was reminded of the lateness of the hour.

Davidson nodded slowly. 'It seems we are assailed by Chinamen. The bank robbery today was planned by a man named Li.' He lifted his hand. 'I know there is more than one Chinaman in Durban, but it seems strange that we are presented with three at once.'

Suddenly the shrill sound of the telephone startled them.

Margaret went out to answer it. The men were silent, listening to the soft murmur of her voice. She came back into the room.

'It's for you, Harry.'

Collins went through to the study. It was his partner, McGrath.

'One of the night-shift men got a call from the police. He rang me at home. You're to ring this number.'

Harry reached for his pen and jotted down the number.

'Thanks, Mac. I'll keep you informed.'

'Do that, but do it in daylight.' McGrath slammed down the phone.

Harry dialled the number on the pad, and listened to the quiet voice on the other end. 'OK,' he said. 'I'll be there as soon as I can.' He went through to the living-room. 'I have to go out to Seaview.'

Davidson looked startled. 'Now? At this time of night?'

'Now,' Harry said. 'There's been a killing at Rydal Avenue.'

Davidson sighed. 'I'll come with you. The night's been shot to hell, anyway.'

CHAPTER SIX

Mrs Eripides sat very still behind the net curtain in an upstairs bedroom. For twenty minutes now she had been sitting in the darkened room, watching the car across the street. When the light sweeping across her bedroom window awakened her, she rose from her bed and crept to the front room to sit behind the curtain. The car appeared to be empty, but her patience was rewarded when she saw the glow of a match and a nebulous drift of smoke, which told her that someone was either watching or waiting.

She had moved upstairs to accommodate a new tenant in the downstairs flat and had spent that day cleaning the rooms. She had left the kitchen light on.

Mrs Eripides was, as Harry Collins so rightly observed, a lot smarter than people gave her credit for. As a small animal watches a snake, so Mrs Eripides watched the man in the car. She was uneasy, sensing danger in the dark shape behind the drifting smoke. She hesitated a moment and then went to a bureau in the sitting-room. From a bottom drawer, she took out a Smith & Wesson revolver. She loaded six rounds into the cylinder. She had not used it since her father died, but she kept it cleaned and oiled. From the top drawer she took a pair of binoculars and went back to the window.

She half-hoped the man had gone, but with a perverse tingle of excitement she saw that he was still there. She saw a movement, and the door of the car clicked open as the man took a quiet step into the street. Her heart thumped when she saw that the short stubby shape in the man's hand was a machine pistol. She had seen enough television to recognize the destructive force of the weapon he held. He made no sound as he crossed the quiet street; it was like watching a silent film. For a moment she felt that she was part of a nightmare, then all at once she was overcome with a surging return to reality. She told herself that this man was carrying a gun that could be aimed at her. Was she his quarry? Why? What had she done to deserve his wrath?

Fear drove at her. Her mind darted back and forth, searching for some means of escape. She stood quite still, thinking. Then finally she felt a growing anger that smothered her fear. She was filled with a furious indignation. For no reason that she knew of, someone had come into her life to take it from her.

She walked quickly through to her sewing-room where she had hoarded the accumulated jumble of decades. There were trunks of clothing, boxes of materials, several old sewing -machines, and three dressmaker's dummies on wheeled plinths. She took an old dress from a cardboard box and slipped it over the one with a faceless head. Then she covered the head with a shawl. Quickly she carried it down the back stairs and, unlocking the back door, pushed it down the passage to the front of the house. She moved it several times before she was satisfied with the position she had decided upon. It was a metre and a half from the door and directly in front of it.

Then she waited, listening. It was still quiet outside, but intermittent rumbles of thunder were approaching from the south-east. She knew the man would have heard her moving about. She looked once more at the dummy. It was not quite discernible in the reflected glow of the kitchen light. She switched on the living-room standard lamp. There. That was perfect.

At that moment the front-door bell rang, throwing her into a moment of panic. She took two deep breaths and called out:

'Just a moment. I'm coming.'

She moved quietly to the left of the jamb, so that the opening door would not hinder her. With the gun in her right hand, she reached across with her left and slid the chain across. Now the key. It took an immense effort of will to let the man in. She turned the key with shaking hand, and then paused a moment before throwing open the door. She was facing the dummy with her back to the wall.

The shattering noise of the machine pistol left her momentarily paralysed. It was the sight of the dummy exploding in all directions that galvanized her. The man was in the doorway, twelve inches from her, but with his attention on the mangled dummy on the floor, he failed to see her in the dark. She heard the bark of the Smith & Wesson and felt the gun bucking in her hands. She saw the man jerk sideways. Then he fell backwards down the steps.

Mrs Eripides' legs collapsed under her. Breathing deeply, she sat for a moment before lifting herself to her feet. She looked at the revolver in her hand and at the bundle on the step. She spoke with quiet venom.

'That will teach you, you bastard. That will show you I'm no dummy.'

*   *   *

Distant lightning flashed within the deep thunderheads piling up in the southern sky. The muffled growls of thunder were almost continuous, and with them came the strong gusts of wind ushering in the summer storm. Davidson lifted his chin from the recesses of his overcoat.

'We're in for it tonight. At least a couple of inches.'

As he spoke the first heavy drops splashed on the windscreen. Within seconds, the water was cascading from the sky. The wipers laboured against the wall of water that bucketed down. Harry slowed at the Bellair

78

roundabout and turned east to Seaview, and five minutes later he drove into Rydal Avenue. Through the driving downpour, they saw the flashing lights of police cars.

As they stopped Davidson raised his voice over the drumming of the rain.

'Tell me about the old woman.'

'Mrs Eripides?'

Davidson nodded. 'What's she like?'

'About sixty-five, with the usual head of grey hair. Good education. Family had money.' Harry turned to look at Davidson. 'Looks like your average senior citizen but don't underestimate her intelligence. She's smart.' He added thoughtfully: 'I think she's lived alone long enough to develop her own set of values.'

Davidson smiled. 'Seems a likeable sort.'

'Definitely. You'll like her. Shall we go in?' As he spoke, two police cars drew away from the house.

The two men hurried across the road and up the steps. Mrs Eripides opened the door, held her fingers to her lips, and ushered them into the living-room. As they entered, a young constable turned from the window.

Mrs Eripides gestured towards him.

'This is Constable Radebe.' The black man nodded slightly. 'Superintendent Blain left him here until you arrived. I told the superintendent my cousin and his son were coming.' Her face was expressionless as she looked at the constable. 'Thank you for staying. There is no need to wait any longer.'

He looked at her with concern. 'Are you sure you are all right?'

'I'm sure.'

'Then I'll go back to the station.' He went into the hall. They heard the front door closing. Mrs Eripides hung their coats on the coat tree.

Mrs Eripides went to her armchair.

'Please sit down.' She sighed. 'I thought they would never leave.' She shuddered. 'At least they had the kindness to wash the blood from the steps. I could not have done it myself.' She looked at Harry. 'It's not like it was with the blood in the front room. I had nothing to do with that.' She paused. 'You're Joe Davidson. Harry told me all about you.'

Harry realized that in spite of her apparent calm, her fingers on her lap were tightly laced.

Davidson smiled.

'I'm sure it was slanderous.' The rain was easing, but a last defiant thunderclap startled them. 'Why don't you tell us what happened?'

'Before I begin, I should offer you some refreshment.'

Sensing that the activity might help her ease her stress, Harry said quickly: 'A beer would be nice.'

She looked at Davidson, who nodded. 'The same for me.'

She went out to the kitchen, returning with

80

a tray of bottles and glasses. As she poured the beer, Harry said quietly:

'You realize, Mrs Eripides . . .'

'Please call me Grace.'

'You realize, Grace, that I am to blame for all that happened here tonight.'

She placed her glass on the small table beside her.

'I guessed it was something to do with Kay Kelsey. But no one could blame you. You didn't know you were being watched.'

Davidson nodded agreement.

'When Harry came here looking for Kay Kelsey, it was like poking a hornet's nest with a stick.'

Suddenly, Harry felt an icy touch of fear. It had never occurred to him that he was being followed. There was no doubt that Mrs Eripides was smart.

The rain had stopped, and the occasional rolls of thunder were becoming more distant. In spite of the receding storm, the tension was palpable. The alien terror that had burst upon this house had invaded every corner, banishing the aura of comfortable security that had lain there for decades. The room, once redolent with the smell of furniture polish, Brasso and musty furniture, was now tainted with the odour of violence. Mrs Eripides knew she would never sleep another night in this house without fear.

Her thoughts returned to Joe Davidson's

81

question.

'Someone tried to kill me and I don't know why.'

Her voice was firm as she recounted every moment from the time the man arrived with a machine pistol, to the moment the body tumbled down the stairs. When she stopped there was a long silence.

At last Davidson spoke.

'I tell you, Grace, that was the most courageous thing I have ever heard.'

She lifted her shoulders.

'It was the only thing I could do. The police asked me why I was attacked. I couldn't tell them.' She paused. 'I told them I had never seen the man before. I don't know if the superintendent believed me.' She frowned. 'I didn't tell them about the couple who stayed here—or about Harry.'

My word, Harry thought, she was smart. She knew that if the police knew, then everyone would know. It was safer if the people who wanted her killed thought she had no idea why she was targeted.

Harry said: 'Who was the man? Had you seen him before?'

She looked at him as though he was half-witted.

'Of course. He was one of the two men who called on the Lindquists. The short bald one.' A tight smile touched the corners of her mouth. 'I heard the super say he knew him.

Said he was Lawrence Hatfield. He had a police record.'

Davidson shook his head.

'Incredible. Three Chinese men and now two men named Lawrence.'

Harry nodded. 'From Three Garnet Road.'

Davidson placed his empty glass on the small table. 'I think it's time to tell Grace what we know. Then we'll lock up here and take her with us.'

Davidson's cellphone tinkled softly. He took it from his pocket. As he listened to the caller, Harry watched him expectantly. Davidson spoke briefly and switched off the phone.

'That was Margaret. She has had two calls since we left. Both asking if she knew where you are.' Davidson looked at his watch. 'Someone wants you badly.'

As they drove away from Rydal Avenue the eastern sky was being tinged with an orange glow, while from the south a light breeze was shredding the clouds, scattering them across the western horizon.

*   *   *

Ramona Gomez was cold and frightened. A grill-covered glass dome high up on the wall lighted the room. The furniture consisted of a double bunk bed, a table, and two chairs. There were two doors, one leading to a flight of stairs with a locked trap-door at the top, and the other to a toilet and shower.

She lay now on the bottom bunk, curled up tightly, her knuckles against her mouth. As she sobbed, her body shuddered with each breath. A black girl was asleep on the bunk above her, her tears still marking her cheeks.

An elderly woman delivered food. She always carried a police truncheon, which was held on her wrist by a leather thong.

Ramona had no idea how long she had been held in this room. When she awoke from a drug-induced sleep, she had been alone. She had slept for a while, and when she opened her eyes a second time the black girl had been on the bunk.

Slowly her sobs ceased, her breathing deepened, and for a few brief hours, merciful sleep enveloped her once more. As she slept, banner headlines in the country's newspapers proclaimed:

**DEVELOPMENT IN MISSING
CHILDREN MYSTERY.**

*   *   *

Georg Gomez stared at the photograph on the desk in front of him. The three people were looking happily at the camera; the father was looking fondly at his daughter; the mother had her head back and her face was creased with laughter, while her daughter was smiling at someone out of range of the camera.

Ramona had disappeared two days later.

Grief took him and shook him in waves that tore sobs from his throat. In her room, his wife heard the sounds of his agony as she woke from a deep sleep in which she dreamt that her child had been found. When she realized she was still in the midst of her nightmare, she cried out in her own agony.

She wondered how long her torment would last, or if it would ever end.

CHAPTER SEVEN

Harry Collins woke at noon, showered and donned a pair of fawn slacks, a cream shirt and a cream-and-brown tie. He looked down at the Marine Parade, and saw the heat shimmering on the macadam and decided against a jacket. He looked in the refrigerator and concluded it was too much effort to prepare lunch. He decided to eat at the restaurant on the ground floor. He walked through to Collins Security and found Mrs Grant alone at the reception desk. She looked up from her computer.

'Jordan Stolz wants you to phone him. The payroll was late again today.' She forestalled his objections. 'He won't talk to McGrath. He's got the shits, and wants to move his business to Brandon-Kelvin Security.'

Occasionally his staid, middle-aged secretary shocked him with her outspoken perspective on company problems. It was her way of demonstrating her disapproval.

He used the telephone on her desk. Jordan Stolz answered almost at once. His voice was harsh and abrupt. Harry spoke quickly.

'Jordan, it's Harry. Mrs Grant said you weren't happy with our service.'

'I'm bloody disgusted with it.'

Before he could continue, Harry broke in. 'Jordan, you're a valuable customer. Here's what I'll do. I'll buy a new vehicle and allocate it exclusively to your company.' He saw Mrs Grant's urgent signal. 'Hold on a moment, Jordan.' He pressed the instrument mute button.

'It wasn't the vehicle. It was standing by. The cashiers were late.'

He nodded and disabled the mute button. 'Jordan, Mrs Grant has explained the problem. I will put an accountant full time on your account.'

'I don't care a stuff what you do, Harry. Be late one more time and the contract is cancelled.'

'Understood.' He replaced the phone. He looked at Mrs Grant's pursed lips and shrugged. 'What could I do. Please let Mac know what I've promised Stolz.'

'He won't like it.'

'So what else is new?'

Mrs Grant sniffed.

'That's a damned silly remark.'

Harry grinned as he left the office. He took the lift to the ground floor and lunched at the Blue Band. He ordered a small plate of calamari and chips and filter coffee. Half an hour later he was crossing the Umgeni River towards Durban North. He entered Grosvenor Place and stopped in front of a house finished with clinker-brick facings and a red-tiled roof. He locked his car and went along a brick-paved path to the front door.

He was about to knock when he heard a raised voice from somewhere in the house.

'I don't want that bastard visiting this house.'

'You've never met him.' The voice was unmistakably Betty Rolands's. 'He's doing me a favour by looking for Kay Kelsey.'

He wondered whether he should retreat and return later, but was aware that the road was visible from the house. He shrugged mentally, and rang the doorbell. The voices were silenced.

The door opened to reveal a maid in a black apron and white cap. She stood aside to admit him.

'Mrs Rolands is expecting you. She is in the lounge.' The maid had a strong Zulu accent.

As he entered the hall Betty Rolands appeared from the passage. Harry paused, and for a few seconds, there were no years of separation between them. Her hair was different, softer, with just a hint of grey, but the lovely face was as young as he remembered it, without a sign of the passing years. Only then did he see the bruise high up on the cheek that marred the perfection of her features. Instinctively she touched her cheek, and just as quickly dropped her hand. She walked forward to greet him.

'Harry! It's good of you to come.' She led the way into the lounge.

He paused inside the doorway, looking curiously at the furnishings, suddenly envious of the man who had provided this opulence for Betty Rolands. Then he realized that no man could have possessed such impeccable taste. The delicate shades of the suite fabrics were repeated in the curtains, while the few carefully chosen ornaments complemented the style of the décor. She gestured to a comfortable chair near the window and sat opposite him on the sofa, her fingers laced and her ankles crossed. For a moment he was disconcerted by the familiar pose. It seemed to him that nothing about her had changed. He was overwhelmed by the familiar emotions that had so nearly destroyed him. As though she sensed what was in his mind, she stood up quickly.

'I haven't offered you anything.'

Harry shook his head. 'Nothing for me, thank you.'

She sank back on the sofa. He wondered where her husband was. Apparently he had elected to stay out of sight. What was his name? Then he remembered. Rupert. That was it. 'How is Rupert?'

In a reflexive action, her hand moved to her face and stopped. Flustered, she glanced towards the bedroom.

'He's well. He's dressing. He's on his way out.' Her fingers became restless. 'Have you made any headway?'

'Not yet. But someone doesn't want us to find her.' He recounted the events of the past three days.

Her hand went to her cheek. 'Oh, I am so sorry. I didn't realize . . .'

Rupert Rolands appeared in the doorway.

'No! You never damn well think.' He stood, hands clenched, his faced suffused with anger. 'I told you this man is trouble. I will not have you involved.' He looked at Harry. 'You will drop this now. Whatever it is, leave it alone.' He turned to his wife, spittle flecking the corner of his mouth. 'I want this man out of my house at once. Get rid of him now.'

Harry looked at Betty. She was white-faced, her knuckles hard against her teeth, naked fear in her eyes. He stood up.

'Look, Rolands. I will do whatever—'

'Harry, no! Do what he says.'

Harry shrugged. 'If that's what you want.'

There was a long silence. Eventually

89

Rolands stalked to the door. He stood for a moment, striving to control himself.

'Pay this bastard off and get him out of here.' He went into the passage, and they heard the front door slam.

There was absolute silence until they heard his car leave the house.

Betty put her face in her hands, her shoulders shaking as she sobbed silently. He went to her.

'Stand up.'

'Why?'

'Just do as I say.'

She watched his face as she stood up. He took her in his arms and pulled her head to his shoulder.

'Now you can cry.' He felt her body shaking uncontrollably. 'Go on. Let it go.'

She relaxed and the tears coursed down her cheeks.

At last she stood back and looked up at him.

'Oh Harry, what have we done?'

'We tried to do an old man a favour. It isn't our fault.'

Her lips trembled. 'I mean us, Harry. How did we let it get away from us?' As her eyes filled once more, she dropped her arms and walked away from him. She went into the passage.

Harry went to the window and looked out at the sun-drenched garden. Several starlings flew up from the lawn into a pink tibouchina.

Harry knew now that he still loved her. He went to the front door, knowing he would have to leave. Her voice called him back.

'Don't go Harry. We have to talk.'

He turned hesitantly and went back to the lounge. She sat opposite him on the sofa.

'I haven't been entirely honest with you. Mr Kelsey didn't approach me. I went to him.' She held up her hand as he began to speak. 'No, Harry, let me finish.' She plucked at her skirt. 'Some months ago, I went to the Blue Bonnet in Cowey Road to meet a friend. I saw Rupert and Kay Kelsey at a table near the back. They were in earnest conversation. They didn't see me and I left at once. That night I asked him where he had gone for lunch.' Her eyes reflected her misery. 'He said he hadn't left the office.'

'So you went to Mr Kelsey for answers?'

She nodded forlornly. 'He hadn't heard from Kay for months, and he hadn't any idea who Rupert was. I didn't enlighten him.'

'And you thought I would turn up something?'

She thought for a while, frowning as she stared at the ormolu clock.

'For a while I believed I was doing it for Mr Kelsey. Then I had to confess that my motives were selfish.' She was thoughtful once more. 'I mentioned her several times in casual conversation. He didn't react at all. He behaved as though he had never met her.'

Harry walked to the sofa and sat down beside her.

'Why did he hit you?'

She looked up, her eyes brimming with tears.

'He never needed a reason.'

He took her hand. 'Do you love him?'

She shook her head. 'I haven't loved him for years.'

'Why don't you leave him?'

'I dare not. You saw him just now.' She touched his face. 'I know now, there was never anyone else but you.'

Harry stood up and walked to the window. All at once, he remembered the words of a poem he had learnt long ago.

True love comes only once,
And all the rest is lies

He smiled wryly. He was becoming maudlin. He turned to find her watching him.

'I love you too, but this is not the time to talk about it.' He went to the door. 'I have to find out what happened to Kay Kelsey.' He turned to leave.

'Harry.' He looked back. 'I'm going to ask him anyway.' She paused. 'For the divorce.'

Harry smiled. 'If he doesn't give it to you, I'll kill him for you.' He closed the door behind him.

CHAPTER EIGHT

The safe house was located in a short cul-de-sac off North Ridge Road on the Berea. It consisted of three bedrooms, lounge, dining-room, and a large, well-equipped kitchen.

Captain Roberts heard the signal from the microwave and took out the scrambled eggs. He took the bowl to the table, and went to the dresser for the plates. He called out:

'Janet. It's ready.'

The girl came out of the bathroom, sniffing appreciatively.

'Looks good. What is it?'

'Don't be sarcastic. It's the same as you had yesterday and the day before. Scrambled eggs, tomato, onion and bacon chips.'

She looked at him with wide eyes. 'What do you know? It *is* the same.' She sat down at the table.

He handed her a plate of eggs. 'Like it or not you'll eat it. The cupboard is bare.' He poured the coffee. 'I'm the best cook in the house.'

'Cheeky too.'

'Shut up and eat.' He finished before she did and carried his plate to the sink. 'The washing-up is your chore. Don't be long. The old man will be here in an hour.' He looked down at her shabby robe. 'And don't forget to dress. I believe that particular uniform is no longer acceptable.'

'Get stuffed.' She ate the last of the egg, finished her toast and coffee, and took her plate to the sink. 'That, Robbie, was the best damn breakfast I've had since yesterday.' She turned on the faucet. 'Don't let it go to your head.'

'If we're here tomorrow, breakfast is on you.'

'What about scrambled egg?'

He glared at her as he carried out the garbage.

The man they called Uncle John arrived promptly at ten o'clock. As he came in the front door, a garden-service crew arrived and made heavy weather of mowing the lawn. Captain Roberts remarked drily:

'Someone had better teach security how to mow.'

Uncle John smiled, pulled out a chair at the head of the dining-room table, and opened his briefcase. He placed a green folder beside it. He wasted no time in getting down to business.

'Gaffney still has no idea that you were the mole. You were lucky that it was his idea that you should remain downstairs during the Florence exchange.' He smiled. Janet thought it was a little smug.

'The letter we allowed him to smuggle out indicated that he thought the Swiss police were responsible.' He opened the green folder. 'His

94

instruction to you to make contact with Victor Piper was a bonus for us.' He looked at the girl. 'Are you absolutely certain that it was Piper you heard in the Florence hotel?'

She nodded quickly. 'There is no doubt in my mind. I could never forget him.'

'And he remains convinced that your smuggling operation is the key to his business?'

'Definitely. He has no alternative.'

Uncle John nodded with satisfaction. 'In the meantime, there are two questions requiring immediate attention.' He held up a stubby forefinger. 'Why was an attempt made on the life of Mrs Eripides.' He added his middle finger. 'Who were the two men who visited her and spirited her away?'

Roberts frowned. 'Relatives perhaps?'

'She doesn't have any relatives. The constable who was left there thought he had seen one of them before. He isn't sure, but he thinks it was a police matter.' He looked at Janet as he dug into the briefcase. He handed her some eight-by-six police photographs. 'Go through this lot and see if you can spot our Chinese friend.' He held up his hand. 'I know he called himself Li, but we want his real name. His name will tell us which triad he belongs to.' He smiled. 'And don't say that all Chinese men look the same to you.'

'This one is different,' she said. 'This one is a cold-blooded killer.'

'We dare not make any arrests until we find

the missing children. If we do the gang will scatter.' He looked at each of them in turn. 'You know what will happen to the children then.'

*   *   *

Harry Collins drove into the car park behind the group of simplexes, turned the car to face the exit, and switched off the engine. Davidson's flat was at the south end, with the entrance facing away from the others. Two doors away a young woman in jeans and a long-sleeved blue shirt laboured in the hot sun. She was planting seedlings in a freshly prepared strip alongside the wall. Her dibble was a wicked-looking tool that could have doubled as a pike. She looked up and smiled as he walked past her. Her face was red with exertion, and her hair had escaped from her headscarf. She had wisely protected her arms from the burning sun, but Harry thought it would have been wiser to stay indoors.

Davidson met him at the door and led him into the living-room.

'Margaret's out shopping. Can I offer you anything?'

Harry shook his head. 'Perhaps later.' He pulled at his lip.

Davidson watched him patiently. He knew the young man was troubled, and he suspected that his visit to Betty Rolands had affected him in some way. He waited for Harry to compose himself. At last, Harry sighed deeply.

'She's changed, Joe. She's defeated, crushed, and beaten into submission.'

He recounted the facts of his meeting with Rolands, and Betty's reasons for sending him to Kelsey. 'I know that sending me to Kelsey wasn't just to uncover an affair. Kay Kelsey really is missing, Joe.' He stood up and looked out of the window. 'That bastard actually beats her.'

Davidson looked at him in surprise. 'Kelsey, you mean?'

'Rolands.'

In the silence, Harry heard the ticking of the clock on the mantelpiece. It seemed a sad reminder of the wasted years. Memories fought for cognizance, things he thought he had forgotten, recollections of a more careless time. He returned to his seat at the window. He was smiling. 'She was loyal, Joe.'

Davidson knew silence was the best remedy for what ailed him. Harry was staring out of the window, reliving something from the past.

'We were about ten years old. Two boys from the school decided I needed a lesson. Before they could begin, this whirlwind came in swinging, beating them about the head with her satchel. They never had a chance. She knocked them both into the gutter, daring them to get up.' Harry smiled. 'From that moment I was known as the kid with a female bodyguard.' His expression changed to anger.

'She has guts, Joe, but Rolands has turned her into a frightened child. Her courage wasn't only physical. She had a moral courage that nothing could dent.'

Davidson nodded sympathetically.

'I understand how you feel, Harry, but you know that external interference exacerbates a situation like that.'

Harry sighed. 'You're right. As Mrs Eripides said, this doesn't get the baby washed.' He smiled. 'Where have you stashed Grace? Not on a banana boat to the Caribbean, I hope?'

'Not bloody likely. I sent her to a secluded spot near Margate.' He laughed. 'When she heard, she threatened to buy a tanga.' Davidson looked at him thoughtfully. 'You know, Harry. I feel that the Durban North house is the key to everything. I feel we should turn it over. Preferably late tonight.'

He stood up and went to the tray on the coffee table. He poured two glasses of fruit juice. He handed one to Harry. 'Did you tell her you suspect that Kay Kelsey's dead?'

'No. I didn't think she was in a state to handle it.' He sipped the juice, then went back to the window. 'And we're not even sure she *is* dead.' His voice trailed off as he peered to the left and right of the garden. 'Your gardening neighbour appears to have given up. Too hot,

I expect.'

Davidson joined him at the window. 'What neighbour?'

'The lady planting seedlings two doors down. Number five.'

Davidson felt the slow prickle of his scalp, and the familiar presentiment of danger.

'That flat belongs to Winnie and Jimmy Conroy. They've been away for two weeks. Margaret checks on things every morning.'

'Perhaps they engaged a garden service.'

'No. We would have known.' He frowned. 'Surely they wouldn't be so blatant.' He frowned. 'But then, why not? She could always claim she had come to the wrong flat. Or even the wrong block.'

'They want me badly, Joe.' The apprehension Harry felt at knowing he was the target of dangerous men was mingled with a burning anger at the insolent malice of people who believed that no one would challenge them.

'She may still be around.'

Davidson went to his study, took the Ghisoni from the gun safe, and put a spare load in his pocket. He led the way to the kitchen, looked through the fine net curtain, and saw the dibble stabbed into the turf at the edge of the strip of garden. There was no sign of the woman.

Harry looked over his shoulder.

'That's what she was using.'

'It belongs to Dorothy. She leaves it under the step.'

Davidson opened the back door. The whole complex was deserted, the silence unbroken except for the distant sounds of traffic.

'Obviously she got what she came for.'

'What do you think it was?'

'Information. I surmise it was to establish our whereabouts. I suspect something has happened or is about to happen.'

Both were aware that the situation had gone beyond a missing girl. The tension wrought by the danger that stalked them would not end until the syndicate was destroyed.

Davidson was clearly angry. 'It's time to go on the offensive. I'm not sitting down for this. How dare they invade my space.' He looked at Harry thoughtfully. 'The only lead we have is the house in Durban North. Meet me here at nine tonight and bring some firepower.'

Harry smiled. 'Right. And a couple of radios from McGrath.'

Davidson smiled wolfishly. 'It's time we gave someone a bloody nose.'

*   *   *

General John Anders walked along the passage from his office to the communications room two doors along the corridor. Although the building that housed his headquarters was pleasant enough, he preferred the solitude of

Rafters Canine Breeders. There, he was Uncle John; here he was General Anders, with all the bureaucracy that the rank entailed.

He went to a console and lifted the headset. He spoke to a spare, grey-haired man at the supervisor's desk.

'An agent will call in three minutes. I'll take it here.'

As the second hand crept around the face of the big clock on the wall, Anders sat immobile in the comfortable chair. Behind him, multicoloured lights flashed on a bank of consoles. The muted voices of the operators impinged on his consciousness as he waited. He knew that at this moment the operation was delicately poised, capable of going either way, and he needed to know that he had covered every eventuality. Code-named 'Asparagus', the man for whom he waited was his ace in the hole. Anders was the sole recipient of the intelligence emanating from that source and, indeed, only he and his agent were aware of the fact that a third person was a factor in the equation. Roberts and La Barre were unaware of the existence of his most skilled operative.

The light flashed in front of him.

'Anders here.'

'I'm at a call box. Number one two one.'

Anders punched the number into the computer. He watched the positioning grid stop, and a red circle appeared at the junction of two streets. 'I have the location.'

'The Kloof bank robbery is definitely linked to Victor Piper. The Chinese man planned it. A man named Davidson stopped the robbery.'

'That information was in my box this morning.'

The agent knew he was referring to a scrambled electronic signal. 'It seems that it was Davidson who appeared at Rydal Avenue after the shooting.'

'Now that is interesting.'

'I have identified eight of the gang members. Their names are in the next box.'

'Well done.'

'I have located two of the girls, but Victor keeps the rest in four groups. They are never together.'

'Then we dare not move in on any of them. We have to get them all at once.'

'I must go. The car has come for me.'

'Try and keep to the schedule.' Anders paused. 'If it is impossible, send me a box.'

'Understood.' The receiver was replaced.

Anders removed the headset. He stretched, stood up wearily, and left the communications room.

CHAPTER NINE

Ramona Gomez sat up quickly in the darkened room, wakened by a pinprick in her right arm. She whimpered as a hand grasped her shoulder.

'Quiet.' The woman's voice was harsh. Ramona could not tell whether she was young or old. She knew only that she was without compassion. In the dark, her captor was just a shape holding her tightly until she felt the familiar creeping lassitude. This was the third time they had drugged her, and she knew it would not be the last, until her father came for her. Throughout her nightmare, she continued to believe he would come for her.

Eventually darkness filled her mind, and she slept, unaware of the arms that carried her up the steps from the cellar. Then they came for the other two, the black girl and the older white girl, and carried them into the night. Outside, the wind howled and the rain beat against the walls of the house.

*　　　*　　　*

By midnight, a wild south-easter had sent louring clouds scudding along the coast, bringing squalls that drove the rain across the city.

Inside the car, their warm breath misted the windows and first Davidson and then Collins rubbed a cloth over the windscreen. In the house a hundred metres away, a solitary light burned behind a curtain on the top floor.

Harry shifted uneasily. 'I wonder if the old bitch ever sleeps.'

Davidson ran the cloth over the windscreen. 'Probably sleeps with a light on.' He smiled wryly. 'Most witches do.' He opened the door, oblivious of the driving rain. The drops rattled on his plastic raincoat. 'I'm going in.'

At that moment, headlights threw a white strip along the drive and a van appeared at the gate. Davidson slipped back into their car. Both men crouched below the windows. Rain on the windscreen splintered the light as the van turned towards them and hissed past through the sodden tarmac. Davidson lifted his head.

'Black van with local plates. Two five six. Certainly false registration. Two people. A man and a woman.'

'White hair?'

'Definitely not.'

'Then the old woman must be in the house.'

Davidson nodded. 'Let's give her another ten minutes.'

They sat quietly. The rain came in sporadic waves as squalls drove it against the windscreen. Above them, branches swayed wildly as the south-easterly gusted to gale force.

Davidson grunted. 'We go in five minutes, storm or no storm.'

They heard the rain ease slightly. The quiet street was dark; no lights showed in any of the other houses. The road was dark between the dim circles of the streetlights.

Davidson started the car and drove forward without lights to a tree on the verge, thirty metres from the front gate. He turned off the ignition.

Harry handed him a small radio. 'I'll give you a level before you get to the gate.'

Davidson got out of the car, removed his raincoat, and walked a few paces towards the gate. When he lifted his arm, his radio clicked several times. He adjusted the level until the signal was barely audible. He lifted his arm and Harry saw him disappear up the driveway.

Davidson made a complete circuit of the property before he was satisfied that he would have to break into the house. It was embarrassing to break in the front door and find the back door wide open. It had happened to him a long time ago.

He walked quietly to a door at the back of the house which appeared to be the entrance to a scullery. His crêpe-soled shoes were silent on the grano surface. He examined the lock for a moment. It was a simple mortise lock. He would have that open in a few seconds. He would have bet a fortune that the front door was a complicated, burglar-proof fitting. A minute later he slipped into the darkened scullery and stood for two minutes listening. He heard nothing above the sound of the rain as the squalls rattled the windows.

He took a small flashlight from his pocket, directing it to the door to his right. He turned the handle to reveal shelves, and rows of tinned foods. He shed his raincoat, hung it over the pantry door, and moved stealthily into the passage. No light penetrated the heavy curtains over the living-room windows, but a faint glow came from the staircase. The ground floor appeared to be deserted, but he made a swift circuit of the rooms before directing his attention to the stairs.

As he moved towards the bottom step, he saw a chink of light coming from a small, partly opened trapdoor under the staircase. He opened the trapdoor fully to reveal an entrance to a cellar. He moved his head cautiously over the edge of the trapdoor until he could see the room below. It was empty.

He went slowly down the stairs until he was standing beside a bunk bed. A red garment showed from under a pillow on the top bunk. He pulled it out and examined it carefully. It was a school uniform with a nametag under the collar. The name on the tag was Ramona Gomez.

For a moment, shock froze him into immobility. The name had been in the

106

headlines in a dozen newspapers around the country; she was one of six children who had disappeared over a period of three weeks. A slow anger was growing within him. He replaced the garment on the bed and went up the cellar steps.

When he returned to the ground floor, he was aware of an eerie silence. The rain had stopped and the only sounds were the plopping of the raindrops and the interminable rolls of distant thunder.

He went towards the staircase. At the top of the stairs he could see a strip of light coming from the partially closed door at the end of the passage, but behind the remaining open doors there was only darkness. He stood for several minutes listening to the silence, his gloved hand on the newel post. He pushed the tiny radio into his pocket and drew the Ghisoni from the holster under his arm. He checked all the empty rooms and then turned his attention to the lighted room. He stood at one side of the jamb and pushed the door open.

He saw the blood first and then the blanketed mound on the bed. The head was turned to the wall, a wound in the left temple from which the life had drained. He felt her pulse, but the woman was dead. She must have been killed just before the van left the house. She fitted the description of the woman Collins had interviewed.

He took the radio from his pocket. 'Harry.'

He heard the soft voice answer. 'I'm here.'

'The house is deserted. The woman is dead. Come up through the back door. I'm upstairs.'

Two minutes later, Harry stood beside him in the bedroom.

'This looks like a clean-up operation, Joe. The son botched the job on Mrs Eripides. The police will be pointed this way, so they have to close up.'

Davidson nodded. 'Which means sweepers will be sent to clean up the evidence.' He went to the door. 'Come with me.' He led the way to the cellar. He pulled out the red dress. 'Look at this.'

Harry examined the garment and read the name on the tag.

'Ramona Gomez.' He looked at Davidson. 'This is one of the missing girls.'

'Right. This is what it's all about.' He took the dress and tucked it back under the pillow. 'This is the kidnap ring. They operated from this house until about an hour ago.'

'The van?'

Davidson nodded. 'They moved the girls away from here.'

'Hell, Joe, I'm beginning to breathe water. We're out of our depth with this.' Harry shook his head. 'I started out to find a girl. Kay Kelsey. A simple little job. And now look what we have.'

'Right. It's too big for us. We have to bring the police in. Take the car and phone from the

Broadway boxes and get out. They're sure to make a fast trace of the call box.' He went downstairs. 'I'll wait down the road in case this lot get back too soon.' They left the door wide open.

As Harry drove away, Davidson took up a position in the driveway opposite the house. The wind had backed to an easterly, scattering the cloud mass, with stars becoming visible in a moonless sky. Morning would bring another hot, sub-tropical day.

As he waited, he imagined the desperate fear of the girls held captive in the house across the road. His anger grew into a hard knot in his breast. He felt no compassion for the woman shot to death in her bed. She had connived at a heinous crime, and he felt she deserved all she got.

He saw the lights of a car turning into Garnet Road. He eased himself back into the shrubbery until he saw Harry cruising slowly past. Davidson flashed his torch and Harry waited for him across the road. They waited at the end of Saint Andrews Drive until they saw the flashing lights stop in front of the Garnet Road house. Harry looked at his watch.

'Three minutes,' he said. 'Not bad.'

Davidson rubbed the fatigue from his eyes.

'Let's go.' He opened the window to clear the warmth from inside the car. 'So we still haven't found Kay Kelsey.'

It was after four o'clock when Davidson

slipped his latchkey into the lock. Margaret had left a table lamp on in the living-room. It was cool and the air-conditioning was off. He walked through to the bedroom to find Margaret sitting up in bed with a book on her lap. He bent over to kiss the top of her head.

'How dare you wait up for me.'

She looked at him with mock indignation.

'How dare you expect me not to wait up for you.' She shrank from him. 'And put away your coat before you come near me.'

He smiled and took his coat to the kitchen, hung it on a hook and returned to the bedroom.

'What sort of a day did you have?'

'I found a first edition someone had mislaid.' Margaret worked in the university library. 'You'd have thought I'd found the Cullinan diamond.'

'How do people lose first editions?' He took off his shirt and went into the bathroom.

'Some ding-dong had put it amongst the regular books.' She heard the bath water running. 'Why don't you shower? It's quicker.'

'I can't see when my glasses get wet.'

'Idiot. You don't wear glasses.'

'They would if I did.' He looked at her from the bathroom. In the subdued light of the reading lamp, she looked warm and comfortable. By the time he had showered, she was fast asleep.

He stood at the window and, moving the

110

curtain slightly, looked across the city at the horizon where a faint glow over the sea marked the beginning of a new day. In spite of his love for Margaret, this was a time that he savoured most, when he was isolated, wrapped in a cocoon of insularity that permitted him to see beyond his own ego. Once, his insularity had been loneliness, when the dark despair of his first marriage had taken him to the brink of self-destruction. It was at moments like this that he realized the insignificance of one man's grief in the context of universal suffering. When he had accepted that, his healing had begun. He had told himself that in a hundred years none of it would matter. It was a kind of fatalism that had supported him through the sad years.

He thought of the parents and the pain of their loss. There would be no easy healing for them. If the girls were not found, their pain would go on, unceasing in the face of diminishing hope and years of tortured uncertainty. His earlier anger had not left him, and he knew he would not sleep until there was surcease.

The sky was brighter, the deep red line on the horizon bleeding upwards until the whole eastern sky reflected the promise of sunrise. He went into the kitchen to brew the coffee.

CHAPTER TEN

When Harry left Davidson at his flat, he drove along Ridge Road, revelling in the fresh early smells of a city swept clean by the storm. It was the hour when the scents of jasmine and honeysuckle had not yet given way to the stink of freeway fumes.

At the tollgate bridge, he left the Berea and took the freeway to the beachfront. A few minutes later he turned into Boscombe Terrace.

It was at that moment that he saw the black van.

It was parked on the centre island about a hundred metres away. It was facing away from him with the cab obscured. He stopped at the kerb from where he could just read the numbers on the plate. The first three digits were two five six. He took a pen from the cubby-hole and jotted the entire number in his small diary. He put the pen and diary on the passenger seat.

He knew without any doubt that the van was parked in front of his office building for reasons that were sinister. Quietly he slid from the car and, watching the street, crossed the pavement in the direction of the van. He moved so that a small shrub on the island screened him. Suddenly a dark shape

112

appeared from his left, and he felt a sharp blow on his head. He fell to his knees and then on to his face as a second blow caught him at the base of his skull. Dazed and unable to move, he felt hands dragging him towards the van. Then the lights went out.

*　　　*　　　*

The whole world was coming apart, she thought. Junkies and prostitutes, muggers and pushers peopled the dark street, all spewing their filth into the once bright city. Depraved specimens of humanity battened on the young, and enslaved them in the chains of bright lights, loud pounding music, drugs, and sex.

From the back seat of the Mercedes, she watched the crowded pavements and teenagers, some just children, swarming into the clubs and bars. She shrank into the corner as she saw a figure emerge from the alley. Then Roberts, in a chauffeur's cap, opened the door and got in. She leant forward questioningly.

He spoke softly. 'He isn't here. The doorman said he hasn't been in the club since yesterday.'

'What the hell is he playing at? He said he would see us here this evening.'

She saw the slight movement in the darkness as he shrugged.

'Who knows. Perhaps he's suspicious.'

'Somehow we have to keep the hooks in. We lose him, we lose the girls.'

A whore in black leather jacket and short red skirt stuck her frizzed hair in at the window. She looked at the girl and giggled at Roberts.

'Wassa matter?' Her drug-slurred voice breathed cheap liquor into the car. 'Can't get anything better? Thassa poor screw you got back there, mate.' She giggled once more, walked behind the car, and disappeared into the alley.

Janet touched him on the shoulder. 'Let's go. We shouldn't look too eager.'

Roberts turned the ignition, spun away from the kerb and drove into Rutherford Street. They passed the Customs House, and at the traffic lights they turned into Smith Street. He drove towards the city hall where he stopped and looked back at a passing car.

Janet turned her head. 'What is it?'

'Victor Piper. Heading towards the Marine Parade.'

'He could have been held up. Think we should have waited?'

Roberts shook his head. 'No. Let him look for you. He knows where to find you.'

He started the car. Under the harsh white glare of the mercury vapour lamps, frozen-faced phantoms loitering under the statues of Queen Victoria and General Smuts touted drugs or sex, made assignations, staggered to

114

the next watering hole or cast predatory eyes on parked cars. Janet looked across the gardens towards the city hall, saddened by the soaring crime rate and the regression of the city she loved.

Reflections from the neons crept up the polished bonnet of the car as they slowed behind a lumbering bus. Then Roberts saw a gap and raced through it into the racecourse tunnel. A few minutes later, they stopped in front of the sumptuous home they had rented in Essenwood Road.

While Roberts parked the car, Janet went into the house. She took off her expensive coat, threw it carelessly on the oak credenza in the hall, and went through to the living-room. She switched on the table lamps, throwing a warm glow on a room furnished in a mixture of styles. There was a Victorian ottoman in an alcove, Windsor chairs scattered about, with small regency tables amongst them.

She looked up as Roberts appeared in the doorway. As she was about to speak, he held his fingers to his lips and cupped his ears. Startled, she looked towards the window, and then she saw that he was pantomiming electronic surveillance.

He walked to the ottoman and sat down.

'Pity Victor doesn't want to do business. His merchandise would have fitted in well with our routes.'

The girl followed his lead. 'Do we really

need it? We're doing a million a month without him. His stuff could clutter our supply lines.'

'We could use the West African route. It's foolproof.'

'Well, it's obvious he's made his choice.' As she spoke, Roberts went to a small escritoire near the cocktail cabinet. He scribbled on a small pad.

She yawned. 'Pour me a drink, will you.'

'Right.' He poured a soft drink, took it to her and slipped the note to her.

Surveillance from van across the road. Must assume bugs as well. Suggest dinner at restaurant.

She crumpled the note, went to the guest toilet under the stairs, and flushed it down the pan. When she returned, she said:

'I'm too tired to cook. What about a table at a restaurant?'

'Good thinking. I'll shower.'

She sat for a moment, sipping her drink, eyes narrowed, looking for signs of surreptitious entry. Nothing seemed out of place, but with skilled burglars, nothing would be out of place. Victor Piper's organization was fine-tuned. Failure would not be tolerated. Lawrence and his mother were examples of his ruthless power.

It was for this reason that the house was bare of individuality. They were careful not to make it too secure. No one was left to guard the house when it was vacant. They had left money and drugs in a safe that anyone could open.

She went through to the bedroom, glancing to the left of the closed door, where she had left a fine hair glued between the door and the jamb. A hair was there, but it was not the same one. The hair she had left there had been her own, but this one was darker. She opened the door, looking at the window before she switched on the light. The curtains were closed, but the slight fold she had left in the left drape was now smoothed out. She smiled inwardly at her small victory. Uncle John's tuition had paid off. If these were professionals, then she had no need to be concerned about her own ability.

Roberts was still showering. She heard the water splashing on the mosaic floor, almost drowning an out-of-tune version of *Moon River*. She looked out at the moonlit garden where manicured lawns sloped for nearly fifty metres to the road. Shrubs and trees were planted in some arcane arrangement that, Janet suspected, was a product of the owner's weird fantasies about what she called her Karma. She had insisted on interviewing her tenants personally, and had talked constantly of her astrological expertise. Janet turned as Roberts returned dressed in charcoal slacks, white silk shirt and cravat. She regarded him with admiration.

'I thought the man about town was into

denim suits.'

'You're way out of date, young lady. Get with it. Anyway, how I dress is my business.'

'It's my business when my escort is improperly dressed.' She looked at him critically. 'Where's your jacket?'

'Too hot.'

She raised her eyebrows and cupped her ears.

'Anyway, I'm tired of this place. We can't do business with these people.' She sat on the ottoman. "We'll go back to Johannesburg early tomorrow.'

'Right. I've said all along this isn't our line.'

'Then we get out at eight in the morning.' She stood up. 'We'll send Bernie Levine to close up here.' She paused. 'Can we still reactivate that Middle East assignment?'

Roberts continued the charade. 'They're just waiting for us to agree.'

She walked to her bedroom door. 'I'll be out in ten minutes.'

Roberts went upstairs to the master bedroom, which looked out over Essenwood Road. Beyond the first streetlight, the small white van still waited. Equipped with a roof rack and two long ladders, these superfluous additions had alerted him. With high-tech communications and street boxes on the pavements, the ladders made it an unlikely-looking Telcom vehicle. Trained to read the intentions of any vehicle remaining immobile

118

for long periods, these discrepancies had led him to believe that the house could have been bugged.

There was no doubt that the surveillance team was in direct contact with Victor Piper, reporting to him minute by minute. In the final analysis, he needed them. It was his caution that made him delay. He was as cautious as a hyena, operating behind several front men.

At that moment, the telephone rang. He knew at once that they had won this round. He heard Janet answer the call in the bedroom.

She came out of the room smiling broadly.

'Victor Piper wants to meet us here tonight. At midnight.'

*　　*　　*

Harry turned on the narrow bunk. His eyes opened a fraction, squinting against the light of a single naked bulb that illuminated the four dirty whitewashed walls. The bed and a small wooden table were the only items of furniture. Steel mesh covered the high window. He swung his legs over the edge of the bed. His head throbbed relentlessly, and his ribs felt as though he had been kicked. He stood up carefully. As the room began to spin, he sat down again and tried to remember what the time on his watch had been. And the diary? He tried to remember what he had done with it after recording the registration numbers.

He couldn't think. All he could think about was Davidson. Images began to drift in and out of his consciousness, moving aimlessly from the present into the past and back without his concussed brain being aware of the absurdity of the changes.

Then certain images became stronger. He was ten years old, sitting on the beach with Uncle Joe as he talked of the creatures of the sea; he learnt that when the mullet gape at the surface of the water, the barometer is dropping and the strong westerly is close. Uncle Joe was telling him about the winds; that the northerly at night leaves no dew in the morning.

Images dissolved and returned. What had he done with the blood sample from Seaview? Then, in his delirium, Davidson faded from his mind and he was back in the home he had shared with Eleanor. He was staring into her face and feeling again the pain of her desertion.

Then the pain, both physical and emotional, subsided as sleep claimed him.

CHAPTER ELEVEN

From his office on the tenth floor of Simcox House in West Street, Victor Piper looked down at the lights of the traffic flowing towards the beachfront. He looked at his watch. It said 8.45. He pressed the button that closed the curtains, went to the desk, and sat in the executive chair behind it.

On the wall behind him, a mural depicting an English country garden, complete with rose bowers and statuary, covered the entire area from corner to corner. Visitors wondered at this incongruous adornment in an office furnished severely in chrome or glass, but by the third or fourth meeting, if there was reason to repeat the experience, the rationale became apparent. Behind the urbanity, the elegance, and the show of refinement, the discerning could detect the straying of the occasional vowel into the accents of Fortsburg, that Johannesburg breeding ground of poverty and crime in the late sixties.

Victor Piper used his wealth in his attempt to mask his origins, surrounding himself with the trappings of culture. He succeeded only in convincing his visitors of his ostentation.

If there were any who believed in the fiction of his urbanity, then his ruthless and unprincipled business practices soon disabused them of their illusion.

He looked at the Chinaman sitting motionless on the sofa.

'I don't like it. On each parcel of twelve, I expect to make a million dollars. I expected to pay at least thirty thousand apiece to ship them out of the country.' He spread his hands. 'Yet she tells me the price is fifteen.' He shook his head. 'What is she? A fool? A police trap?'

The Chinaman's face was expressionless. 'She owns property all over the country. In her safe is enough drugs to send her down for life.' He shrugged. 'If she is police, then there is very strange police in South Africa.'

The third man, sitting in a leather recliner, placed his glass on the small table beside him. His small eyes in a face layered with fat, looked at Piper.

'We've watched her since she arrived in the city. Nothing.' He stood up, ran a hand over his bald head, tugged at the lapels of his charcoal suit, and walked across to the liquor cabinet. 'I didn't put a bug in until I was sure they had swept the place a couple of times.' He poured a shot into a clean glass. 'All I got was what we heard today.' He walked over to the window.

Victor looked at the Chinaman. 'That's good enough for me. If Grundling says the girl is clean, then she is.' Grundling walked back to the chair. Piper went on: 'Your people have received the South American shipment.

The Indian shipment arrives in Bangkok tomorrow.' His voice grew hard. 'The South African shipment must leave within a week.' He looked at the man called Li.

The tension in the room grew in the silence. The Chinaman's eyes were expressionless as he stared back. When he spoke, his tone was mild, but there was no mistaking the contempt in his voice.

'Indian girls available every day. Poor people sell their family for a few rupees. My people want girls from here.'

Piper pointed an angry finger at Li. 'The Sun Ki Son triad will take what I bloody well send them.' He stood up and spread his palms on the desk. 'And they will pay the same price for every shipment.'

The Chinaman nodded. 'My people will pay.'

Piper sat down, mollified. There was another long silence. Grundling sipped his drink. His thick features were shining with perspiration in spite of the air-conditioning.

Piper walked to the window, moved the curtain aside and looked down into the street.

'I'll see the woman tonight. At her place.' He turned, looking directly at Grundling. 'I want the whole place covered. Back and front. And I want two men to accompany me into the house.' He sat in the executive chair. 'Use the best people.'

'What about Collins?' Grundling looked

into his empty glass. 'I'll have to delay his disappearance until tomorrow.'

Piper nodded thoughtfully. 'That might be more convenient. I can deal with him personally.'

'Not a good idea. It's too risky.' Grundling began to pace.

'Perhaps you're right.' Piper fiddled with a letter-opener.

The Chinaman watched the exchanges impassively. Grundling was Piper's man, body and soul, he mused. He was a man who enjoyed hurting people, and even more so when it pleased his master.

Piper looked at Grundling. 'And stop pacing, dammit.'

Grundling sat in the recliner. 'Are you ready to go yet?'

'Let the woman wait. We'll call her later.' Piper dropped the letter-opener. 'What made Collins look for the girl?'

Grundling frowned. 'He'll tell me when I work him over tomorrow.'

'What about Davidson? I still think we should deal with him. Put a good man on him.'

Grundling stood up and began pacing once more.

'Leave security to me.' He was becoming irritated. Li wondered if it was the reference to Davidson. The Chinaman had seen Davidson's handiwork. The man would intimidate anyone.

Piper smiled sardonically. 'I want my pound

124

of flesh. The man cost me half a million on that Kloof job.' He paused. 'But if you're afraid of him, we'll say no more.'

Grundling said irritably: 'I won't say it again. I'm not afraid of him. I respect him. That's why I'm the best. I know my enemies, and their strengths and weaknesses.' He sat on the edge of the desk. 'Leave Davidson alone until he interferes. If we attract his attention, we don't know where it will end.'

'I hope you have a good man on him. We don't want any surprises.'

'He's the best we've got, but if Davidson makes him, then God help him.' Grundling was irritated enough to retaliate. 'And I think it was bloody careless to let the girl look at our security.'

Piper went to the liquor cabinet. 'You know why I did that. She insisted on knowing how secure we are. Otherwise, it was no dice.' He poured himself a soda water. 'Anyway, she didn't learn much, and I can handle her if she becomes a problem.'

The Chinaman wondered how these two men could ever work together.

'Why do you need this woman? Why not move the shipment yourselves?'

Piper looked at Grundling. 'You tell him.'

'The borders are too tight. Gunrunners and smugglers have forced Customs to beef up the borders. They even have army patrols. It's murder. We can't find out how the girl does it.'

He stood up and paced across the room. 'Her security is too good. 'We've used her a few times, running stuff into the country for us. She is efficient and fast.' He smiled coldly. 'Once she gets the cargo, we're out of it. If she slips, it's her neck, not ours.'

The telephone shrilled through the office. Grundling answered it. He listened for a moment, grunted twice and cut the connection.

'It's the van. She's talking about leaving in the morning. She's backing off.'

'Call her. We'll meet her at midnight.'

* * *

Davidson opened his eyes when the sun was bright enough to filter through the heavy bedroom curtains. Margaret had already left for work. He sat up and threw aside the covers just as the telephone rang.

McGrath's agitated voice came to him down the line.

'Joe. Mack here. Have you seen Harry?'

'Not since early this morning.' Alarm bells rang in his head.

'One of the guards reported that Harry's car was standing near the entrance to the building. The door was open and the key was in the ignition.'

'What time was this?'

'The man came on duty at six this morning.'

126

Davidson suppressed an irritable comment at the oblique answer. 'What time did you hear of it?'

'When I arrived at seven.'

Davidson sat for a moment picturing the scene, seeking inspiration from Harry's habits. He had complained that Harry never parked a car. He abandoned it. But certainly he would not leave a car in the way McGrath had described.

'Are there any signs of struggle?' He pictured the interior of the car. '*Where* were the keys?'

'Still in the ignition. The guard brought them up after he'd closed and locked the door.' There was silence for a moment. 'Oh yes. There was something else. I searched the area around the car, and in the island. There were tyre tracks on the island, and I found Harry's diary near them.'

Dear heaven, he thought. The man must have been behind the door when brains were issued. Davidson sighed.

'And where is the diary now?'

'Here in front of me.'

'And what, if anything, is recorded against today's date?'

McGrath heard the veiled sarcasm. 'Nothing. I looked.' His tone was resentful. 'There's nothing significant. Only his appointments.'

Davidson spoke quietly. 'Did he make a

127

note of a car number anywhere in the diary?'

'Hold on. I'll look.' McGrath came back a few seconds later.

'There's a number inside the front cover.'

'Read it to me.'

'Have you got a pen?'

'Mack, just read it to me.' His voice was calm, but his exasperation was evident.

Mack read the five-digit number. The first three were two five six.

'Right. Send the diary up to me at once. Harry's in trouble.' He replaced the receiver before McGrath could speak.

Davidson took his keys from the bedside table, went to a cupboard built into the alcove between the master bedroom and the second bathroom, opened it, and then opened a small steel cabinet fixed to the lower shelf. It was crammed with electronic equipment. Its primary function was to detect the presence of bugging equipment. Tired of constantly calling in the technical firms to sweep his house, he had ordered this sweeper as a permanent fixture. When it was switched on, it swept over every frequency, stopping instantly when replying oscillations indicated the presence of a bug. It was wired to every room in the house and to the casual eye it appeared to be wiring and speakers for an elaborate hi-fi installation.

He switched it on, listened impatiently for the stop signal that indicated that it had completed a sweep. He locked the cabinet and went through to the study. He picked up the telephone and dialled. Margaret answered at once.

'I'm going out. Don't cook for me and don't wait up.'

'Murder and Robbery phoned. They said you could call for your gun.' She paused. 'I left the message on your desk.'

He looked down at his blotter. 'I've got it. Thanks. I love you.'

'Thank you. You know my thoughts.' It was her stock reply if there was someone near her desk.

He skimmed through the post, discarding the junk mail and opened the only envelope that wasn't. It was a letter in which the manager of East Coast Banking thanked him for his services. He thought the wording inappropriate for killing four men. The manager also said that a cheque was in the post and assured him of their attention at all times.

He thumbed quickly through his private directory, found a number, and dialled. The voice that answered sounded like a load of stones rotating in a drum.

'Parker.'

'Roger. It's Joe.'

'Whatever you want, it's got to be worth a dinner at the Royal.'

'The Royal Hotel it is. Name the night, as long as it isn't between Monday and Sunday.'

'That's you. Cheap.'

'The Royal. Any time.'

'That's better. Gimme the number. I'll give you the car.'

'You must be clairvoyant.'

'You could get it yourself by filling in a simple form, presenting your ID and paying two rand.'

'I haven't got two rand.'

'My newspaper told me a different story. About a bank robbery.'

'Newspapers don't have anything to do with real life.'

'Crap. I believe everything I read in the papers.' Davidson heard the sound of a computer keyboard. 'Ready. Gimme the number.' Davidson read off the numbers. He heard Parker clear his throat.

'You still there?'

'Of course.'

'I thought you'd gone off to the Royal to book a table.'

Under the badinage Davidson's thoughts kept turning to Collins. He felt a rising impatience, but he knew he could never hurry Roger Parker.

The man coughed. 'Here it is. It's registered to Mr James Martin at Six Swan Place, Mayville.'

'Thanks Roger. I owe you one.'

'You do. At the Royal, and bring the two rand.'

Davidson searched quickly through the city directory and dialled once more. His call to the university serological department elicited the fact that there was enough blood in Collins's small sample to work on, but the analysis was not yet complete. Sorry. Try tomorrow.

Davidson looked at the address that Roger Parker had given him. He knew the area around Swan Place and remembered that the low numbers were at the Cato Manor end in an area of factories and warehouses. He thought it likely that the registration was false, but it was the only lead he had.

Above the whisper of the air-conditioning, the dull sound of the freeway grew as the traffic poured into the city. All at once he felt the familiar sense of claustrophobia, born of his need to act on a seemingly insoluble problem. Fortunately, it was always a transient emotion, a fleeting reminder that he was not invincible.

As he considered the difficulties facing him, he realized in fact that he was facing three different problems. There was Kay Kelsey, missing or dead; there was the missing Harry Collins who could also be dead; and there were the missing girls, who could already be out of the country. He was convinced that all three problems were linked, and that if he found Harry Collins alive, he was part of the way to solving the other two.

131

As he considered the alternatives open to him, he felt his confidence growing. He knew that in spite of his preference for working in isolation, he was not alone. This was his city, where over the years he had built a web of contacts with informants at the extremities of the strands, which vibrated to the tread of his enemies.

He decided to begin at Swan Place. For the moment, there was nowhere else to go.

CHAPTER TWELVE

Janet La Barre and Captain Sam Roberts took the lift to the fifth floor of the hotel where a private room had been booked for them. As the lift door opened, a man in a dark suit confronted them. He was carrying a transmitter, and he nodded as he recognized them.

'Along the passage. Second left.'

The girl led the way to the room where they found Uncle John seated at a table laid for three. The lighting was subdued and alongside the window, which was covered with velvet drapes, stood a long table with a smorgasbord ready for the diners. Uncle John was alone, and it was evident that he had arranged matters so that the hotel staff were not required to wait on them.

He waved a chicken drumstick at them.

'I didn't wait. I have to leave as soon as I have briefed you.' He waved towards the smorgasbord. 'Stay as long as you like. This is my personal gesture of appreciation. The meals up at North Ridge Road were abominable. But that's the bureaucratic way.' He smiled and touched his lips with a table napkin. 'And I can't let the uglies see you at a greasy spoon.'

No wonder this man is the best in the business, Janet thought. He'd had a brilliant career in army intelligence and when the new inept Minister of Defense decided to discard him, the new head of National Security appointed him to lead a new special operations team. He accepted the appointment on condition it was a secondment and not a transfer. That way he could keep his rank.

This gesture today was typical of the ways in which he built respect and loyalty.

He looked at Roberts. 'Think you were followed?'

Roberts nodded. 'Oh yes. The full treatment. Blind runners, switched cars, and radios. The lot.'

'Good. Means they're still in the game. If they had ignored you, we'd have had something to worry about.'

Janet and Roberts carried their plates to the table. They had both chosen the prawns and salads. Roberts poured wine for all of them.

He looked up. 'They've bugged the house too. There's a van down the road.'

'What do they propose?'

'Piper wants to meet me tonight at midnight.' Janet spoke quietly, but Anders sensed the tension in her voice.

'They must be damned sure of themselves. Probably bringing in an army.' He speared a piece of tomato from his salad. He thought for a moment. 'Looks as though we're going into the sensitive phase. You'll both have to be very careful. This man will kill without compunction. Especially if he thinks you have no support.' He was silent for a moment. 'Hindsight tells me I should have given you an impressive bodyguard.' He shook his head. 'No, I think not. He would not have given you the time of day if he suspected that you could trump his best tricks.'

She nodded her agreement. 'We've been more effective this way. He is under the impression there's just the Captain and me. He still believes that the bulk of my organization operates from Botswana.'

Uncle John took a small sip of wine.

'From now on, every step must be examined with care. That killing in Durban North was the first inkling we had of the whereabouts of the three girls abducted ten days ago.'

As Uncle John looked at his notes, Roberts caught the distinction. So, the general knew the location of some of the girls.

The general continued. 'A dress belonging to the Gomez girl was found in the basement. We kept the lid on it. We gave the press a description of an alleged prowler.' He paused. 'We knew about the house and its tenants, but we had no idea there was a cellar.'

Janet pushed aside her wine. 'Then the girls must still be in the city.'

'Not necessarily. We must presume that Victor closed down part of his organization that was exposed by the botched assassination attempt at Seaview. He chose to dispose of the evidence, including the woman.' He smiled sardonically. 'I am confident that someone was in that house and made an anonymous call to the police.'

Roberts replaced his wineglass on the table. 'What about fingerprints?'

'Only three sets of prints. The mother, the son and one other. That set has not been identified.' He looked at Roberts. 'How were the prawns?'

'Nice. I like them skinned.'

Janet frowned impatiently. 'Sir. We're talking about girls whose parents are living in hell.'

Uncle John looked at her with sympathy. 'Yes. They're always uppermost in my thoughts.' He nodded. 'And in yours. I figured you needed a distraction for a moment.'

'Of course. I'm sorry.'

'I understand. You've done magnificently up

to now, but don't get emotionally involved.'

She looked at Roberts, who was sitting back with his eyes closed. All at once, she realized how fortunate she was to be working with these two men. They had needed a woman for this operation, because a woman would be more acceptable to the wary enemy, but they had supported her with the department's finest.

Uncle John observed her carefully, shrewdly judging the moment when her objectivity was restored.

'You must make it clear that the girls are to be delivered to the farm in a single batch. The area has to be cleared of all his men. He must understand that you will not move while you are under surveillance.' He paused. 'He will accept all those conditions because he will disregard them. But it won't matter when we have the girls.'

'I would like to insist that he must have three nurses with them.'

Uncle John shrugged. 'I don't think he will object to that. It's in his interests.' He made a note on his pad. 'As soon as you signal us that the girls are safe, the immediate families will be spirited away and taken to the farm. They must understand that they must remain incommunicado until all the arrests are made.' He looked down at his notes. 'It should not be more than a few hours.' He stood up and touched her arm. 'Good luck.' He walked towards the door. 'Wait half an hour before you leave.' He turned. 'And Sam . . .'

'Sir?'

'Take good care of her. We need her.'

*   *   *

Harry Collins opened his eyes and saw the rough whitewashed wall. A strong wave of emotion, compounded of fear and anger, swept over him. He turned over to face the door, and looked around the room. Except for the tin plate and mug beside the bed, nothing had changed. He looked with revulsion at the ants crawling over the cold mashed potato and the thickened scum on top of the coffee. He sat up, probing gingerly at the lump at the back of his head. His headache had diminished to a faint throbbing. He stood up, stretched and touched his toes three times before he felt the pain increase.

He sat on the bed and considered his position. Firstly, he was in the hands of an organization that wanted him dead. That much was obvious from the ruthlessness with which they had attacked Grace Eripides. Secondly, he was being held here until it was convenient to take him to where his murder could be accomplished without his body being found until the kidnapped girls were out of the country.

He went to the door and tried the handle

without believing for a moment that it was unlocked. It was a reflex action born of desperation. He stood listening to the sounds coming through the high window. There was the screech of the ubiquitous mynah birds, the occasional rumble of traffic and the distant hum of machinery.

Then suddenly he heard another sound. From behind one of the walls came a soft sobbing, followed by a muffled voice as though someone was speaking comforting words. The slanting sunlight told him that the window must be in the west wall. The sounds were coming from behind the east wall.

He picked up the mug from the floor, flung the contents under the bed, and began to tap softly against the whitewashed brick. The voices were silent. He tapped once more. Then he heard a voice speaking softly and the words were clearly audible through an incomplete bond in the rough brickwork.

'Who are you?'

'My name is Harry. Who are you?' There was a long moment of silence, some muffled whispering, and another long silence. 'Don't be afraid. Who are you?'

A second voice, sounding older than the first, spoke with hopeful urgency. 'Have you come to get us out?'

Harry felt a surge of helpless rage.

'You may have to wait a little longer. But someone will come soon.'

'It will have to be today. They are taking us away tomorrow morning.'

'How many of you are there?'

'There are four of us in here, but there are others in the next room.'

Harry paused for a moment. 'Have you come across a girl named Kay Kelsey?'

He heard a swift rustling, the creak of a bed. The older girl spoke softly. 'Someone's coming.'

A steel door clanged loudly. Harry lay down on the bed and feigned sleep. A key turned in the lock. The door opened. There was a moment of silence and a voice spoke from the passage.

'He's still out. He won't give us any trouble.'

The door closed and footsteps retreated along the passage. A door clanged, and silence descended on their prison.

Harry heard the bed creak and the soft voice.

'What was the name of the girl?'

'Kay Kelsey.'

Harry heard soft whispering once more. 'No one has heard of her.' The whispering stopped and once again their prison was silent.

*   *   *

Victor glanced at the notes on his desk. He looked up at Grundling.

'The girl is no fool.' He stood up and

139

walked to the window. 'We'll have to be careful. We got nowhere last night. We need Li at the next meeting.' The waters of the bay sparkled in the sunshine. 'Where the hell is Li? How the hell can I operate if I don't know where my people are?'

Grundling heard the rising tones that preceded Victor's bouts of rage .

'He's at the warehouse organizing the trucks. We need two, but I told him to get four. The false compartments have to be welded in.' He smiled disarmingly. 'It all takes time.' He refilled his glass at the cabinet. 'We're still on schedule. The drivers are ready.'

'Who's in charge of them?'

'Ed Wharton.'

'He's the best.' Victor turned and went back to his desk.

Grundling watched him cautiously. 'I always use the best. You know that.' He sipped his whisky. 'The girls will be on the road by tonight.'

'I think you're wrong about Davidson. I want you to see to him.'

Grundling knew that Victor was beyond the point of reasonable persuasion. He stared at him for a long time. Then he shrugged.

'I'll get on it now.' He walked to the telephone.

*   *   *

General Anders walked to the communications room, sat in the supervisor's chair, and donned the headphones. He waited for three minutes before the signal was activated. He heard Captain Roberts speaking.

'I'm ready when you are.'

The general switched on the recording equipment.

'What happened?'

'Piper put nothing on the table. He came at midnight and stayed for half an hour listening. Then he said he would get back to us and left.'

'Is it your opinion he will come back?'

'Definitely. He was playing for a superior position. He's looking for an advantage. Janet was great. He will come back. We're meeting again today.'

'You make it sound good.'

'It is good. I believe he's hooked. He will accept terms today. He has to. He has to get the girls on the road.'

'Capital. Don't take chances, but brief me as soon as a deal is on the table.'

'Tonight at eight.'

'At eight then.'

The general disconnected and swivelled his chair to face the supervisor.

'Signal Asparagus to sign in as soon as possible.'

CHAPTER THIRTEEN

Davidson stared at the address Parker had given him. In the silence he heard the refrigerator motor cut in. He thought fleetingly about getting a new model, went through to the living-room and, moving the curtain slightly, looked down at the city and the sea beyond. A heat haze shimmered over the bay and the green ridge of the bluff, while from the bayhead a pall of smoke hung over the dockyards and railway workshops. He looked north, where the Umgeni River poured its muddy waters into the ocean, staining the coast with a brown streak. The sun was very bright in a clear blue sky, but far to the south, a smudge of grey hung over the horizon, an augury of the unsettled weather to come.

Davidson considered the options open to him, calmly assembling the facts of the problems. Over the years, he had learnt that time spent in analysis was more valuable than fruitless action. The strategy prevented the mistakes for which precipitous action was responsible. In any event, he knew he would have to go with what he had.

He went through to the study, picked up the phone, and dialled. The voice of his attorney's receptionist answered him.

'Mathew Hallowes and Partners.

'Mr Greig please.'

'I'll put you through.'

There was a brief moment of recorded music.

'Greig speaking.'

'Dennis. Joe Davidson. Have you a minute to spare?'

'A minute is all I've got, Joe. I'm due in court.'

Davidson glanced at his watch. 'It's a small enquiry. Can you spare one of your juniors for a while?'

'I can do that. What is it you want him to do?'

'Two things. Who owns the premises at Six Swan Place, and if it's a corporate ownership, who are the directors?'

'Is that all you want?'

'The problem is, I want it yesterday.'

'I'll put young Smythe on it.'

'You have my undying gratitude. Ask him to call me at home. Do you have my number?'

'Somewhere. Give it to me again.'

Davidson read off his number, replaced the receiver, and went into the kitchen. He switched on the percolator, put bread in the toaster, and took an egg from the refrigerator.

He was sitting at the breakfast table sipping the last of his coffee when the phone rang.

'Mr Davidson. Bill Smythe here. I have the information you want.'

'I'm ready.'

'Proctor and Berry, a subsidiary of Charlestown Holdings, own the Swan Place property. Both are Close Corporations and the directors are the same for both. They are P.R. Grundling, and A.J. Kenny. I haven't been able to find an address for either yet. Charlestown is a holding company with several properties in the city. Proctor and Berry is a company that imports tea and coffee.'

Davidson was writing furiously. When Smythe stopped speaking, he said: 'Can you get a list of the properties held by Charlestown? And the addresses for the directors?'

'I can have the list of properties in about twenty minutes. The addresses may take some time, unless you're prepared to settle for the addresses recorded at registration.'

'What's the difference?'

'Directors are supposed to notify the registrar of changes of addresses, but some directors are sloppy about the regulations.' There was a pause. 'However, I might get them from other sources.'

Davidson smiled, and thought it wiser not to comment.

'Whatever it takes. How long?'

'A couple of hours.'

'I won't be here.' He thought for a moment. 'Phone Collins Security. Ask for Mrs Grant and give the information. Tell her it's for me.'

'It's as good as done.'

144

'Thanks. Get back to me as soon as you can.'

'Right. Twenty minutes.'

Davidson was showered and dressed before Bill Smythe came back with the information.

'Charlestown owned fifteen properties in Durban. If you give me a fax number I'll put them on line.'

Davidson read off his number. 'I don't suppose a balance sheet or financial statement came with that lot.'

'No, but I can get something for you by tomorrow.'

'No need. I can't imagine how a balance sheet will help me at present.' He was silent for a moment. 'I think that's all for now. Thanks.'

'My pleasure.'

Davidson opened his gun safe and took out the Ghisoni. Before he had strapped on the shoulder holster, the fax was chattering.

He went back to the study, took the list of properties and, ignoring the blocks of flats and hotels, concentrated on those that appeared to be industrial and commercial businesses. There were four of those, one of which was the one in Swan Place. He listed the remaining three on a pad.

Ritson Transport, 50 Godsell Avenue.
Ritson Transport Hire, 75 Godsell Avenue.
Burrows Printers C. C. 14 Augustine Avenue.

He looked up the telephone numbers and jotted them down against each entry. Then he dialled the number for James Martin at Swan Place. An operator answered him.

'May I speak to Mr James Martin please.'

'One moment.'

There was a long silence before the operator returned. 'I'm sorry. No one by that name is employed in this business.'

Bingo. Davidson replaced the receiver and sat for a moment, savouring his elation. Now he knew where he was going. He dialled the next number on his list.

'Ritson Transport. Thank you for calling.'

'Mr James Martin, please.'

'One moment, please.'

Davidson listened to music. It stopped abruptly to be replaced by a voice that could have been male or female.

'May I help you?'

'Yes. I would like to speak to Mr Martin.'

'What is your interest in Mr Martin?'

'This is the Metro Protection Service. I have a summons for a traffic offence that has to be served on him.'

'Mr Martin is no longer with this company.' There was a brief pause. 'I believe he is travelling in Europe.'

'I see. Thank you.' Davidson replaced the receiver. There was no doubt in his mind that someone in the Charlestown company was

146

involved in some dubious enterprise, and while their protection of the elusive James Martin was not evidence, Davidson knew he had taken hold of one of the strands of the puzzle.

His thoughts returned to the directors of the company, his subconscious nagged by a feeling that he had overlooked something important.

Then he remembered what had been eluding him. He should have recognized the name immediately. Seven years ago he had been involved in a shootout on the Mozambique border. He had prevented the proceeds of a diamond robbery from being smuggled out of the country. He had apprehended the man with the gems, but the other two had escaped. The police had named Piet Grundling as one of the smugglers, but there was no evidence to link him with the robbery. If he had needed confirmation of the link between Charlestown and the abduction of the girls, he had it with the name Grundling.

From the house at Durban North, to the black van, Charlestown and Grundling, the chain was being forged.

It was time to find James Martin. Hang in there, Harry, he thought, I'm coming.

*   *   *

When Davidson left his simplex there were four cars parked in the street, two of which he recognized as belonging to residents of his block. The other two, a white Mercedes and a red Toyota, were unfamiliar. It was not unusual for strange cars to be parked in this quiet street, but each time he saw one, he made a mental note of the type, colour and plate number.

He drove north on Ridge Road, crossed the tollgate bridge, and turned right into Berea Road. He glanced in the rear-view mirror. A red Toyota was turning, three cars back. He stayed in the left lane until he was behind a municipal bus. The three intervening cars swung past him, leaving the Toyota exposed immediately behind him. A glance in the rear-view mirror told him it was the same car. The driver was a bald man with tinted glasses. It wasn't the first time his innate caution had paid off.

He should have felt a sense of satisfaction that his vigilance had been rewarded, but it was one of his bad days. He was weary, and he felt only despondency. His whole life was being spent in an aura of mistrust and disillusionment. Suspicion had become a conditioned reflex, souring his relationships with all but his closest friends. Yet he knew that suspicion was as much a part of his armoury as the weapons he carried.

At the bottom of Old Dutch Road, he turned into Warwick Avenue where the sprawl of the bus depot covered several blocks. It was

148

an area teeming with black and Indian shoppers, where white people entered at their peril and where muggings were commonplace. Pedestrians on the Station Overpass were often robbed at knife-point while crowds pushed past, too afraid to intervene.

Davidson drove on down to the fish market, where he parked the car, locked the doors and activated the audible alarm. Behind him, the driver of the red Toyota was parking fifty metres away.

The odour of fish and the babble of voices assailed him as he entered the main doors of the sales hall. Marble counters covered with fish and ice lined both sides of the market. Customers crowded the stalls, arguing over non-existent bargains. Davidson slipped through the throng, making for a stall in the far corner, where the Indian proprietor watched his assistants cutting and wrapping fish and giving change. He was a small man in a blue striped shirt and blue trousers. He saw Davidson, nodded to a door in the back of the stall and preceded him into a small office. Davidson sat on the desk as the Indian watched the shop through the one-way glass in the door. He spoke without turning.

'There is a short bald man out there with no coat and lemon shirt. He's looking very puzzled.' He kept watching the hall. Then he turned, his eyes as dark as coffee beans. 'He's a bad one, Joe. Beater Thompson. His name has something to do with his profession. Do you want to lose him, Joe?'

Davidson smiled. 'No. I'll deal with him when I'm ready.'

It was always a source of wonder to him how the Indian community knew so much about the city and its underworld. It was a defence mechanism, developed through the years of apartheid. Dispossessed and compelled to live in cheap community housing estates, the result was a pot-pourri of diverse groups. It included both the respectable and well bred, and the criminals and thugs who preyed on them. There was no escape for the honest ones unless they learnt who their enemies were. A grapevine developed, each tendril an informed element of the community. Through his friendship with the community, Davidson could call on an invaluable pool of knowledge. They trusted him. He had been there when they needed him.

'You been busy, Joe.' He sat on the chair behind the desk.

'So the papers tell me. Somehow, it seems none of them report the same robbery.'

Abdul Docrat looked at him quizzically. 'You want something, Joe? Just ask.'

'Thanks, Doc. I'm looking for a man named James Martin.'

'Martin? Do you want to find him or just learn something about him?'

'I want to find him. My friend Harry Collins

150

has disappeared. I think he's in trouble. Martin is involved somehow.'

Doc nodded. He went to the door. 'Wait here. I'll be back in a few minutes.'

Davidson looked through the glass as he disappeared into the crowd around the counter. He watched the assistants as their knives cut deftly through the fish, slicing, filleting, weighing and wrapping, all to a continuous flow of badinage and good humour.

Doc was away for about ten minutes, and when he returned, a large obese man with a head of thick, black hair and a full beard accompanied him. He was wearing black trousers and a black alpaca coat.

'You know Vishnu, Joe.'

Davidson nodded. 'Hullo, Vish.'

The man put out his hand. 'Long time, Joe.'

'About five—six years.'

'About that.' Vishnu took the only other chair. 'Doc said you were looking for Jimmy Martin.'

Davidson nodded. 'Did Doc tell you why?'

'He said Harry Collins was missing.' He shook his head. 'Bad. If Martin's crowd is holding him, I don't give much for his chances. Martin is working for a man named Kenny. Kenny's boss is Piet Grundling; no one knows who he is working for.' Vishnu shrugged. 'There's a race meeting at Greyville today. If he's true to form, he'll be there. Look for Biggie MacFee. He'll point out Martin for

151

you.'

Davidson looked surprised. 'Is Biggie involved with Martin?'

'Only at the races. Biggie is a runner for five or six punters. At the end of the day, they slip him a note.' Vishnu shrugged. 'You know Biggie.'

Davidson nodded. 'I know Biggie.'

Doc went to the glass look-out.

'Why chase Martin, Joe? Why not start with Beater? He's still out there.' He flashed a glance at Vishnu. 'It wouldn't take much to make him talk.'

Davidson looked thoughtful. 'I have to do whatever is quickest.'

His eyes reflected the strain he was under.

Vishnu tapped Davidson's shoulder. 'Grab Beater. They've delivered him to you. Martin might not be at the races, and you'd have wasted a day.' He went to the door. 'I have to get back to my shop.' He went out.

Davidson looked out of the office to where the sun slanted through the high window. Steel girders topped by a concrete domed roof stretched above the dust that hung in the sunlight. He breathed the smell of fresh fish, the dank redolence of the sawdust, and listened to the clamorous voices of the buyers.

He was aware of Doc behind him.

'Go for Beater, Joe.'

Davidson sighed. He felt a hundred years old.

'I'll take Thompson. It seems the quickest way.'

'Let me do it for you.'

'No. I can't put you in danger.'

'I'll farm the job out. Stay here until someone phones. They'll tell you where to go.'

'As long as you don't get involved.'

'I won't. You know my people, Joe. We get things done.'

'Right. Do it.'

Doc went to the door. 'I'll send someone to the course. See if Martin's there in case you draw a blank with Thompson.'

*   *   *

Harry Collins looked at the grime on his hands. His clothes felt gritty, the stubble on his chin prickled and he felt like hell. He looked around the cell. The small two-by-three table was of cheap pine; worn and scarred by years of misuse. He placed his hand on it and felt it sway. The legs were solid but ill fitting, and the only reason it stayed upright was because it was propped against the wall. The daylight was fading. He looked up at the ceiling and saw that the light was weak and almost ineffective.

He wondered if anyone had discovered his absence. He thought of Joe Davidson, Betty Rolands and Grace. He found himself staring at the darkening window and remembered that no one had looked in on him since early afternoon. Someone would be coming soon.

He looked at the table, turned it on its side, and took hold of one of the legs. He levered it back and forth until it came free of the nails that held it in place. He replaced the table, leaning it against the wall so that it remained upright. Now he had a weapon, a solid table leg, just less than two feet six inches long.

The bare mattress on the bed was covered with three grey blankets and two pillows. He stripped the covers, folded two of the blankets, added a pillow to resemble a body, and covered the bed with the third blanket.

He sat on the bed and waited.

Silence.

Nothing disturbed the quiet of the early evening. There was no sound from the girls. He wondered if they had been drugged.

It was dark now. Once the sun had dropped behind the hills to the west, night came rapidly to the city, with only the humidity remaining as a legacy of the hot summer day.

Suddenly he heard voices in the passage. He moved quickly, positioning himself so that the opening door would mask his body. He heard the key in the lock, and the door opened. He saw the dim shape in the glow of the ceiling light and swung the table leg. He heard a satisfying crack, and the body crashed to the floor.

Then he heard the voice behind him.

'Put that down and turn around slowly.'

CHAPTER FOURTEEN

The goons came first, quietly, without ceremony, peering into the bedrooms, pushing open the doors of the bathrooms, satisfying themselves that Victor was safe from the police, competitors, hit men or just his own demons. Janet La Barre sat on the ottoman, magazine on her lap, apparently oblivious of their arrogant presence. Roberts leant against the jamb in the open doorway, his demeanour professing his own arrogance and contempt. Their awareness of his contumely was evident in their expressions of resentment.

When they were done, one of them took up a position outside the back door, leaving it ajar. The other spoke softly into a radio and listened to the reply. He spoke to Roberts.

'Please close all the curtains. Stand away from the front door and you are both to remain seated. Keep your hands in plain sight.'

Roberts shrugged, closed the curtains, and sat beside the girl on the ottoman. She continued turning the pages of the magazine without looking up. She could have been alone on the peak of a mountain for all the attention she gave to his announcement. Hell, thought Roberts. *Keep your hands in plain sight.* It was

James Cagney at his worst.

When he arrived, Victor's entrance was equally endowed with melodrama; it was the scene where the big shot arrives. Roberts wondered if Victor had been watching the Edward G. Robinson entrance in *Key Largo*. It was all a bit ridiculous.

He came in quickly, followed by Grundling, who closed the door behind him. It was a replica of the previous day except for Victor's garb. He had on a pair of dark glasses and, incongruously for the time of day, a felt hat with the brim turned down. He was dressed in a pair of grey suede slacks, a silk shirt without a tie, and a pair of grey shoes. As soon as he was in the house he removed the hat and glasses. The goons went into the kitchen.

Victor looked at the girl, who had dropped the magazine to the floor. Then he turned his eyes on Roberts, who knew he was anything but ridiculous. The silence stretched to almost a minute before the two men moved to the big chairs on either side of the room. Roberts watched Victor, comparing the man before him with the facts contained in the police dossier, which described him as a ruthless killer. He saw only the face of a petulant hoodlum. But when he turned his attention to Victor's companion, he knew it would be a mistake to underestimate the depths of that man's depravity.

Victor was the first to speak.

'How many of your people have you brought in since last night?' His tone was bellicose and steeped in suspicion.

Janet stood up, her back stiff with displeasure. She walked to the liquor cabinet.

'How good of you to get here on time. Will you have a drink?'

Victor's face was suffused with anger. He clicked his fingers impatiently.

'I asked a question. I'm not here for social chit-chat.'

She continued pouring from the whisky bottle. Roberts watched her, admiration for her composure mingled with faint misgiving. If Victor walked out on them, the girls would never be seen again.

She looked at Roberts and held up the bottle. He nodded. She poured a drink for him.

'No one else?' She shrugged, handed Roberts his drink, and returned to her seat. She looked directly at Victor. 'There are just the two of us.' She sipped her drink. 'Oh, and, of course, Botha, my chauffeur. You saw him cleaning my car in the garage.' Her voice hardened. 'We're here to discuss business. Not to attack you or shop you. I'll do business with you, only on conditions of mutual trust. I have too much invested to risk working with people I can't trust.' Her voice softened. 'You trusted me enough to see your security.'

Roberts saw Victor visibly relaxing. His

admiration for his colleague grew as he watched the reaction of the two men. She had adopted exactly the right approach, refusing to be intimidated, leading them to believe that she had as much to lose as they did.

Oddly enough, Grundling was conciliatory.

'I'll have a whisky.'

Janet began to rise, but Roberts forestalled her. Grundling took the drink from the captain. 'It isn't that we don't trust you, but Victor wants to be sure that no one but you two will see him.'

Victor grunted impatiently. 'I want to get the girls off my hands. And quickly. I've made the shipment up to ten. What's the deal?'

Janet placed her drink on the small table beside her.

'I gave you a figure. I get half the money when you deliver the girls to me at the farm. The other half when I deliver them to the buyer.'

Roberts listened to the negotiations, his loathing for the two men masked by a bland expression of interest. He listened to his partner manipulating the two men, taking them skilfully along the path she had prepared for them. Listening to her, he began to believe for the first time that the operation could end within the next few days.

He was beginning to feel he had lived his whole life in this past year with Uncle John. He had spent less than three months at home in that time. The tension was getting to him; it was like living on the edge of a volcano. He wanted to get his life back. He was desperately tired. He was concerned too for the girl for whom he had been protective for so long. Yet, he wondered if she was not the stronger one, motivated by an all-consuming hatred of the monster who called himself Victor Piper. Day by day, she lived with the awareness of her responsibility for the safety of the missing girls; yet not for one moment did she betray the slightest evidence of nerves.

The sound of a dove calling, and the muted screeching of mynah birds, interrupted his reverie. His concentration had slipped.

He saw that Janet's glass was empty and he stood up to replenish it. She was speaking with authority.

'The girls must be delivered dressed in the clothing they would be wearing on a luxury holiday. Each must be equipped with a suitcase containing two changes of clothing, including underwear, and a complete cosmetic bag.'

Victor looked at her with contempt.

'You'll take them as they are.' He waved a hand. 'What is this? A Cook's tour?'

She stood up angrily. 'Either you accept my conditions or the deal's off.' She turned to Roberts. 'I don't need this shit. What the hell are we into here?' Her voice rose. 'I'm not doing any deals with a bunch of amateurs.'

Roberts took his cue. He looked at Victor and frowned angrily.

'She's right. We know exactly what conditions are necessary for a successful run.' He shrugged. 'We can't do the job unless all the elements are right.' He watched the girl sit and take a sip of her drink. 'Another thing. The girls must be in perfect health when they are handed over to us. If we lose any, we're responsible. If we guarantee delivery, we must start with healthy girls.'

Grundling stood up to hand his empty glass to Roberts. 'OK. OK. We accept your conditions.'

Victor shook his head angrily. 'No. I won't accept any conditions at all. We didn't have this crap with the South Americans. Or with Gaffney.'

Roberts felt a surge of triumph. Janet had told him about Victor's meeting with Gaffney and his complaint about the girl who had died. He handed a whisky to Grundling.

'And I'll lay you a hundred to five that you lost some of them.' He watched Victor closely. Then he said casually, 'We lost a few before we found the formula.'

Victor looked up sharply. Then he looked away, drumming his fingers on the arm of his chair, unwilling to concede their superior expertise.

Janet knew it was now or never: Victor's vanity must not be allowed to cloud his judgement. He was unpredictable and dangerous, prepared to sacrifice a deal rather than lose face. It was time to sweeten the pot, to feed his ego and make him feel he had won the round. She spoke quietly and persuasively.

'And I am prepared to accept payment on delivery.' She smiled. 'The only way I can be fairer than that is to do the job for nothing.'

She's gone too far, Roberts thought. She's thrown it away. There was a deep funereal silence in the room, reminiscent of the moment before the organist sits down, and the tail-coated ushers have intimidated the mourners into quiescence. Roberts realized then that they had won. If Victor had been about to refuse, he would have been abusive and contemptuous. Without his comprehending it, he had been negotiated into the best deal he could get, at the same time having been led to believe that he had forced the issue.

Victor nodded. 'I'll take it,' he said grudgingly. 'They will be delivered to you on those terms. But remember, if you lose one of them, you don't get paid.'

Janet thought that it was time to tighten the screws just a fraction. He might begin to believe the victory had come too easily.

'As was said, the girls must be delivered in perfect health. When they arrive I will have every one examined by my own tame doctor.'

'Agreed.' Victor was magnanimous in victory. It was not an unreasonable condition.

He could not have expected less.

Grundling smiled disarmingly. 'I think we should drink to that.' He knew that this was a one-off deal. Victor had no intention of paying anyway.

For the rest of his life, Roberts would remember the minutes that followed. The interruption came from the kitchen where the two thugs were waiting. They heard a tinny, agitated voice on the handheld radio. The four people in the room sat frozen into silence, waiting for a word from the men at the back. Grundling went into the kitchen, his voice coming inaudibly as he spoke into the radio.

He returned and looked down at Victor, his face a terrible mask of anger.

'It's Davidson. We have to put everything on hold until we've dealt with him.'

Victor was insane with rage.

'I told you,' he shouted. 'I told you, and you wouldn't listen. He must have found the printing-works.' He stood up. 'Now do as I say. Deal with him, but before you do, kill Collins.' He stood up. 'Kill the interfering little bastard.' He walked to the door.

Janet stood up quickly. 'What about our deal?'

He stopped at the door.

'The deal's off until I've solved this problem.' He went out followed by his men.

Roberts watched the girl sink on to the ottoman.

162

'Hell,' he said. 'What do we do now?'

* * *

Davidson watched the patch of sunlight move higher. The tables had been scrubbed and the assistants had gone to lunch. All hail to the new labour laws, Joe mused. He looked at his watch. Twelve-thirty. The whole morning was wasted. At that moment, he saw Doc enter the main door of the market hall. He came into his office, sat at his desk and looked directly at Davidson.

'From now on Joe, I want you to be very careful. I know you are not afraid of anyone, but be careful.'

'You're wrong, Doc. I'm afraid of everyone. That makes me respect everyone I'm up against.'

'Good. Be careful of this man. He is the worst.' He paused. 'If he ever gets out of this, he will come after you.'

'I look forward to meeting him.'

Doc's dark eyes looked at him with concern.

'It won't be a pleasure.'

Davidson nodded. 'Where did they pick him up?'

'As he was about to leave through those big doors out there. It was neat and quick. They had Beater cuffed and in the van before he knew they were behind him.'

'How long before they call?'

163

'Not long.' Doc began working on the ledger in front of him. In the main aisles of the sales hall, cleaners with wide squeegees hosed down the floor ready for the afternoon customers. In Warwick the midday traffic grew until the waterfall roar of it appeared to be in the office with him.

The telephone rang. Both men looked up. Doc hesitated before he lifted the receiver. He listened with eyes closed, grunted a few words in his own language, scribbled on a pad and tore off the page. He scrawled a rough map on the back and pushed it across the desk.

Davidson nodded wordlessly, picked up the paper and touched Doc on the shoulder. He walked out of the office.

*   *   *

The address was west of the city, beyond its urban sprawl. Davidson drove along the N3 to Hillcrest. There, leaving the lights of the village behind him, he turned east towards Inanda Road. At the old spice-works, he stopped and consulted Doc's map. Then he took a dirt road that wound into a valley, circled a grove of trees and climbed to the top of a ridge. He stopped at a dilapidated fence that enclosed a smallholding. A large sign, streaked and rusted, was nailed to an open vehicle gate.

185 THORNHILL ROAD KEEP OUT

Two rows of blue gum-trees lined the drive behind the gate. The fields beyond the trees were wild and overgrown with rank grass and oleander, milkweed and lantana. A cluster of buildings was just visible through the trees. Signs of neglect were everywhere.

It was quiet but the shrieks of Christmas beetles disturbed the silence. A slight breeze rustled the tops of the gum-trees, and far away a dog barked at imagined enemies. Bulbuls clustered amongst the thick bushes, endlessly twittering their liquid notes to one another.

Davidson drove slowly along the rutted drive. A black man carrying a shotgun waited on the stoep of the dilapidated house. He checked the number plates, lowered the gun and motioned him inside.

'They're waiting for you. Second door on the left.'

The house was bare of furniture, light fittings were ripped out, and the smell of damp and decay permeated the whole place. A lantern illuminated the main bedroom. Two Indian men watched over Thompson who was handcuffed to a window guard. His hands were behind his back, and his face was marked by red weals.

Davidson looked at the older man who stood just inside the doorway. The man stared at him impassively. He was huge, about two

165

metres in height, his muscled body bulging in a yellow tee shirt. He had a small cut over one eye. The other man was smaller but with the same look of a wrestler or weight-lifter. Davidson knew him as Cassim.

'Did he give you any trouble?'

The big man answered him. 'A little. But he soon calmed down.' He touched the cut over his eye.

Davidson looked at Thompson. 'I'm in a hurry. I want some answers. Where is Harry Collins?'

'Go to hell.'

Cassim stepped forward, ripped the man's shirt to the waist and held a knife to his stomach. Thompson spat at him.

'You stupid bastard. You're dead. You're all dead. Do you know who I am? Don't you know who I work for?'

Before Davidson could stop him, Cassim slashed at Thompson, slicing a gash from his chest to his navel. Thompson looked down in horror.

'No. Don't. Please don't.' He looked at Davidson. 'Don't let them do this to me. Please.' Words spilled from him. 'They've got Collins at the printing-works. Augustine Place. Stop them. Please. I'm bleeding to death.'

'How many people are guarding him?'

'Two men and two women. The women are there to look after the girls.' His voice rose hysterically. 'Please. Get me to a doctor.'

166

Saliva drooled from his mouth. Sweat gleamed on his bald head.

Cassim observed Thompson with detachment.

'What do you think, Joe? I would say that's the exact tone his rape victims used when they begged for mercy.'

Davidson nodded with contempt. 'I would say so.'

Thompson looked at them uncomprehendingly. Then all at once, it became clear to him that he was about to end his life in this stark, ill-lit, dirty room. He moaned once and sagged to his knees, his cuffed arms above his head.

Davidson turned and walked out of the room. Cassim followed him to the front door.

'Who owns this house?' asked Davidson.

'Doc's brother.' Cassim looked across the dark fields. 'He had to leave. It was too close to the shack settlement. He was burgled five times, his dogs were killed, and his family was threatened.'

Davidson nodded towards the room. 'What will you do with him?'

Cassim shrugged. 'Leave everything to me.'

As he walked towards his car, Davidson heard a scream, and then silence.

CHAPTER FIFTEEN

The printing-works stood in its own grounds in what had once been a garden factory. The driveway beyond the chain-link fence was rutted, gardens were weed-covered, and the outbuildings had the dilapidated look of premises long abandoned. The only incongruities were the pristine chain-link fence, the new steel gate, and the smart black security guard in the small gatehouse. In the dying early evening sunlight, Davidson could see the door of the main building with its shuttered windows on either side.

He stopped the car two hundred metres from the gate and turned it to face the main road. He sat watching the main building, where the only light glowed at the far end. Daylight was fading rapidly and soon he could no longer see the gatehouse. Quietly he opened the car door and walked to the boot, opened it and took an assault rifle from clips fitted to the spare wheel. It was a FA-MAS rifle of bull-pup design. It was equipped with an infra-red aiming spotlight and goggles. The French manufacturer had delivered a batch of these to an African country from which Davidson had acquired one through some inspired persuasion that had included some bribery.

Davidson detached the sight and goggles, and returned the rifle to its clips. He sat down to watch, slowly sweeping the front of the building with the aiming spot. Nothing moved beyond the fence. He was becoming impatient, constantly aware of Harry's predicament, but he knew that only patience could reward him now. From time to time, he made a slow sweep, staring through watering eyes at the green images behind the fence.

Eventually, he was rewarded by a slight movement at the corner of the building. A man armed with a shotgun walked slowly towards the security guard at the gate. He heard voices, but the words were inaudible. Then the man walked to the main door, opened a smaller Judas-door, and disappeared inside.

Davidson checked the Smith & Wesson in his holster and slipped a cosh into his back pocket. When he was sure the shotgun guard was not returning, he picked up the infra-red spot and goggles, took Doc's map and, holding it in front of him, walked noisily to the gatehouse. The guard watched him approaching. Davidson held the map in front of him.

'Do you know where this firm is?'

The man stared at the paper.

'Wait.' He took a key from his belt, unlocked the gate, and switched on his torch. As he took the paper, Davidson hit him behind

169

the ear, and caught the torch before it fell.

He dragged the guard behind the gatehouse, switched off the torch, and closed the gate. He left it unlocked.

He donned the man's cap, hoping for a few seconds' advantage if anyone confronted him. He walked purposefully towards the main entrance, opened the Judas-door, and slipped inside. He stood quite still until his eyes were accustomed to the dark. He donned the goggles, switched on the infra-red sight, and made a slow sweep of his surroundings.

He was in a spacious work area. Bare concrete plinths, once supporting heavy machinery, were spaced along the factory floor, while overhead, brackets and pulleys left over from the archaic system of centralized power, hung from the concrete ceiling. Parts of discarded machinery were piled in the corner. There was a door opposite him, and one to his left.

He stood listening to the malevolent silence, hearing the scrabbling of rats and the creak and shift of the roof timbers. Then he heard the distant sound of laughter coming from the passage ahead of him. Surmising that the lighted room was in that direction, he moved forward softly, avoiding the plinths, loose iron, and abandoned timbers. He left the pistol in its holster, knowing it was a weapon of last resort, for a body with a hole in it would be a major inconvenience in this place. He had no desire to attract attention to himself so soon after the Kloof affair. He was still waiting for the summons to an inquest for those deaths.

The lighted room was the one furthest from him, at the end of the passage. He moved forward cautiously, trying the door handles as he passed them. Only one was locked. His infra-red spotlight illuminated a piece of two-by-three timber about a foot long. He lobbed it into the work-area behind him where it bounced against a plinth and struck an old bucket. He stepped into one of the open rooms and waited.

The men were silent for a long moment. Then one of them spoke.

'What the hell was that?'

'Probably Joshua.'

'He shouldn't be inside. He should be watching the gate.'

There was a sound of approaching footsteps. The man with the shotgun passed him. Davidson stepped out behind him and clubbed him behind the ear. He caught him as he fell, but he could not prevent the shotgun clattering to the floor. He picked it up, felt for the slide and saw that it was an Auto 12-gauge with a shortened barrel.

A chair scraped in the lighted room. Davidson lifted the shotgun as a man appeared in the doorway and saw the peaked cap.

'Joshua?' He paused. 'Hell, you're not

171

Joshua.'

Davidson took off the cap and dropped it to the floor.

'No, I'm not Joshua.' He cocked the gun. 'What's your name?'

'Ford.' The sight of the man on the floor mesmerized him. 'Is he dead?'

'No. He's just joined Joshua in a little nap.'

'Who the hell are you? Do you know who owns this place?'

'I don't particularly care. Just shut up and listen. If you move, no one will hear the bang when this goes off.' He moved a step closer. 'Now look in all your pockets and tell me if you feel a weapon of any kind.'

'You're crazy. Grundling will kill you.'

'I'm sure he'll try, if I don't kill him first.' His voice hardened. 'Now do as I say.'

The man was very short, about five feet two with small mean eyes. He took a pistol from his jacket pocket, hesitated, bent over, and placed it carefully on the floor.

'Now the rest of it. Don't be a hero. Beater tried to be. It was just before he died.'

The man was appalled. 'You killed Beater?'

'My friends did. They're waiting outside, so don't be a hero.'

The man bent over, took the ankle gun from his left leg, and a knife from the small of his back. Davidson kicked them into the empty room.

'Good. Now, where's Collins?'

172

Ford nodded to the locked door. 'He's in there.'

'Open it.'

Ford's hands trembled as he inserted the key. He opened the door and stepped into the room. As he did so, a piece of table-leg struck the little man on the back of the head. Davidson saw Harry with his back to him. He spoke firmly.

'Put that down and turn around slowly.'

Collins dropped the table-leg.

'Joe.'

Davidson grinned with relief. 'I thought you were going to whack me with that thing.' He looked at Ford. 'You saved me the trouble.'

'Have you found the girls?'

'No. Are they here?'

'They were this morning.'

Ford stirred and sat up.

'Before we kill this little worm, let's see if he'll tell us where they are now.'

'I don't know.' The man began to babble. 'I really don't know.'

Davidson pointed the shotgun at his legs.

'Stand aside, Harry. He's lied to me once already. Let's see if he can walk on stumps.'

The man sank to his knees. 'Don't shoot. Please. If I knew, I'd tell you. I'm not lying now.'

Davidson nodded. 'No. I don't think you are. Come on, Harry. Let's go.'

The radio announcer was experienced. He knew which stories made dramatic radio, and which were ordinary, but it needed no special skill to recognize the dramatic significance of the story on the next page of his bulletin. He sharpened his voice and raised the tempo slightly.

At a news conference this morning, a police spokesman confirmed that there is a common factor linking the ten missing girls. It is understood that an important breakthrough has been achieved in the last few days.

In the meantime, more than a hundred convicted sex offenders have been questioned, borders, airports, and harbours are being watched, and roadblocks are being set up on a random basis. A reward of two million rand has been offered for information leading to the arrest of the kidnappers.

Anyone with information that can assist the police, is asked to call their nearest police . . .

The driver snapped off the switch that cut the voice in mid-sentence. There was a long silence in the cab. They were parked in a lay-by forty kilometres from the city centre. The co-driver looked out of the window at the sugar cane growing cab-high in the fields alongside the removal van. The driver looked at him occasionally, began whistling tunelessly, thought better of it, and watched the traffic whipping past him on the N2 to the north. Ahead of him was the long haul through Mpumalanga Province to Pietersburg. Each knew what the other was thinking, and each wondered when the subject would be raised.

Crowther licked his lips. Two million, he thought. It was a hell of a lot of money. More than he would ever earn as a co-driver for Grundling. He glanced at Spargel. His driver was looking straight ahead, seemingly oblivious to the news on the radio, but he knew. He knew. They had been driving together for months, and he could read his colleague like a book. The cliché seemed to give him some satisfaction. I can read him like a book, he thought happily. He wants it as much as I do.

Spargel cleared his throat. 'It's a hell of a lot of . . .' He stopped. 'I wonder when these bastards are coming.'

'That's not what you were going to say.'

'Yeah. Well.' Spargel was ill at ease. He looked up at the clear sky. 'At least we'll have good weather for the trip.'

Crowther shifted in his seat. 'No. Say it. Something about a lot of something.'

Spargel was suddenly filled with bravado.

175

He said harshly:

'It's a hell of a lot of money for someone to pay for the four girls we got in the back here.' He looked out of the window. 'I wonder where the others are.'

'Maybe in the rig we're waiting for.'

'Yeah.' He looked directly at Crowther. 'A million each.'

The silence stretched interminably, each man thinking his own thoughts, identical thoughts. Thoughts of a million each, and what he could do with it.

A slight breeze waved the top of the cane field. A truck roared past, whipping up the dust, the turbulence of its wake causing the van to twitch briefly. They looked down the valley to the sea stretching away to the horizon. They heard the drone of a plane dropping down to Virginia Airport.

Spargel sighed. 'A hell of a risk.'

Crowther nodded a reluctant assent. 'Nowhere to hide.'

Spargel scratched his chin. 'Wish these bastards would get here.' He frowned. 'Why do we need someone to show us the way?'

Crowther nodded. 'All they had to do was draw us a map.'

Spargel looked over the sea to where a Cessna was droning towards the airport.

'The pricks don't trust us. Or mebbe we're not going where they said.'

Crowther nodded slowly. That could be it,

he mused.

'They kept the destination secret until the last minute.' He realized the bastards were ahead of them. Reading their treacherous minds.

*　　　*　　　*

Ramona Gomez looked up at the small aperture through which light seeped into the cell where she and three other girls were confined. The cell had been constructed by enclosing six feet at the front of the van. Furniture was stacked in the remaining space so that the cell and its door were effectively camouflaged. A chemical toilet, a water-dispenser, and four bunk beds were the only concessions to comfort. Mercifully, an air-conditioning unit had been installed high up on the front end of the van.

All four girls wore the same drab uniform, a blue cotton frock, although Rowena Smith still had the ribbon she had been wearing when she was abducted fifty metres from her home. At sixteen, she was the oldest of the four, well built, pretty, with flaxen hair and blue eyes. The other girls, Candice Epstein and Sharon Witbooi, were fifteen and thirteen respectively. They were both on their bunks in a drug-induced sleep.

Ramona thought of her family. Tears sprang to her eyes.

'I'm frightened, Rowena. I know my father is coming to fetch me, but I'm frightened.'

Rowena stood beside her bunk and patted her shoulder.

'Hush. If you keep believing he will come, I know he will.'

CHAPTER SIXTEEN

Grundling unrolled the one-in-fifty-thousand scale map on the boardroom table, weighted the corners with four ashtrays, and glanced up at the inadequate lights in the ceiling. He spoke brusquely to the man at the end of the table.

'Put the spots on, Pearson.'

The man reached out to the switch. The office took on a sharp, businesslike ambience, the off-white walls throwing the light back into the centre of the room, giving the illusion that the ceiling had suddenly become a little higher. It was a tribute to the décor specialists, but the single painting on the wall was Victor's choice. It was a print of De La Tour's *Cheat with the Ace of Diamonds*, which was perhaps more a Freudian choice than an aesthetic one. It was in contrast to the stark environment. The room could not have been mistaken for anything but what it was, a workplace for those whose thoughts transcended the functions of daily living. It was a place where the pursuit of business interests predominated.

Victor stalked into the boardroom, removed his jacket, and threw it over a chair-back. Pearson took it and hung it on a coat-tree in the corner.

'You can leave us, Pearson.' He began to undo his shirt cuffs. 'Stay close. I may need you.' He gave Pearson a slight nod. The man looked at Grundling's back, gave Victor a slight nod, and went out quietly, closing the door behind him. He went directly to a small office down the corridor, unlocked a small safe, took out a pair of headphones, and listened intently to the conversation in the boardroom.

Victor spoke without looking up from the map.

'Have you found Thompson?'

'No. It doesn't look good. His car was found in Warwick Avenue.'

Victor looked up, his face dark with rage.

'You leave three people at the printing-works, and Davidson walks right through them.' His fist struck the table. 'Then he takes Collins from under your nose.'

'Ordinarily three would have been enough.'

'That's why I told you to deal with him.' Victor walked to the water cooler and filled a glass. 'I'm not going to say it again.' His voice rose. 'Deal with him at once.' He sipped the water. 'I want Davidson, Collins and

179

Davidson's wife.'

'Davidson isn't married.'

'Li says there is a woman in the flat.'

Grundling shrugged. 'You know how it is.'

'Don't split bloody hairs. She must be important to him. I want her too.'

'We'll have to take her first. And take him when he comes for her.'

'I don't care how you do it. Just get it done.' He ran his finger over a map feature. 'Where is she now?'

'At her office at the university. He's at his flat with Collins.' Grundling spoke calmly but his resentment was growing; it was resentment born out of Victor's failure to acknowledge that whatever Grundling had done, he had done it with his employer's approval. He resented the tantrums, and Victor's assumption of his own inerrancy.

Victor ran his finger along the N2 North. He grunted.

'Where are the girls now?'

'They're all in two pantechnicons, on their way north. They'll be at the Kwambonambi farm tonight.'

Victor's finger moved. 'That's only a hundred and eighty kilometres.'

'It's far enough. Remember, the minibus has to be ten kilometres ahead to signal roadblocks.'

Victor nodded. 'As long as they rendezvous with the La Barre woman on time.'

'You're forgetting that we left things in the air.'

'But we closed a deal.'

Grundling felt a rekindling of his resentment. 'We agreed on terms, but we never closed the deal.' He was aware that Victor's precipitate exit had created unnecessary complications. He wondered whether La Barre was still in the city. 'I'll set up another meeting.' He spoke with thinly disguised reproach. 'I think we should remember that she doesn't need us all that much, but we certainly need her.'

'She'll sign.' Victor went back to his study of the map. 'The place we rented is just a hundred kilometres from her farm outside Pietersburg.' He looked up. 'The girls will be out of the way until we hand them over.' He looked up at Grundling. 'Unless the stupid cretins get lost. Get them started. I won't be happy until they're on the road.' Grundling turned to leave the room. 'And Piet . . .' Grundling paused. Victor's face was a mask of hatred. 'Deal with Davidson.'

*   *   *

Uncle John's attitude expressed a confidence he did not feel.

'Victor will be back. He needs us.'

Roberts turned and looked out at the neat garden of the safe house. He turned abruptly

181

to face Uncle John.

'Hell, we were so close.'

Uncle John nodded. 'You were closer than you knew.'

Janet looked at him questioningly. 'Oh? How?'

'I went over the tapes several times. Just before he left, Victor referred to the printing-works. We know he was once owner of a printing-works in Augustine Place.' He spoke quietly. 'We could not identify any of his properties in which the girls could have been held. The reference to the printing-works led us to the building in Augustine Place.' He turned a page of the file in front of him. 'I sent in a team.' He waved a hand. 'Forensics, finger print staff—the works.' He stood up to relieve the stiffness of tension. 'We will know by tonight what we've got.'

Janet was uncharacteristically inelegant.

'It's a right bastard. We know who Victor is, we know who his top men are, and we can't lay a hand on them until we have the girls.' She poured coffee from the tray on the table. 'I was too damned concerned over the loss of the deal to listen to what he was saying.'

The general shook his head. 'No regrets, now.'

Roberts turned from the window and touched her on the shoulder.

'Remember, I was there as well. I should have listened too.'

She smiled gratefully, shook her head, and took her coffee to the sofa. She watched the general over the rim of her cup.

A stiff breeze whipped through the chinks in the old house, whining on a rising note, and then dropping to a quiet moan to the accompaniment of the soft tapping of a mango-tree on the window. Opposite her, the high sideboard, all angles, shelves and knobs, towered over the rest of the furniture. She wondered what the department would do with the house when its usefulness was at an end. The general refused to use a safe house more than once. Each house was bought for a single operation and then sold, usually at a profit. Womanlike, she began a mental refurbishing; what pieces she would buy and where she would place them.

Then all at once she was seized by a miasma of melancholy, occasioned as much by uncertainty as the prospect of a final confrontation. She had never considered herself as someone who was especially heroic, but she knew without conceit that at no time of her life had she tested the boundaries of her fortitude. She had no qualms about what lay ahead. She knew it was banal to attribute this to her training, for she was always aware that the core of her fortitude existed within her own individuality.

Janet placed her cup on the side table. As she watched Uncle John consulting the file in front of him, she wondered idly why he had chosen that code name. Then she realized how apt it was. He was the quintessential wise uncle, ever present, tolerant, and protective. He turned a page and looked up at them.

'We have ten men from the local stations near the farm. To avoid suspicion, they will continue their normal duties until we signal them to move in. We have two helicopters on standby and a platoon from a special service battalion within radio distance, in case there is an armed confrontation.'

Roberts smiled inwardly. Armed confrontation indeed. If the Old Man meant a bloody shootout, why didn't he just say so?

The general shuffled some pages in the file. 'Charlestown Holdings was the key. Once we had that, we had Victor.'

Roberts frowned. He looked at Janet. 'Victor appeared to be very angry with a man named Davidson.' He turned to the general. 'Do we know a man named Davidson? Could it be Joe Davidson?'

The general smiled with his lips. His eyes remained as hard as basalt.

'It could indeed. He is causing us considerable inconvenience. He was one of the two men who spirited away Mrs Eripides before the investigation was finalized.' He tugged his ear, frowning as though it had caused him pain. 'Someone was at the printing-works before our men arrived. I'll lay odds it was Davidson. I believe he went there to get the second man away.'

Janet picked up her coffee. 'Do we know who the second man is?'

'Collins of Collins Security. I've sent a team to pick them both up. They'll be charged with obstruction of justice.' His voice hardened. 'I'll have them both put away until we have Victor.' He closed his file and stood up. 'I'm sick and tired of interfering freebooters endangering the lives of these girls.'

CHAPTER SEVENTEEN

Davidson woke when Margaret left for the library, went back to sleep, and woke at eight o'clock to the sound of frantic ringing on his front-door bell. He hauled himself sluggishly out of bed, donned his brown towelling dressing-gown, and went to the front door. Mrs Eripides, in dark-blue dress and dark-blue voile headscarf, and carrying a cardboard suitcase, pushed past him into the living-room. As he shut the door, he glimpsed a taxi driving away.

'For God's sake, Grace, I thought I told you to stay out of sight.'

Silently Mrs Eripides took off her scarf, folded it neatly, and put it on the arm of the sofa. Her hair was neat, pulled back into a severe bun, her cheeks lightly touched with blush, and her lips had the faint trace of some deep shade of lipstick. She looked as though something—or someone—had encouraged her to take pride in her appearance. Davidson saw nothing of the dowdy old woman from Rydal Avenue.

She sat down, folding her hands in her lap.

'Dammit, Joe, that is the dullest place I've ever visited. A bunch of old people, looking as though they were in God's waiting-room. There was only one person there I could relate to.'

Davidson smiled. 'A man? Right?'

'Go to hell.' She looked away and smiled. 'But you're right. He was a very nice fellow, but he was married, and a woman couldn't have a conversation without some people butting in.'

'His wife?'

She looked away, refusing to meet his eyes.

'Right. But I wasn't trying to steal him away. He was an interesting talker, and he had so much to say that was fascinating to hear; about the mines and about the sea. He had been involved in both.' She shrugged and looked at him. 'Some people thought he was a bore, but they were only interested in recipes or knitting.' Her voice reflected her scorn. 'And she was the worst. Kept telling him to stop being a bore.' Her voice grew soft. 'She didn't realize he just wanted to remember the time

186

when he was young and happy.' A smile touched her lips. 'And he was so pleased to find someone who was genuinely interested in what he had to say.'

Her voice stopped abruptly.

Davidson went to the chair opposite her. 'Would you like breakfast? Tea?' She shook her head. 'How did you get here?'

'I took the morning plane from Margate.' She looked up at him. 'Anyway, I didn't come back because I was bored. I came back because I got to thinking about the people who tried to kill me.' She looked at him defiantly, her eyes reflecting her anger. 'I've a home and furniture, and those bastards aren't going to keep me out of it. If they come back, I'll deal with them.'

Davidson shrugged. 'What do you want me to say? Bravo? Good for you?' He leant forward. 'Grace, these men are vicious killers. They won't be satisfied until they shut your mouth permanently. If one fails, they'll send another.'

'I don't care,' she said stubbornly. 'I'm not prepared to live like this, running from my own shadow.' She frowned. 'That's another thing. What the hell have they got against me?'

'You saw two of their men. And you probably know too much about Kay Kelsey.'

She looked at him reflectively. 'No. That doesn't hold water. I can't prove anything. I never saw anyone killed.'

187

As Davidson looked at her, he saw the stubborn chin, the eyes, honest and intelligent, and the integrity that dominated her whole life. He suspected that it was a reluctance to come between a man and his wife that drove her from Margate. So, she left. It said much for the probity and dignity of this lonely old woman. Others as lonely as she was would be attracted to her repose and ability to listen.

'Grace, these people don't need a reason. They are part of a despicable and dangerous business, and killing is the least of their crimes.' He went on to tell her about the missing girls, the killing at Durban North, and the kidnapping of Harry Collins.

'How is Harry?'

'He's fine. He's in the other room. He's still asleep.'

'The hell I am.' Harry appeared in the doorway, showered and dressed. 'Hullo Grace. Was it your symphony concert on the doorbell?'

Grace stood up. 'Well, this is a lovely surprise.'

Harry hugged her. 'You're surprised? What are you doing here?'

'I'm not going through all that again.'

Davidson stood up. 'Harry. Make some coffee. I'll be out as soon as I'm dressed. Then we'll see if Grace's house is safe.'

While he dressed, he heard the muted voices, loud laughter, and the clatter of coffee cups.

The telephone rang in his study. He finished strapping on his watch and answered it. He heard Mrs Grant's voice asking for him. She had the addresses of the directors of Charlestown Holdings. He asked her to fax the information to him.

A note on the desk from Margaret caught his eye. She had taken a message from the serio lab, asking if he was certain that the bloodstained carpet in the front bedroom was the one that he wanted analysed. He frowned. It seemed to him a peculiar enquiry. How many bloodstained carpets did Grace have in her house?

Davidson dialled a number from memory. Doc's deep voice answered his. Davidson dispensed with formalities.

'Doc, where can I find Biggie at this time of day?'

'If you're not in a desperate hurry, I know where he'll be at lunchtime.'

'No great hurry.'

'He lunches at the Beldam.'

'Every day?'

'His brother, Sam, left money . . .'

'I remember now. The trust.' Biggie was simple. You couldn't trust him with a cent. He would have blown his entire inheritance on a rank outsider, so Sam put the money in trust, and all Biggie's bills were sent to the MacFee Trust.

'He used to lunch at the Central, but when that closed down he shifted his business to the Beldam.'

'Thanks, Doc. I owe you one.'

'Any time.'

Suddenly, Davidson was aware of an ominous quiet in the flat. He went into the living-room, where he saw Harry and Grace at the window. Grace put her finger to her lips.

'Police. Four coming up the drive, two around the back.'

Davidson shrugged. 'I don't think they're coming in for coffee.'

She pushed him towards the bedroom. 'Get what you need, and let me handle them.' She went towards the door. 'Be ready to leave in a hurry.'

Davidson smiled. 'You'll handle . . .' He stopped and looked into her determined eyes. Who else, he thought? He went through to the study, took the Ghisoni and a nine-millimetre Browning from the gun safe, and put money into his wallet. He picked up his cellphone and threw some toilet articles into a valise. He paused as he heard the front-door bell.

'Yes, officer? Can I help you?'

A deep voice answered her. 'I would like to speak to Mr Davidson. Mr Joseph Davidson.'

'Oh, you would, would you. Well you can just go down to number one, where you'll find the son-of-a-bitch with his girlfriend.' Her voice rose to a screech. 'Not content with taking her to the Edward for dinner, the bastard stayed the night. And now they're off to Mauritius.'

'Mauritius, ma'am?'

'You're damn right. They're booked on the eleven o'clock flight.'

'From Durban International?'

'Do you know what he looks like?'

'No, ma'am.'

'I have a picture in my bag.' There was a moment of silence.

'Here. That's him.' A pause. 'No you can't take it. It's evidence.'

'Thank you, ma'am.' His voice rose to a shout. 'Van Wyk. Go to the back of number one.' He heard some confused shouting and then silence.

Grace hurried into the study.

'Quickly. The car keys.' She went through to the garage and started the car. Collins came from the bedroom, his face creased in a delighted grin.

Davidson growled at him. 'What are you laughing at?'

'Stayed the night, did you?'

'Get off my back.' He picked up Grace's bag. They heard the car start and the gears grate. They caught a glimpse of a uniformed back at the far end of the complex before they coasted down the drive. Grace looked over her shoulder. 'Keep your heads down.'

'Evidence, Grace? Evidence of what?'

'Evidence of obstruction if I had let him keep it.'

'Whose picture is it?'

'Omar Sharif in *Lawrence of Arabia*.'

Harry laughed. 'Complete with burnous?'

'Is that's what it's called? Anyway, his mind wasn't on the photo. He was excited about Flat One.'

'How did you come to have a photo of Sharif?'

'He's a great actor,' she replied with dignity. She smiled as she slowed for a traffic signal. 'And he's handsome. Besides, his photograph came with my new bag.'

Davidson contained his laughter with difficulty. 'What made you think up that outrageous tale?'

'The more outrageous the lie, the more believable it is.' She turned into the freeway. 'Hitler taught us that.'

'They might have come to see me about something quite innocent.'

She glanced at him with scorn. 'Delivering a paper marked *Warrant of Arrest*.'

'I hope Mrs Crain can convince the police that I'm not hiding in her flat.'

Davidson remembered Thompson. There would be others. He dialled rapidly on his cell phone. 'Margaret can't go back there tonight.' He looked thoughtful. 'I wonder what the police want me for, this time.'

From a block roof high up on the ridge, the Chinaman focused his binoculars on Davidson's car as it left the complex, and then turned his attention to Victor's watchers as the car passed in front of them. Victor's surveillance team saw the woman driving and went back to their magazines and radio programmes. He smiled contemptuously. These were the types that the philosopher called the perfect pebbles. *Better,* he said, *a flawed diamond, than a perfect pebble.* Victor's disasters would continue as long as he employed idiots. Li had no intention of allowing any more disasters to ruin his success. He would see this consignment on its way to Hong Kong, and get out before the roof fell in.

He had appointed himself the secret guardian of the operation. The surveillance team had failed their assignment at the first test. They saw a woman driving Davidson's car without him. Ergo. Davidson had not left the building. The sight of policemen rushing to Flat One meant nothing to them. To him it was clearly a ploy to escape while they searched the wrong flat.

He went down to his car, drove the short distance towards the complex and parked a few metres from the back gate. He waited patiently until the frustrated policemen had retreated from the complex before he got out

193

of the car. It took him only minutes at Davidson's flat to establish that the doors and windows were impregnable. Given the right tools, he could break in anywhere, but this flat showed all the signs of sophisticated security.

Next door, however, it was a different story. He knocked, waited a full minute before knocking for a second time. When no one answered, he picked the simple mortise lock and let himself in. He smelt the slight mustiness of an empty house. He took up a position at the front window from where he had a clear view of the flat next door and would see when Davidson's woman returned.

Li was a slightly built man, intelligent and wily, with an animal's ability to sense imminent danger. He knew that there was danger in the continuing instability of Victor's plans. Nothing he had seen of Victor's organization made him confident of the outcome. Most of the men Grundling employed were lazy and incompetent, and it was only Li's ability that had taken them this far. He knew the triad wanted the girls, but if they did not get this consignment, there would be others.

It was his pride that was at stake here. His father had sent him to complete this assignment, and he had no intention of losing face through the failure of the shoddy talents waiting outside the gate. He wondered when they would discover that Davidson had long gone. Even the police had small expectations of Davidson's return. A solitary constable had been assigned to watch the flat. It would not be long before he would begin to wonder about the two idiots parked outside the complex.

Now Li was baiting his own trap for Davidson.

From the roof of a block of flats high above Ridge Road, the man called Pearson watched Davidson's complex through a pair of powerful binoculars. He saw the watchers in the road, and noted the Chinaman's entry into the neighbour's flat. He sighed.

It seemed no one trusted anyone. He dialled Victor on his cellphone.

CHAPTER EIGHTEEN

The call came when Margaret was out of the office. It was taken by Joan Cope, a woman without too much intelligence and less common sense.

'Miss Ryan's office.'

'Is Miss Ryan in? This is Joe Davidson.'

'Margaret isn't in, Mr Davidson. She's at a meeting of the Purchasing Committee.'

'Will you see she gets an urgent message?'

'Of course.'

'On no account is she to go home. She is to go to the Paris Hotel. She is to book in and wait for me there.' He paused. 'Have you got all that?'

'The Paris Hotel. Right.'

She replaced the receiver, pulled a pad towards her, and wrote the message.

Don't go home. Mr Davidson wants you to meet him at the Paris Hotel. Book in and wait for him.

She continued filing documents.

When Margaret returned, she saw the note, smiled, and threw it into the wastepaper basket. She wondered what the occasion was. From time to time they had celebrated some special occasion at the Paris or the Royal. She decided she would dash home first.

She called to Joan at the cabinet.

'If Joe calls, tell him I'll meet him after I've fetched an overnight bag.'

*   *   *

Davidson replaced the receiver and walked to the window overlooking the Marine Parade and the beach. The Paris was located at the north end of the Parade. Grace, to her delight, had been installed in a room that faced north. It had a view along the coast as far as Umhlanga Rocks.

Davidson stared out beyond the breakers, where yachts drifted sluggishly in the light airs. On the horizon ships waited for a berth in the overcrowded port. He walked out on to the small balcony to catch the slight breeze.

A luxurious cabin cruiser was passing the north pier, heading for the open sea. He thought he recognized her. He shaded his eyes against the shifting sparkles of the sea and nodded happily. The smart white cruiser with black-and-gold trim was the *Allure*. Some months ago he had gone out for marlin with the owner, John Williamson. He was willing to concede that it was only through John's expertise that he had taken a magnificent specimen. He watched longingly as the beautiful cruiser turned seawards and her silhouette disappeared towards the horizon. Not the least of the ingredients of his memorable day out were the wonderful gourmet meals served aboard.

There was a discreet knock at the door. He went back inside as Harry entered without waiting for a reply.

'I'm ready when you are.'

Davidson shook his head. 'I'm not hungry, Harry.' He picked up his coat. 'Bring Grace in here, and order from room service. I'll go across to the Beldam and wait for Biggie.'

'The manager says they don't expect him until one o'clock.'

'Biggie may be early.' He pulled on his coat. 'And Harry,' he paused at the door, 'Margaret should arrive about one. She works half-day today. Leave a message at the desk for her.' He waved an impatient hand. 'My room number; don't go out until I come back. That sort of thing.'

'Right.' He watched Davidson close the door behind him. He stared down at the busy Parade, wondering if he should ring Betty Rolands. He thought of her as he had seen her last, cowed and frightened with the marks of the beating still on her face. He knew he had to get her away from Rupert Rolands.

Kay Kelsey.

His search for her appeared to be a lost cause. He should let Betty know that. He should tell her to expect the worst. He suspected Davidson thought as he did, given the man's preoccupation with the kidnapped girls. He wondered whether it was wise to become involved in that. The police were swarming all over the place, following every lead, watching the borders, airports and harbours. What could two people accomplish that they could not?

He glanced at the telephone and back to the distant horizon where the sea shimmered in the late morning sunlight. Should he ring Betty Rolands and tell her that he had no more leads to follow? Wouldn't it be kinder to let her know that finding Kay Kelsey was a task that was beyond him? He sighed. He would give it one more day.

He phoned down to reception, left Davidson's message for Margaret and redialled the number for his own offices at

Collins Security. He needed an update on the alterations and some other minor problems. All at once, he realized how bored he had become with the daily routine. He compared his dull lifestyle with that of Joe Davidson's. Then he wondered if the uncertainty would suit him; but he decided finally that his own lifestyle would be ideal if he could share it with Betty Rolands.

An unlikely prospect.

The ringing tone stopped. He heard Mrs Grant's voice.

'Collins Security.'

'This is Harry, Mrs Grant.'

'Oh, Harry. I'm glad you called.' As her calm voice came through the earpiece, his uncertainties vanished. This was his *métier*. 'There are some messages for you. Mr Stoltz thanks us for the improvement in our service.' He heard a paper rustle. 'Mac wants to spend a few thousand more on the alterations.'

'Did he say how much more?' Then his caution vanished. 'Oh hell. Tell him to take another ten grand. It'll calm him down and keep him happy.' He paused. 'I'll sign the requisition when I get back to the office.'

'Oh. And when will that be?'

Harry smiled at the rebuke. 'Later today.'

'You'd better phone first.' Her voice dropped and her tone became conspiratorial. 'The police have been here.'

'What did they want?'

199

'Answers to some questions.'

'I think perhaps I'll stay away for a while until I've cleared up a couple of things.'

'I hope you do.' She chuckled. 'I hate prison visiting.'

'Did I hear you laughing?'

'Well, why not? Harry Collins on the run from the police. Don't you find it funny?'

'Excruciating.'

'It's not as funny as a Marx Brothers movie, but I can't think of anything more salutary. Perhaps you'll keep your mind on business in future.' Harry heard the rustling of paper. 'There's one more message for you. A Mrs Rolands wants you to call her.'

There was a long silence. 'Harry. Are you still there?'

'Yes. I'm still here.' He wondered if by some paranormal phenomenon her call had prompted him to think of her. He shrugged. He was getting weird. Recent events had inspired a chimerical unreality. 'Thank you, Mrs Grant. I'll call her.'

'Harry.' Her voice was soft, almost pleading. 'Be careful.'

'I will. And thanks.'

He broke the connection and began dialling.

'Rolands and Bannen.'

'Mrs Rolands, please.'

'She is in conference now. May I tell her who called?'

'Harry Collins.'

'Oh, Mr Collins. She left instructions to put you through if you called.'

He listened to music for a few seconds before Betty answered.

'Harry?'

'It is. You wanted me to call.'

'Yes. I must see you. Now if possible.'

The urgency in her voice made him uneasy. 'I'm sorry, Betts. If it's about Kay, I haven't been able to trace her yet.'

'It isn't about Kay. I know it's too early.' There was a pause. Harry heard the sound of a door opening. Betty spoke to some one in the office. 'I won't be a minute. Carry on with the fashion spot. I'll be out in a minute.' He heard a door close. 'Sorry about that, Harry. We're just wrapping up an issue. I must see you.'

Harry thought for a moment. 'I'm at the Paris. Can you come here? Suite four.'

'The Paris? What are you doing there?'

'It's a long story. Suite four.'

'In ten minutes.'

Harry depressed the cradle and dialled Mrs Eripides' room.

She answered at once.

'Grace. I won't be able to meet you for lunch. Get room service to send up something for yourself.'

He heard her laugh. 'You've made my day. I've always wanted to call room service.' She rang off.

201

It was a little more than ten minutes before Harry heard the soft tap at the door. When he opened it, he was filled with the same sense of loss he had felt so many years ago. She stood for a moment, smiling nervously. She wore a light summer blouse, white with a blue scarf to add a businesslike touch. With it, she wore a plain blue skirt. Her hair was a soft, shoulder length, caught at the back with a blue bow.

She craned her head to look past him. 'Is there someone with you?'

'No. Come in.' He stood aside, motioning her to the sofa. He moved towards the telephone. 'Can I order something for you? A drink? Coffee?'

She shook her head. 'Not right now.' She dropped her hands to her lap, twisting her ring nervously. 'I spoke to Rupert last night. About a divorce.'

He nodded. 'And?'

'He said that if I left him, I would regret it.'

'Oh? How?'

She shrugged. 'He has ways of punishing me.' He saw the glistening tears. 'At least a dozen ways.'

'But if you left him . . .'

'You don't know him, Harry. He's vindictive and insanely jealous.' She looked down at her hands and up at him. 'Were you serious, Harry?' Her eyes were pleading. 'About us.'

'Of course. I have never stopped loving you. If I didn't realize it before, I know it now.' He

202

saw gladness in her eyes and on her lips. He went to her and lifted her to her feet. He held her close. 'Leave him, Betts. Even if he won't divorce you.'

As she hid her face against his shoulder, he thought he heard a small chuckle. She looked up and smiled wickedly through her tears.

'Is this the part where we go into the bedroom?' Suddenly he felt a sense of *déjà vu*. She was repeating the exact words she had spoken years ago when they had been alone in her house. He remembered his adolescent reaction. He had felt the moment called for chivalry, and he had regretted it all his life.

'If you think I am going to give you the chivalrous answer again . . .'

She laughed. 'I would have dragged you kicking and screaming.' She took his hand and pulled him towards the bedroom.

*   *   *

They lay on the bed, lazily content. She stroked his hair away from his forehead.

'I can't live without you, Harry. I have to leave him, whatever it takes.'

He smiled. 'I've said it before. Even if I have to kill him for you.'

She sat up frowning. 'It wasn't funny then. And it isn't funny now.'

He sobered. 'I know. I just want you to know how much I love you.'

'I'll talk to him again tonight. I'll make him understand I'm serious.'

As he caressed her, he looked into her eyes. 'I've never known such happiness. What stopped us, Betts?'

She coloured slightly. 'I wanted to, remember, and you didn't.' She sighed theatrically. 'What a waste. We could have kept ourselves busy every day after school.' She giggled.

'I don't believe what I'm hearing.' He laughed. 'Anyway, I wouldn't have known how.'

'That wouldn't have been a problem,' she said airily. 'I'd have shown you.' She threw back the covers and walked towards the bathroom just as a pillow sailed over her head. He heard her laughter as she slammed the door.

* * *

The Beldam was a small comfortable hotel catering to the retirement trade. Elderly guests found it quiet, with reasonable rates and a dining-room that provided appetizing meals without the pretensions of the more luxurious establishments. It was in Gillespie Street, half a mile from the Paris.

Biggie had not arrived for lunch. Davidson went through to the bar where he ordered a Castle. The beer was cold, the glass frosted, and the first two sips were like nectar. The only other occupant was a small swarthy man who was writing rapidly on red cards that Davidson recognized as computerized betting cards. All at once, he felt the familiar prickling of his scalp. He drained his glass and surreptitiously moved to the corner of the bar where he was hidden from the man by an angle of the wall. He did not have long to wait.

He heard Biggie before he saw him. He bustled into the bar, calling out as he saw the swarthy man.

'Hey, Jimmy. Have I got a good thing for you today? Twenty to one and past the post.'

Davidson hadn't seen Biggie in five years, but he remembered the same hoarse voice, the white open-neck shirt, the grey baggy trousers, and the inevitable good thing at twenty to one, that usually came in at two o'clock. If he hadn't heard Biggie's greeting, he would have guessed that the swarthy man was James Martin.

Davidson watched as he filled out the cards, opened his wallet, and took out a hundred-rand note. 'Seventy-two for the pick-six, and the rest for you. Make bloody sure you get it on.'

'I'll guarantee it. Have I ever let you down?'

'There's always a first time.' He stood up. 'And Biggie,' he pocketed his wallet, 'don't carry the bet because your good thing isn't in it.'

Biggie looked pained. 'I wouldn't be so stupid.' He stacked the cards and tucked the money in his back pocket. 'When do you leave?'

'Tonight. I'll miss tomorrow's meeting.' He went towards the door. 'Remember to get my bet on.'

'I guarantee it, Jimmy.'

Martin ambled from the bar. Davidson watched him through the window as he paused for a moment on the hotel steps before stepping out into the street. Davidson waited for Biggie to hitch himself on to a barstool before he spoke.

'Hey Biggie. No time for your old friends?'

Biggie looked confused for a moment, peering shortsightedly into the shadowy corner. Then he beamed.

'Joey. Hey, man.' He walked over. 'Haven't seen you in years. Where you been keeping yourself?'

Davidson shrugged. 'Here and there.' He knew Biggie didn't read the papers. 'I've been out of town.' He nodded towards the door. 'Who's your friend?'

Biggie's voice took on a note of pride.

'That's Jimmy Martin. He's a big wheel in the race game.' Biggie smiled happily. 'Him and me're friends.'

'I see that. I haven't seen him around. Where does he live?'

'He's got the penthouse at Gatehouse

206

Mansions.'

Davidson spoke for a while of old friends, good times and bad, and of trainers Biggie had known. He heard his own voice making comments, answering questions, and found himself listening to Biggie's rambling stories about his gambling coups. He knew that Biggie had already forgotten his interest in James Martin.

Davidson stood up.

'Biggie, it's been great. I have to run.' He paused. 'I suppose Martin has an expensive car too.'

'A big green Mercedes,' Biggie said proudly.

In the street, Davidson flinched as the heat enveloped his body and drew the perspiration from his skin. Before he had reached the sanctuary of the air-conditioned lounge on the first floor of the Paris, he could taste the cold, crisp beer he was about to order.

But first he had to speak to Margaret.

At the desk, the receptionist had no knowledge of Miss Ryan's arrival. Yes, she had been given a message for her. She produced it from the key box behind her, but Miss Ryan had not been in to claim it.

Uneasy now, he went to the telephone in the foyer. He dialled the number for the university. Joan Hope answered.

'Miss Ryan's office.'

'Is Margaret there, Joan?'

'No, Mr Davidson. She left early today.'

'Did she get my message?'

'To go to the Paris Hotel?'

'That one. Did she get it?' Davidson found it difficult to disguise his exasperation with this dull woman.

'I put it on her desk.'

'You told her that on no account was she to go home?'

'Only to get her overnight bag.'

'Then she did go home first?'

'That's what she said she would do.'

Hiding his anger with difficulty, Davidson rang off. He went up to his room, wondering if Margaret had been intercepted by the police. He discarded the idea. They wanted him, not Margaret. He switched on the air-conditioning and went into the shower. He would give her half an hour. He would have to know she was safe before going up against Martin.

The police. What the hell did they want him for? They had shown Grace a warrant of arrest, and that meant it had to be something serious.

As the cold water streamed over his body, he felt the tensions draining away, taking away the uncertainty and misgivings, and leaving him confident that he could handle any crisis that faced him.

So, why was he so uneasy about Margaret?

*   *   *

Margaret was one of the fortunate ones on the university staff. She had been allocated a parking bay under a giant fig-tree, probably because no one coveted one that was occasionally the focus of attention of the mynah birds in the neighbourhood. She considered that the rare splash of birdlime was infinitely preferable to a car that had an interior temperature of a hundred and twenty degrees in mid-summer.

She stowed her briefcase on the passenger seat and drove on to the university motorway, descending the hill towards South Ridge Road. As she drove into the back entrance of her flat, she noticed a Nissan standing in front of the entrance to the Conroys' flat. She looked at it uneasily. It wasn't their car, and they weren't due home until Monday. Her uneasiness raised her awareness of her surroundings. She looked around her, noting familiar details with a heightened sentience, conscious of the quiet and the loneliness of the complex in the sleepy afternoon. She felt a frisson of fear, wondering if she was about to cross the frontiers of Joe's alternative lifestyle. She knew he often ventured into danger, but the perils had never reached out to her before; the danger had never shown her its menacing guise.

She looked at the blind kitchen window, curtained by prosaic red and white drapes. She saw the closed and presumably locked back door. She looked down at the red grano step.

There, faintly showing on the red polished floor, was a footprint.

Her cellphone was still on her office desk.

She touched the accelerator and realized that the motor was still running. Quietly she backed the car out of the driveway, turned in the street, and drove to the post office in South Road. She inserted a coin and dialled rapidly. Her hands were shaking so badly, she wasn't even sure if it was the right number.

'Paris Hotel.'

'Mr Dav . . . Mr Da . . .' Margaret took a deep breath and exhaled slowly. 'Mr Davidson please.'

She waited a moment.

'Davidson speaking.'

Her relief was overwhelming, but she forced herself to speak calmly.

'Joe. It's Margaret. There's someone in the Conroys' flat.'

'Where are you?' His voice was soft. He was maintaining his composure with an effort.

'At the South Road post office.'

'Wait inside near the tellers. Can you see the manager's office?'

'Yes.'

'Good. If you feel threatened in any way, go in there and scream for the police.' He paused. 'Do you understand?'

'Yes. I'll be fine now, Joe.'

'Good.' He broke the connection and dialled.

'Doc's Fishery.'

'Doc. It's Joe. I'm at the Paris. I need some people and I need them now. Cassim and his friend if possible.'

'Is it heavy?'

'Very heavy.'

'I'll call them, but you'll have to negotiate with them. If it's the big one, it means money.'

'There's no limit, Doc.'

'Wait for the call.' Doc broke the connection.

Davidson dialled Harry's room.

'Harry. I want you at once. Come down.' He replaced the receiver and paced impatiently, his whole body tense with the seething anger that drove him.

The phone rang just as Harry opened the door. Davidson motioned him to a chair. He picked up the phone.

'Davidson.'

'Cassim. Someone said you want help.'

'Yes. It's the big one. It can get hairy.'

'How much?'

'A hundred grand.'

'Each? For three of us?'

'Done.' He explained Margaret's predicament. 'I want someone there to watch her at once. I'll meet you outside the post office.' He replaced the receiver. He looked at Harry. 'You heard all that?'

'Yes, I heard.'

'I want you to stay here and look after

211

Grace.'

'Done.' He went out.

Davidson went down to the parking garage below the hotel, checked under and around the car, and drove to South Road.

Cassim was parked about fifty metres from the post office. He found Margaret inside, sitting on a bench in the corner. She stood up and hugged him.

'I was so frightened.'

'What happened?'

She described the car waiting in the driveway and the suspicious footprint on the step. He nodded slowly, his anger building.

'Do you think you can come back with me to the flat?' He touched her lips before she could answer. 'You don't have to.'

'I want to go with you.'

He nodded. 'Wait here. I have to brief someone.'

He walked over to Cassim, spoke rapidly to the three men. Cassim looked at his companions. They nodded. Cassim turned to Davidson.

'We'll do whatever it takes, as long as it's only a disposal.'

Davidson's eyes were bleak. 'That's all I want. I'll do the job. This is personal.' He knew what he had to do, and he would do it without compunction. Someone had threatened the life of a woman who meant everything to him. Margaret had come into his

212

life and turned something cold and inhospitable into something he now cherished. He would not allow anyone to destroy that. It was intolerable, an insupportable insolence. More important, this man had invaded the lives of dozens of people, causing immeasurable suffering for tortured parents. Summary execution was the only appropriate punishment.

'Wait at the back gate. Come on my signal.'

'You got it.' Cassim put the car into gear and drove away.

Davidson went back to Margaret.

'Give me three minutes. Then drive in at the front gate and come in the front door.' He thought for a moment. 'When you walk in the front door, go straight out of the back door to my car. Get in and drive to the Paris Hotel. Register and go up to suite four.'

She touched his hand on the windowsill.

'I love you. Please take care, Joe.'

He bent down, kissed her, touched her hair, and went back to his car. He stood for a moment looking back at her. Behind him he could hear the roar of the traffic and from the garage the dull thump of an idling engine. He waved and started the car.

He drove slowly towards his home, turned into the back gate of the complex where he saw Cassim's empty car parked a few metres from Flat One. There was no sign of the three men. He parked his car in front of number two, and checked the loads in the Ghisoni. Keeping close to the wall, he moved quietly towards his own flat. He kept his profile below the level of the window as he passed the Conroys' flat, noting with approval the faint footprint on the red grano that Margaret had described.

He reached his own back door and turned the key in the lock. The oiled wards retracted silently. He eased his way into the kitchen, leaving the door slightly ajar before he went to the window from where he could see the front door. He checked the Ghisoni once more, returned it to his holster, and screwed the silencer on the Browning.

There was an eerie quiet in the flat. Even his ancient refrigerator was silent. He had the uneasy feeling that every inanimate thing in the flat, everything he owned was waiting breathlessly for some cataclysmic event. He shook off the feeling, recognizing it as a sort of pre-action syndrome. It was the tension most soldiers feel before a major battle. He took several deep breaths, relaxing each muscle in turn until his composure returned.

He heard Margaret's car before he saw it enter the front gate. She parked in their bay, locked the car and, looking completely relaxed, let herself into the flat. She left the door slightly ajar. She smiled at him, walked through the kitchen, and disappeared behind the garages.

At that moment, Davidson heard the Conroys' front door open and close. From his angled view through the front window, he saw a shape, blurred by the net curtain, walking towards his front door. A few seconds later the door began to swing wider.

Davidson waited. Silence.

He wondered if the man had sensed his presence behind the front door, but eventually he heard the scrape of a footstep and the doorway darkened for a moment before the man stepped into the house. Davidson pushed the door shut. The man spun round, saw Davidson with his silenced weapon and knew he was about to die. He knew of Davidson's reputation and his ability to kill swiftly and efficiently. He knew Grundling feared him.

Davidson watched the slimly built Chinese man as his eyes flicked from side to side seeking an escape. He lifted the Browning.

'You've come for me?'

The Chinaman nodded briefly. 'Yes. I have come for you, but you have me at a disadvantage.'

Suddenly Davidson felt the cold clutch of wariness. The man was too calm, too submissive. He tensed, his whole being concentrating on the Chinaman's eyes, hands and feet. Unarmed, Davidson was no match for the smaller man, and he knew it. He knew too that Li would seek some small advantage in an attempt to resolve the impasse, for the

Chinaman was aware that Davidson would not kill him until he made that attempt.

At that moment, Cassim appeared in the kitchen doorway, a Walther PPK in his hand. Sensing someone behind him, Li lifted his chin slightly, then in one lightning-fast movement did the one thing neither of them expected him to do. His body moved into a *mae geri* on Davidson, followed by a *mawashi geri* on Cassim. The roundhouse kick caught Cassim below the chin and, following through, sent the Walther flying across the room. The Chinaman landed, went into a turn and dived for the Walther. Davidson, confused for a moment by the unexpected direction of the karate attack, swung the Browning towards the new threat.

As Li grasped the butt of the weapon, Davidson fired once. A red stain began to spread on the man's chest as he collapsed to the floor.

Cassim shook his head, picked up the Walther and checked the action.

'I'll get him out of here before he bleeds on your carpet.' He pulled on a pair of grey cotton gloves.

Davidson nodded. 'One moment.' He went to the bedroom, returned with a spare blanket and threw it to Cassim. 'Put that over him. Load him in the trunk of his Nissan.' He picked up the ejected case from the floor. 'I want to make a call before we visit Martin.'

Cassim peered cautiously from the door and

carried the blanket-wrapped body to the Nissan.

Davidson went through to the study, stood beside his desk, and breathed deeply to contain his shaking nerves. He knew there had been sufficient justification for using the Browning, but the knowledge was not enough to assuage his regret that it had been impossible to avoid. He told himself that the man was guilty of the worst form of criminal activity, but his feeling of guilt remained undiminished.

He closed his eyes for a moment, then picked up the telephone, and dialled the number for the Paris Hotel. He asked for suite four.

Margaret answered. 'Joe. Is that you?'

'It's me.'

There was a pause. Margaret said with calm dignity, 'I knew it was you the moment I heard the phone ring.'

'Then you weren't worried at all?'

There was another long pause. Then her tearful voice cried out to him. 'Of course I was bloody worried, you idiot. I was terrified from the moment I saw you behind that door.' He heard a stifled sob. 'Talk to Harry.'

'I love you too.'

He waited a few seconds and Harry came on the line.

'Joe?'

'I'm going to need you, Harry. With a bit of

217

luck, we can make the ungodly feel uncomfortable.'

'What have you got?'

'The Chinaman is no longer with us. We have one more thread to pull. James Martin.'

'Oh? How can he help us?'

'I heard him tell Biggie he would be away for a couple of days. I think things are moving.'

'Sounds like D-Day. Where shall I meet you?'

'Come to my flat. We won't move before four-fifteen.'

'We?'

'Cassim and his lads.'

'The police?'

'No sign of them, but there are a couple of dummies sweating it out in the road. They look like your erstwhile guards from the printing-works. Come in the back way.'

'Fifteen minutes.'

'Let me speak to Margaret.'

Her tone was lighter and restrained. 'Yes, Joe?'

'Are you OK?'

'I'm fine, Joe. And I want to tell you; your Mrs Eripides has been keeping me company. Joe, she's a gem.' He heard her laugh. 'I told her I wouldn't mind if you proposed to her. She said she wouldn't have you unless you came with a half-pack.'

Davidson laughed. 'That's my Grace.' He spoke more quietly. 'I'm going out again. I'll be out all night, but don't worry.'

'I won't, Joe.' But he knew she would.

Davidson went out to the courtyard where he found Cassim leaning against the Nissan.

'Where is he?'

Cassim inclined his head to the back of the car.

Davidson smiled wryly, reflecting that he had never heard Cassim utter an unnecessary word, a trait that could be downright irritating.

'Right. Take him out to the farm. Put him where you left Thompson.' Cassim nodded. 'I'll wait here for Harry. Meet me outside the Gateway Mansions at precisely four-thirty. No earlier. Don't be seen waiting around.'

Cassim drove away in the Nissan.

Davidson went back inside, went to the front window, and pulled aside the curtains so that the approaches to the complex were visible. He did not intend being caught unawares.

He moved the easy-chair around and sat wearily, avoiding his shadowed reflection in the mirror on the wall alongside him. He was doing that a lot lately, reluctant to admit to himself that the tired lines on his face were growing deeper, accentuating the bald truth of his age. He was beginning to realize that he no longer liked what he was doing. What was important to him twenty years ago now appeared to be a conditioned reflex without the enthusiasm that had accompanied earlier appeals for help.

At that moment, as though nature had decided to match his sombre mood, a cloud darkened the hard white sunlight. He looked to the south and saw the black shape of the gathering storm. He got up and went to the kitchen window just in time to see Harry alighting from a taxi at the back gate.

*   *   *

When she thought about the two men in her life, Betty Rolands wondered how she could have accepted Rupert as an adequate substitute for Harry Collins. Harry had always been thoughtful and generous, never disagreeable or unpleasant to her. While this was a retrospective judgement, it was one that held true through the years. In the beginning, Rupert had presented a similar façade, but it had soon become evident that it had become just that; when the veneer was peeled away, he was exposed as an unpleasant autocrat.

She looked at the ormolu clock, and realized that the hands had scarcely moved since the last time she had looked at it. Her nervousness was apparent in the restless movement of her hands and the tense expression in her lovely face. Her nervousness increased as she remembered the message she had left on his office machine. She wondered if he would ever bother to call her back.

The shrill ring of the telephone startled her.

She put her hand out to answer it, withdrew her hand, and then snatched up the receiver.

'Yes. What do you want?' It was Rupert.

Her nerve almost failed when she heard the anger in his voice.

'I want to talk to you, Rupert.'

'I'm very busy. You know that. What do you want to say?'

'No. Not on the telephone. I want to see you.'

'Can't it wait? I'm in the middle of a conference.'

She heard the rising inflection in his voice, and recognized his growing fury, but she knew she was ready for this moment.

'No, Rupert. It can't wait.'

'You'll have to wait until I get home.'

'When will that be?'

'How the hell do I know? Don't you realize I have things on my mind that are more important than your trivial problems.'

'Then we'll settle this now. I'm seeing my attorney tomorrow about a divorce.'

'I've told you what will happen if you go that route.' His voice was hoarse with anger.

'Don't threaten me, Rupert. If that's your attitude, I have nothing more to say.'

'I have plenty to say. You have no grounds. That bastard Collins can wait until hell freezes over.'

Betty paused for a moment. 'I have grounds.

What about your women?'

'Don't try that on me. There are no women and you know it.'

For a moment, she was tempted to cut off the connection and wondered why Rupert had not done so already. She decided to call his bluff.

'You denied you knew Kay, but I saw you lunching with her.'

There was a long silence. Then he spoke softly with ominous overtones.

'We had this out before. Where did you see us together?'

'At the Blue Bonnet in Cowie Road. Late last year.'

The silence was longer this time. Betty heard his hoarse angry breathing, and the occasional sounds from his office. When he spoke, his voice was subdued.

'How well do you know Kay Kelsey?'

She felt a surge of triumph. Her voice held a touch of scorn.

'We were school friends. We grew up together.'

'And you're certain it was me you saw lunching with her?'

For a moment, she was puzzled, more by his change of tone than the question. She hesitated, conditioned by years of fear-induced caution.

'Of course. How could I be mistaken about that?'

'Stay where you are. I haven't time to debate this now. I'll get back to you.'

'Rupert.' But the phone was dead.

*   *   *

As Harry walked into the flat, he held the noon edition of the evening paper. Davidson read the banner headline.

BODY FOUND
IS THIS ONE OF THE GIRLS?

A police spokesman had told the press that the girl found in the bushes behind the Snake Park on North Beach was fair-haired and was between fourteen and sixteen years old. There was no evidence of sexual assault. The remainder of the story was a rehash of library material. It was obvious that nothing new had emerged.

Davidson looked thoughtfully at the stark, black headlines.

'Evil doesn't whisper, Harry, does it.' He threw the newspaper on to the sofa. 'It can't. Piety whispers because nobody cares about the good people. Evil can scream out its message because all humanity is fascinated by it. Not even piety's clamours can drown the sounds of its whispers.' He walked to the window and looked across the lawn.

223

Harry smiled ruefully. 'Philosophical today, aren't we?'

'This murder has nothing to do with the other girls.'

'You can't be sure.'

'I'm sure. It doesn't fit the pattern. This is a random murder. A stupid murder. The culprit will be arrested in a week.' He looked at his watch. He went to the study door. 'I'm taking the assault rifle. Are you armed?'

Harry nodded. He patted his shoulder holster. 'I've got the Browning.'

Davidson glanced at the front gate. 'Hullo. Our watchers have gone. See if they've moved to the back.'

Harry looked through the window, left and right. 'No sign of them.'

*   *   *

The small dark man was Ford. The big heavy one was Harrison. They were known to their friends as the Graffiti Twins, from *American Graffiti*, in which Harrison Ford made an appearance. It was Victor who gave them the name. It was one of the few jokes he had ever made.

Ford looked towards Davidson's flat.

'Hey. There's someone in there.'

Harrison got out of the car. 'There is too. The curtains are open.' He looked down at Ford in the passenger seat. 'There must be a

224

back way. Get out of the car and wait here.'

Harrison drove slowly until he found the back gate to the complex. Collins was just getting out of a taxi, which was standing in the courtyard. Harrison inched his car forward until it was effectively blocking the gate. He left the driver's seat and leaned nonchalantly against the front mudguard. He waited until the taxi stopped a few feet from him.

The driver, a small coloured man, leaned out of the window. He put on a soft plaid cap and looked carefully at the big man a few feet away. Streetwise and experienced in the ways of the city's underworld sub-culture, he knew this was no accidental obstruction. The big man wanted something and he knew it was more than his pitiful takings. The hollow feeling in the pit of his stomach told him it would be unwise to demur.

'Let's get it over with, man. Tell me what you want.'

Harrison's smile was mirthless.

'That's my boy.' He moved his jacket so that the little man could see the gun. 'Where did you pick up the fare?'

The driver smiled nervously. 'Hell, is that all you want? He came from the Paris Hotel.'

'You sure he was staying there?'

'The hotel reception booked the taxi for him.'

'Good man. Now you keep your mouth shut. Hear?'

'I got good ears.'

Harrison drove to the front of the complex, picked up Ford and made for Berea Road.

'Now,' he said. 'We deal with the woman.'

Ford grinned. 'I'll teach that bastard Davidson to stick a shotgun in my face and make me kneel.' The humiliation and his own craven behaviour still rankled.

Harrison grunted, and rubbed his neck. 'I'll get him for that rabbit punch.' He stopped the car in front of a stationery shop on the beachfront.

Ford looked surprised. 'What you stopping for?'

'A get-well card for Davidson's woman.' He smiled cruelly. 'She's going to need it.'

Ten minutes later he drew into the parking lot behind the Paris Hotel.

'Wait here.' Harrison took the lift to reception and smiled at the clerk. 'Message for Mr Davidson.' He handed her the card.

She nodded, reached behind her and pushed it into the pigeonhole for suite four.

Harrison went to the bank of telephones on the other side of the foyer. The voice that answered him was one he knew well.

'Yes. Who is this?'

'Harrison, Mr Grundling.'

'Speak. I'm busy.'

'I've located the woman. Davidson's woman.'

There was a momentary pause. 'You have? Good work. Where is she?'

'Suite four. Paris Hotel.'

'Stay there. Both of you. If she leaves, one of you follow, the other must get on the phone to me. Keep in touch with each other. Has Ford still got his cellphone?'

'Yes. How long must we stay here?'

'As long as it takes me to get things organized.'

'I can handle her, Mr Grundling.'

'I don't want anyone to handle her, you idiot. I want her to draw Davidson. Now do as you're told.'

On the tenth floor of the Simcox building, Grundling replaced the receiver, went through to Victor's office and sat on the edge of the desk.

'I know where Davidson's woman is.'

Victor looked up, startled. 'How did you find her?'

Grundling laughed. 'The Graffiti twins. Would you believe it? That dumb pair got lucky when everyone else came short.'

Victor shrugged. 'We have to get lucky sometimes. Where are they?'

'The Paris Hotel. I told Harrison to stay there.'

'Send Pearson and Gadsby.' He looked thoughtful. 'I can trust those two. It was Billy Pearson who told me that Li was at the Davidson flat.'

Grundling stared at him. 'Did he indeed? I didn't know he was reporting directly to you.'

He seemed irritated. 'I sent Billy Pearson to go with the look-out car.'

'You were out. Then send Lindsay with Gadsby.'

Grundling nodded. 'Good choice.'

He stood up to go. Then he looked at Victor. 'We'd better deal with La Barre today.'

Victor's lips twitched in a tight smile. His eyes remained cold. 'Make the arrangements. And find Li.'

Grundling nodded and left the office. Victor stood up, walked to the big window overlooking the Bay and stared across to the Bluff where the dark green promontory loomed over the harbour entrance. He watched a container ship move slowly into the bay, while beyond the breakwater a freighter lay at anchor. Victor looked at all this, yet saw none of it. His thoughts were fixed on his next move, and the three people to be killed in the next twenty-four hours.

CHAPTER NINETEEN

As Davidson emerged from the study carrying the French assault weapon, he heard the phone shrill behind him. He handed the weapon to Harry and went back to answer it.

'Davidson.'

'Mr Davidson, this is Grondien.'

'Oh yes, Mr Grondien. You have news of the bloodstain?'

'I have, but you won't like what I have to tell you.'

'Indeed? Why not?'

'The stain is not human.'

'Not human?' Davidson's voice reflected his disbelief. 'Then what is it?'

'It's chicken blood.' Grondien chuckled. 'I take it you don't want to know whether it's a Rhode Island Red or an Orpington.'

'Chicken blood? What the hell is going on?'

'I'm sure I don't know. Do you still want the report?'

'Send it on anyway. And thanks.'

Grondien laughed. 'My pleasure.'

Davidson went into the living room.

'We've been had, Harry. The bloodstain at Rydal Avenue is chicken blood.'

'Then it had nothing to do with a murder?' Harry sat on the sofa. 'That's a relief. Then Kay could still be alive?'

'Somehow, I didn't think she was dead.' Davidson looked out of the window at the louring sky. 'The whole thing seemed too pat. I think Kay was leaving some sort of confused trail. She was probably in some danger and used a fabricated murder to enable her to disappear.'

'What about the man in the raincoat and fedora?'

'I think it is possible that it was Kay, dressed

229

as a man to confuse anyone who was keeping her under surveillance.'

'Hell, Joe, it all fits.' Harry was silent for a moment. 'No.' He shook his head. 'No. She could not be involved with those bastards.' He looked up at Davidson. 'Could she? Not the Kay I knew.'

Davidson shrugged. 'Who knows. People change.'

He watched the first heavy raindrops spatter the window. He was filled suddenly with an almost intolerable depression, which seemed to flood his mind with a sense of helplessness. He sighed heavily.

'When you get an opportunity, read Robert Lifton's book *The Nazi Doctors*. In it he chronicles the path towards the acceptance of evil that even the most benign and apparently incorruptible of men take.' He turned from the window. 'It's incredible how easy it is for the human mind to adapt to a course of action, if sufficient justification is invented for its acceptance.'

'But Kay? I just don't believe it.'

The telephone rang in the study. Davidson went to answer it.

'Davidson.'

'Is that room service? This is suite four.' He recognized Mrs Eripides' voice. She sounded calm, without a hint of tension.

'Please cancel that order I gave you. We'll re-order later.' She disconnected the call.

Davidson replaced the telephone. He called out: 'I think we've got trouble, Harry. The ungodly have found the women at the Paris. Put the assault rifle in the boot.'

*   *   *

Margaret smiled wanly at Mrs Eripides as she replaced the receiver.

'I've been trying to call the flat to remind him to lock up the Conroys' flat. He'll be away all night.'

'And you're worrying about him?'

Margaret shrugged. 'I've had to accustom myself to what he does.' She stood up and walked to the open balcony door, closing it to the gusts of wind that swung the heavy curtain into the room. 'I'm conditioned to a kind of acceptance of the fact that there is danger in most of what he does. But worry?' She stared out at the turbulent sea, now curtained with heavy rain. 'No, I don't worry. If I agonized over what might happen, I couldn't live with him. He made it clear from our first moments together that if what he did destroyed my peace of mind, he would give it up. I learnt to live one day at a time, and believe each day that he will come back to me.'

Mrs Eripides nodded briskly. 'You're a sensible woman, Margaret. He's strong-minded, but sensitive to your needs, and you know that.'

231

Margaret looked up quickly. 'That's very perceptive, Grace. Most people believe the macho image. They see him as some sort of Superman. He isn't like that. He's kind and caring. That is why he will never stand aside when people need him.'

Mrs Eripides walked to the window and drew the curtains. 'That rain is heavy. We're in for a gale tonight.' There was a soft knock at the door. She looked at Margaret.

'Are you expecting anyone?'

Margaret shook her head. 'Probably linen service.' She went to the door and turned the key. As the lock was disengaged, she was flung violently backwards on to the floor. Two men came in with drawn guns. The door slammed, and Mrs Eripides was thrown on to the sofa. As one of the men searched the suite, the other motioned with a silenced weapon.

'You.' He pointed to Margaret. 'Sit next to her on the sofa.'

Margaret stood up and looked at him defiantly. It surprised her that she was not in the least afraid of him. Her anger at the indignity that he had perpetrated swept away her fear. He waved the gun at her. She obeyed, her discretion overcoming her fury.

She studied the two men as they moved through the suite. They were alike as two steel nails. Both were tall, both had fair hair, and both were dressed in dark-blue suits. She looked at the first man who had gone to the bedroom.

'What do you want?'

He paused in the doorway.

'Are you expecting anyone?' Neither woman answered.

The second man went behind them and glanced into the bathroom. He nudged the back of her head with his silencer.

'You heard the question. Are you expecting anyone?'

Grace looked towards the telephone. She spoke before Margaret could answer. 'Only room service.' She glanced at Margaret and looked at the man in the bedroom doorway. 'Margaret ordered tea and scones for both of us.'

Both men walked to the front of the sofa. Margaret noticed that one had a small scar on his right cheekbone. She thought the detail might be useful later. She knew at once that this was linked to something Joe was working on. She was surprised that both she and Grace were more angry than nervous.

Scarface waved his pistol. 'Where's Davidson?'

Margaret raised her eyebrows. 'I don't know. He rang a while ago and said he would be away for a while. He didn't say where he was going.' She paused. Her voice assumed a tone of bravado. 'You know he'll kill you for this.'

Scarface shifted uneasily. 'We'll wait and see

who kills who.'

Grace sniffed. 'Whom.' The two men gave her puzzled looks. She stared back defiantly. 'It's who kills whom, you ignorant slob.'

'Shut up.' Scarface appeared to be the leader. 'You need a good slapping around to teach you manners.'

Grace was undeterred. 'You can't stay here, you know. Someone will be here in a minute.'

He smiled coldly. 'Oh yes. Who for instance?'

'Room service for a start. With tea and scones.'

Scarface looked apprehensively at his partner. 'We'll have to deal with him.'

Mrs Eripides said quickly, 'We don't want anyone else hurt.'

'Yeah. It's too dangerous.' He pointed a forefinger at Mrs Eripides. 'You. Cancel the order. Now.' She nodded and walked impassively to the telephone, exulting inwardly as she picked up the receiver. 'I'm watching you. No tricks.'

She looked at him scornfully. 'The room service is a single digit.' She pressed the redial button, calling the number that Margaret had dialled earlier.

She heard the ringing tone and then the voice in her ear:

'Davidson.'

*   *   *

The general paced thoughtfully across the room, stopped at the window, and stared out at the mango-tree. He watched the branch swinging in the wind, tapping continuously against the fascia.

'For heaven's sake, get that branch trimmed.' He turned and looked at Roberts. 'What exactly did he say?'

It was Janet who answered. 'We are to meet him at the Virginia Airport at eight tonight. From there we will fly to the place where he will hand over the girls.'

The general frowned. 'He said *the place*? Not *the farm*?'

'He said *the place*. He was definite about it.'

'And this is the first mention of flying?'

'He hasn't mentioned it before.'

The general's frown deepened. He tugged at his ear.

'I don't like it. The original plan was for you to go independently to the rendezvous in the Pietersburg area. Now he wants to take you there.' He looked directly at Janet. 'How did he sound? The tone of his voice? Could you guess at his frame of mind?' He gestured impatiently. 'Did he sound tense? Suspicious?'

'He sounded tense. I wondered about that.'

Anders spoke impatiently. 'Well? What do you think? Do you think he suspects something?'

'Not so much suspicious as wary. Something

has spooked him.'

Roberts sighed. 'I don't know that any of this helps us. Whatever we think, we have to do whatever he suggests. It's the only way we can get close to the girls.'

'That's a simplistic analysis. His frame of mind will tell us what precautions to take.' Anders paced back to the window. He was silent for a long time, staring at the waving branches. His subordinates watched him tensely. Eventually he spoke, without turning. 'I'm going to let you go along with him. There is no other way.' He turned to them, his face lined with fatigue. 'I have two hours to plan surveillance on you both.'

Janet leaned forward anxiously. 'We have to be careful. The safety of the girls is paramount.'

'I'm not unmindful of that, but I have to be certain of your survival. I'm not prepared to lose you through any fault of mine.'

Unmindful. Survival. Roberts covered a smile with his palm. The old bugger could be irritatingly pedantic at times. He followed Janet's lead.

'Miss La Barre is right. The girls must be the primary objective.'

The general sighed. 'You're both right. There was never any doubt about that.' He went to the table that held the files. 'We still haven't found Davidson. Our intelligence indicates that a Chinese national planned that

236

Kloof bank robbery.'

Roberts frowned. 'And Davidson was involved in the shoot-out.'

The general's mouth twisted with distaste.

'We don't need that kind of civilian interference. We have to find him and put him away.' He gestured impatiently. 'I'm positive he is moving towards Victor as fast as we are.' He began slipping the files into his briefcase. 'We have to stop him before he jeopardizes the operation.'

Janet said quietly: 'From all accounts, he's a good man to have on your side.' Both men looked at her askance. She said quickly, 'I know. He could be a threat to our operation, but it's a pity we can't recruit him.' She paused. 'Him and his friend Collins.'

The general was astounded. 'You're not serious?'

'Of course not. It seems a pity that he is such a wasted talent.'

The general said explosively, 'He's a loose cannon. I have five men looking for him, and if they find him, I'll deal with him.'

'Of course. I know he's on the wrong side of the fence, even if he is on the right side of the law.'

'Yes indeed. There is a difference, and Davidson must be made to understand that difference.'

*   *   *

237

Victor turned away from the view of the bay and the falling rain. He stared coldly at Grundling.

'It's a right bastard, but we're on top of it.'

'We were lucky.' Grundling stubbed out a cigarette morosely.

'Luck had nothing to do with it. It was my interpretation of one little fact that put us ahead of the police.'

Grundling looked troubled. 'It means a hell of a lot of extra work for all of us.'

Victor laughed. 'What is a little more work if the bitch is exposed.' He sobered, but his voice still held a hint of elation. 'We were suspicious, right?'

Grundling nodded. 'Right. And your information was accurate, I grant you that. Who—'

'Exactly.' Victor interrupted sharply. 'So I give her new directions, and she reacts as I knew she would if she wasn't kosher. She arranges a meeting with her boss to brief him.' He laughed out loud. Victor was enjoying himself. 'She leaves her house and loses our surveillance. That was a dead giveaway.' His lips curled. 'She's stupid enough to think I can be trapped by a couple of idiotic cops.' He strutted to the window and glanced at the swollen leaden sky. He turned and pointed an accusing finger at Grundling. 'And you thought I was stupid.'

Grundling frowned. 'Trouble is, we've got a whole new ball-game.' He lit another cigarette and waved the match to extinction. 'We have to abort the whole operation and do an extensive clean-up job.'

Victor returned to his desk, patting Grundling on the back as he passed him.

'Everything's under control. Gadsby and Lindsay have the women at the Paris, and they'll soon have Davidson. Roberts and that woman will soon be under control, and the girls will be disposed of.' He sat at the desk, opened a jade cigarette box, and took out a brown cigarillo. 'After that there is nothing to link us to the kidnapping.' He blew a cloud of smoke. 'We still have enough business ventures to stay healthy. This is a minor setback.' His voice hardened. 'I've a good mind to send that bitch's head in a box to the nearest police station.'

Grundling looked alarmed for a moment. Then he smiled.

'You're kidding.' He paused. 'Aren't you?' Even as he said it, he wasn't really sure. The man was weird.

Victor laughed. 'Of course, I'm kidding. But isn't it an attractive idea?'

*   *   *

Davidson did not have to force himself to remain calm. He knew that his rage would reduce his efficiency both in thought and deed if he allowed it. It was now, more than ever, that a disciplined response to the dangers was the only way to defeat his enemies.

He opened the gun safe, discarded several choices, and selected three weapons, a Browning nine-millimetre, a Mateba, and a Star BKM. Neither the Browning nor the Star was registered to him; both were purchased from illegal sources in the townships, and both came equipped with silencers. He locked the safe, returned to the living-room, and handed the Star to Harry.

'If you deal yourself in, you'll need this.'

'Of course I'm in.' He took the weapon, released the magazine and checked the action. He looked quizzically at Davidson as he replaced the magazine. 'Illegal?'

'Of course. Unlike yours. You can't use yours.'

'How are we going to do this?'

'First, we prepare the hardware. Here.' He handed Harry a pair of grey cotton gloves. 'Put these on.' He handed Harry a pile of face-tissues. 'Strip the gun completely. Take out the bullets and wipe every part with the tissues. Then wipe the bullets. Then reassemble it and load up.'

The two men worked swiftly and efficiently. As Davidson rubbed metal parts with tissues, he thought of Margaret. He knew she would be safe until her captors could get their hands on him. Working with the weapons and thinking of her helped him keep his anger under control. At last they were ready. The tissues were bundled into a paper bag to be burnt.

He gave Harry a clean pair of gloves. 'Keep them on at all times.'

'Right.' Harry holstered the weapon, handing his own to Davidson. 'What's the plan?'

'I don't have one. I won't until I assess the situation. Are the women still in suite four? How many men? That sort of thing.'

The telephone shrilled. Davidson motioned to Harry to answer it.

'If it's for me, say I've just gone out to fetch a car that was impounded by the police. You expect me back in forty-five minutes.'

Harry picked up the phone and repeated the message. He replaced the receiver. 'For you. Sounded tough.'

Davidson nodded with satisfaction. 'That will give us some breathing-space.' He picked up his car keys. 'Let's go.' The rain had eased a little. He looked around carefully from the kitchen window, but he was unable to discern any surveillance.

Davidson drove the car. In spite of his apparent calm, his anxiety was reflected in the set of his lips and his impatient drumming on the steering wheel at the traffic lights. Arriving at the rear of the Paris Hotel, he looked around carefully, but could not discern any evidence of surveillance. If he had been five minutes earlier, he would have seen the Graffiti twins just as Grundling was recalling them. Davidson guided the car cautiously into the entrance to the underground car park. He glided to a stop in one of the bays in the nearly empty garage. While Harry waited, Davidson took a pair of white overalls from the boot and left his coat on the back seat. He drew on the overalls and closed the zip, leaving a space large enough to slip his hand on to the butt of the Browning.

Harry raised a questioning eyebrow.

'Either you had a plan after all, or you've been giving this some thought.'

'A little. I'm going in through the balcony. This needs perfect timing from both of us.' Davidson looked around the quiet garage. 'There are usually some mobile laundry skips around here somewhere.'

'Can't see one.' Harry frowned. 'You're not going to use that old laundry gag. They'll be waiting for something like that.'

'They're not to get us in, but to get someone out.' He would say no more until they were in the service elevator, where an empty laundry-skip waited as though it had been provided for their benefit. Davidson smiled, though his eyes remained cold. 'See. We've got everything going for us.' He pressed the button for the top floor. 'Now to find another player for the game.'

The elevator doors slid open to the empty service passage on the top floor. It led to a door into the main corridor. They pushed the skip into the passage, leaving it a few metres from the lift. Cautiously he pushed open the service door. The corridor beyond was quiet and empty. The door to his suite was at the end of the corridor, while Harry's suite was opposite the service entrance. The odd-numbered suites were on his right.

Davidson whispered: 'We'll need the keys to your suite.'

Harry smiled. 'Everything's coming up roses.' He produced the key from his jacket pocket. 'I didn't hand it in.'

Davidson smiled happily. 'I knew that. You never do.' He took the key. 'Saves me phoning down for it. Wait here.'

Inside the suite, he dialled Doc's fish market.

'Doc? Joe. I want a small favour.' He looked at his watch. 'This is life or death, Doc, so get the timing exactly right. In exactly five minutes, phone the Paris Hotel.' He gave Doc the number. 'It's a direct line. Tell whoever answers that someone is climbing through their bathroom window.' He grinned. 'Make it sound like an emergency.' He chuckled. 'You never know. You could get a Best Performance Oscar.' He listened for a moment. 'Big trouble, Doc. The bastards are holed up in my suite with Margaret. Thanks Doc. It's another one I owe you.' He listened once more. 'I'll ring just as soon as I get her out.'

He looked out of the window as the sun broke through the clouds. He went back to the service lift where Harry waited.

'In about four and a half minutes, the phone will ring in my suite. Take up a position where you can hear it, but not where you can take a bullet through the door. Count to three when you hear the phone answered, then hammer as loudly as you can on the door.'

'What will you be doing?'

'I hope to be stepping into the suite through the balcony doors.' He paused: 'That is if all goes well.'

'What do I do if they open the door?'

'I don't expect them to be in any condition to do that.' He paused. 'But if they do that, start shooting the hell out of them.'

Davidson went back to Harry's suite. He opened the balcony doors and looked down at the surf foaming on the white sand. The weak sun was casting the shadow of the building across the Parade, while slightly to the north, the crowds at the Snake Park queued at the ticket window. He picked up a glass ashtray and pushed it into the back pocket of his overalls. He stepped out on to the small balcony.

His own balcony was separated from him by a gap of four metres. The architect had heard of hotel thieves, but had nullified his precautions by adding a foot wide coping between suites. It was a simple matter to climb on to the coping and to sidle cautiously to the adjoining balcony. When he came in sight of the door he saw with relief that the curtains were closed.

He looked at his watch, clambered on to the balcony and slowly turned the door-handle. When he pulled, the door came a few inches towards him. He froze as the curtain moved in the breeze. He waited a moment before peering through the small gap between the curtains.

There was no sign of the women, but two men occupied the living-room. One was seated on the sofa with his back to the balcony door; the other was leaning against the door to the corridor. The bedroom door was slightly ajar. Margaret's blue chiffon scarf trailed half in and half out of the doorway.

Davidson smiled. Good girl. He was certain that it was her way of letting him know where the women were. She knew he would come and, all at once, he was warmed by her faith in him.

He looked to his left at the bathroom window. It was open. Harry was right: everything was coming up roses.

He looked at his watch. Another two minutes.

In the service entrance, Harry stared

245

impatiently at the minute hand of his watch. The fluorescent lights above him glared down at the white walls. He started at the sound of a loud snap of relays engaging, and relaxed as the lift began its slow descent to the basement. The sound of its motor died, leaving only the distant hum of other motors, so faint that they were felt only in the vibrations. He tensed as the minute-hand moved to its appointed time. He moved cautiously towards the corridor entrance, opened the door, and went swiftly to suite four.

On the balcony, Davidson glanced at his watch. Then he peered into the room where the two men still waited. As he watched, the one on the sofa looked up at his companion.

'Get the bitch in here. Davidson must be home now.'

Davidson smiled as the second-hand of his watch passed the appointed time. In a few seconds, he reckoned, there would be a moment of massive confusion. He had learnt the ploy a long time ago. If a man is suddenly confronted with two or more options to bedevil him, there was bound to be a few seconds of disorientation. It was enough time to gain a quick advantage.

At that moment, the telephone rang.

The man at the door picked up the receiver, listened to the excited voice and looked towards the bathroom. Suddenly there was a thunderous knocking at the door and a crash as Davidson hurled the ashtray through the bathroom window. The men looked at one another and then stared indecisively at the bathroom door. They had their backs to him.

He stepped into the room.

'Hey.'

Both men turned swiftly towards him and lifted their guns.

Davidson fired twice, the noise of his silenced weapon loud in the confined space. As they fell, he walked to the door and opened it to admit Harry.

'Quickly, Harry. Bring the skip.' He turned towards the bedroom door as Margaret walked into the living-room.

She looked at the still figures on the floor and then up at Davidson as she put her arms around him. Her voice shook.

'Damn me, Joe. You *are* good.' Then she fainted, collapsing against him as Mrs Eripides appeared in the doorway.

'Take over, Grace. We have a hell of a lot to do.'

He swung Margaret on to the sofa. Harry pushed the skip through the door.

'Right Harry. Into the trolley with them.' He began stripping the weapon in his hand.

Grace brought a damp towel from the bathroom and dabbed gently at Margaret's cheeks.

'She was great, Joe. She told them just enough to prevent them beating the hell out of me. All the time she was acting the Harry Casual, as though she believed every word she was saying.' She dabbed Margaret's forehead. 'I guess the tension got to her.'

'You don't have to sell me on her courage, Grace.' His hands moved deftly over the weapon he was stripping. 'Give me your weapon, Harry. Damned waste of a good unused illegal Star.' He looked at Harry as he holstered the weapon. 'Find the car keys and take the skip to their car.'

Harry found the car keys and two wallets, and tumbled the men into the skip. He looked up questioningly.

'How do I know which is their car?'

Davidson stared at him. Harry smiled sheepishly.

'Click the remote and see which car answers.'

Harry shook his head. 'I'm not thinking straight. I never do when I'm putting bodies into laundry skips.'

Davidson pressed the fingers of one of the men on to various parts of the stripped weapon. He looked up at Mrs Eripides.

'I never wanted to involve her.' He threw the reassembled weapon into the skip. 'Dainmit, Grace, I wanted to keep her out of anything I was doing. These bastards had to bring her into it.' He took out the holstered weapon and repeated the stripping and fingerprinting. Harry closed the lid of the skip.

'What now, Joe?'

Margaret made a soft whimper. Davidson went to the sofa and stroked her hair. 'I need a place where the ladies can be safe until this job is over.'

Harry thought for a moment. 'My flat is secure. I can put a twenty-four hour guard on them using some of my best men.' He smiled wryly. 'Mac will bleat a bit, but I'll handle him.'

Davidson held Margaret as she stood up, took her in his arms and kissed her forehead. 'You were great.' She smiled wanly. 'Get her things please, Grace. Harry will drive you to his flat.' He turned to Harry. 'After you drop them, pick me up at the Metro Bar near the St Albans Grove parking garage. I'll put these two in the boot of their car and leave them in the darkest corner of the garage. With luck they won't be found for days.' He picked up the two silenced weapons, unscrewed the silencers, and stowed them in various pockets of his overalls.

He looked around the suite. 'I don't think we'll check out. There may be others interested in our welfare.'

They all left through the service passage. Davidson came behind with the laundry skip. The employees they passed showed no interest in a man in overalls pushing a skip.

*   *   *

Spargel watched the rig in his rear-view mirror as it pulled up behind him with Harrison at the wheel. He sighed. Perhaps they would be moving at last. At that moment, a car pulled up behind the rig. A few seconds later Grundling appeared at his cab window. He slapped the side of the door.

'All OK?'

'All OK, Mr Grundling.'

'You'll follow Harrison and Ford in the other rig. Remember you will have Pearson in the look-out car for the first hundred kilometres, and Jimmy Martin will pick you up at Mtunzini. We'll be changing every hundred.' He looked towards the back of the truck. 'Hullo. You've got a bad tyre there.'

'I didn't notice, Mr Grundling.' Spargel climbed down from the cab with Crowther close behind him.

Grundling patted his shoulder. 'Don't you fret. Harrison can go back for a new tyre. You take over his rig and he can follow with this one as soon as he puts on a new tyre.'

The two men fetched their bags and went to the second rig to take over. Harrison nodded as he passed them, but Ford made no sign. The Graffiti twins watched sullenly as Spargel started up the motor, pulled into the traffic lane, and settled down for the hundred-kilometre haul to Mtunzini.

Spargel watched a car closing up, then pass him on the long straight.

'Why Mtunzini?'

'What?'

'Why Mtunzini? It was never on our schedule.'

Crowther nodded sagely. 'It wasn't. And that cut in the tyre was new.'

There was a long silence. Finally, Spargel heaved a heavy sigh.

'We'll never know why.'

'And like the Six Hundred, ours not to reason why.'

CHAPTER TWENTY

The stuttering roar of the big diesel engine starting up awakened the girl. She looked across at her three companions; two were in a deep, drugged sleep and the third, Ramona Gomez, was in an exhausted, yet restless slumber.

They were beginning to move again. She wondered how long it would be this time. The first trip was very short before they halted for about two hours. She had lost all sense of time, but the faint orange glow in the small square of sky visible through the aperture above her told her it was nearly sunset.

She began to pray. She prayed for someone to free them, for she had no illusions about their eventual fate if they were not found. She thought of the agony that her wise, gentle mother was suffering, and her father's pain. She began to sob softly in the darkening cell.

* * *

Davidson stopped the car a hundred metres from Gatehouse Mansions. He got out and looked around him, paying special attention to the black, white and Indian pedestrians who made up Desmond Tutu's Rainbow Nation. Then he looked at the cars parked in the street. There were three that caught his attention, a green VW Jetta, a white Toyota and a black Mercedes. The Jetta and the Mercedes were empty, but in the Toyota a couple huddled close together in the front seat. While he did not suspect anything sinister about the courting couple, lovers were occasionally used as a surveillance team.

Harry looked in the direction of his scrutiny. 'Suspicious?'

Davidson glanced at him. 'No, but I think we'll watch them for a minute or two. If they become aware of us, they'll do one of two things. If they are real lovers, they'll move on. If not they'll stay.'

'What if they just don't care?'

'Illicit lovers wouldn't be that stupid.'

'Illicit?'

'Do they look married? Out here. In the street?'

'Silly me.'

Davidson unholstered his gun and held it on his lap. They waited, making no secret of their interest in the couple. Finally, the woman whispered to the man, who drove off in the direction of the beach front. Davidson got out of the car and looked up at the sky. The flash storm had moved north, taking with it the ragged cloud mass that lay on the horizon. He looked across the boundary wall of the building in which Martin lived. In the centre of the lawn was a massive fig-tree, which hid the lower floors of the sixteen storeys, but Davidson could see the windows of Martin's penthouse apartment. Multicoloured shrubs grew on the edges of the lawn.

At that moment, Cassim stepped from behind the fig-tree. He glowered at Davidson.

'You're late.'

'Sorry, Cass. Something unexpected came up. Victor's men had Margaret. I had to go and get her.'

Cassim grunted. 'Need any disposal?'

'We handled it.' Davidson's mouth twitched with wry humour. 'Besides, your funeral service is too expensive.'

Cassim ignored the thrust. 'Martin went up twenty minutes ago. He's wary. He took at least five minutes to check out the street before he went upstairs.'

'Did he see you?'

Cassim did not reply, but his pitying look was

eloquent enough. Davidson smiled inwardly at his own stupid question, but the habit of reviewing every detail was hard to break.

Cassim's voice was soft. 'The frontal approach is out. The man is too suspicious. He will make you before you can get to him.'

Davidson thought for a long time. He snapped his fingers.

'I need a pencil and a big sheet of writing paper.' He turned to Harry who had been watching the exchanges. 'There's a shop two hundred metres down the street. I . . .'

'I know just what you want. Be back in five minutes.'

As the twilight deepened, the two men waited silently in the shadow of the big tree. Cars sped by in the street, and occasionally they heard a whirr of wings as the fruit-bats took to the darkening sky.

It was only a few minutes before Harry returned. Davidson took the pad, scrawled across it in big childish letters, and tore the page from the block.

'This should make him angry enough to bring him out.' Harry looked over his shoulder.

Dear Jimmy
The fifty fell out my pokit. I can't get your
bet on. Sorry.
  Biggie.

'Pocket is misspelled.'

254

'I know that, and you know that. But does Biggie know it?' He folded the paper. 'Where are your boys?'

'Right behind you.' As he raised his arm, Jack, Pili and Seddie emerged from behind the dense shrubbery.

'Right. What's the layout?' He knew Cassim would have done his homework.

'The green Mercedes and the black van are parked downstairs. Both are locked, but that's no problem. Ten minutes ago he brought a bag down and stowed it in the Mercedes. I think he is planning to make a trip.' He thought for a moment with a match between his teeth. He removed the match. 'There are four lifts. Three green lifts serve all floors but the fourth, a red lift, serves only the top three floors.'

Gatehouse Mansions was built on stilts. Three rows of massive columns left an open parking area on the ground floor. If a power failure occurred, a staircase was provided in an enclosed section at the remote corner. Cassim led the way to the bank of lifts. He pressed the fifteenth-floor button on the red lift. Davidson nodded approvingly. A lift stopping at his floor would alert Martin. From the fifteenth floor, they went quietly up to the vestibule of the penthouse. Davidson motioned Harry to stay just out of sight below the top step. Cassim, Jack, and Seddie went to the left of the door, and Davidson and Pili to the right.

He slipped the note half-way under the door

and knocked twice.

They heard footsteps, and the paper was withdrawn from their side of the door. They heard the roar before the door crashed open.

'Biggie. You lying shit. Come back here.' Martin appeared dressed in a pink silk shirt, and a pair of lime-green slacks. He was barefooted. He saw Cassim first before he felt the end of Davidson's silencer in his ear.

Davidson spoke quietly. 'OK, Jimmy. Who's in there with you?' His voice was coldly menacing.

Martin's startled gaze glared at him. 'No one.'

'Cassim. You and Seddie go through the flat. If there is anyone there, kill them. Then we'll kill this bastard for lying to me.'

'Who the hell are you? Who sent you?' A note of bravado crept into his voice. 'Victor will kill you for this.'

Davidson sighed. 'Dear me. We must have heard that at least four times in the last twenty-four hours.' He held up his free hand and counted off with his fingers. 'Thompson. Gadsby. Lindsay and Li. They all told me Victor will kill me. And here I am. Still hale and hearty.'

'Holy shit. You're Davidson.' Martin's eyes began to show a trace of fear.

'A coconut on the first try.'

Martin's reaction took them all by surprise. As Cassim and Seddie entered the flat, the little man shoved at Davidson and rushed for the stairs, only to return backing up with Harry's gun jabbing his stomach.

Davidson regained his poise. 'Well done, Harry. I didn't think he was stupid, but I thought he might try something like that.' Harry, who had thought that Davidson had left him on the stairs to keep him out of the firing line, looked admiringly at the older man.

'Margaret was right. Dammit, Joe, you *are* good.'

Davidson smiled coldly as Cassim appeared in the doorway.

'All clear?'

Cassim nodded. Davidson nudged Martin with his gun.

'Move.'

They all went inside. Davidson looked at Seddie.

'Bring up the bag.'

While they waited, Seddie left the flat and returned a few minutes later with a black tog-bag.

Inside the flat, Davidson grimaced at the black steel and glass furniture, and the garish modern prints on the wall. He walked through from room to room, opening wardrobes and closets, and glancing into the bathrooms. Cassim watched sardonically, but knowing Davidson's habit of checking everything twice, forbore to comment.

Davidson went into the living-room, glanced

at Martin on the sofa, and then stared at the view across the racecourse and the city beyond. He spoke without turning.

'Are you going to tell us what we want to know?'

'Piss off.'

Davidson nodded. 'Ask a stupid question.' He walked back to the window. 'I'm not wasting any time on you. If I don't get answers in two minutes we'll begin the treatment.'

'Then I'll be dead.'

'Probably. But if you're not, you'll wish you were.'

'Go to hell.'

'If that's how you feel. Right Cass, do it.'

It took only a few minutes for the four men to bind and gag the little man. As Davidson watched impassively, Cassim made a hole in the gag into which he shoved a funnel, forcing his captive's lips apart.

Harry's expression was impassive, but his emotions were in turmoil. He had heard of this form of persuasion. Indeed, it had been described in a book on the holocaust and the Gestapo horrors. He knew what would happen next. The man's nose would be blocked, meths or benzine would be poured into the funnel, and he could only breathe if he swallowed the liquid. Then a match would be lit.

Harry began to question the morality of their actions. There was no doubt about the morality of their purpose. Davidson wanted the kidnapped girls freed, but should it be at the cost of his own self-respect. He wondered at the two sides of the man; the quiet, gently sensitive man who had been his mentor and guide, and the man who stopped at nothing, even death, when faced with a threat to himself, his loved ones or to those who needed his intervention. He knew Joe sometimes abhorred the lengths to which he was forced to go, but he hated criminals more, and his concern for the plight of the girls gave him the motivation to deal with criminals on their own terms.

He watched Martin squirming as Cassim tilted the bottle over the funnel. Then the little man nodded frantically. Davidson touched Cassim on the shoulder.

'I think he wants to talk.' He tugged viciously at the tape.

Martin began to babble as soon as his mouth was freed.

'I have to meet a man named Spargel at a place called the Forest Inn.'

Cassim slapped his face. 'Bullshit. There's no such place.'

'I swear. It's true. It's a hundred miles up the coast.'

Seddie spoke from the door. 'I know it. I've been there.'

'This Spargel. Does he know you?' Davidson watched the man for any hint of evasiveness, the narrowing of the eyes, the

259

hesitations and uncertainty of speech patterns, but Martin appeared eager to talk.

'I don't know any of this crowd. I was brought in for a special job. Grundling told me to stay under cover.' He shifted uncomfortably. 'Can't you take the ropes off?'

'After you bare your soul.' Davidson looked thoughtful. 'They told you to stay under cover, and then use your van to kidnap Harry.' He shook his head sadly. 'What is your part in all this?'

'I have to deliver the money.'

'What money?'

'The payoff for the girls.' He moved his legs. 'To pay the woman. The one who shifts the merchandise.'

Davidson looked up at Cassim, who raised his eyebrows. Cassim said: 'Who is this woman?'

'Janet La Barre.'

Harry became animated. 'Do you know Kay Kelsey?'

'Never heard of her.'

Cassim loosened the bonds on his feet, but kept the hands bound.

Martin stretched his knees. 'Victor's just found out she may be a police plant.'

Davidson's eyebrows went up. 'Why does he think that?'

Martin shook his head angrily. 'Hell, I don't know. He doesn't confide in me.' He raised his wrists. 'Either let me go or kill me.' Davidson

260

knew it was mere bravado. 'I don't know where the girls are. I can't tell you any more.'

'Oh yes, you can,' Cassim insisted. 'You can tell us how much money there is and where you stashed it.'

'I haven't seen it yet. Someone is bringing it.'

Harry looked at Cassim. Cassim saw the look. 'We're not hijackers. Leave us out of this. We'll take what we're being paid.'

Harry stepped forward angrily. 'He's lying, Joe. To hell with the money. Where are the girls?'

'I swear I don't know. Believe me, if I knew I'd tell you.'

Martin's swarthy face was running with perspiration. 'Please. Loosen the ropes.'

'He's lying, Joe. Make him tell us where the girls are.'

Davidson spoke quietly. 'He doesn't know, Harry. Only Grundling and Victor control their whereabouts. And you can be sure they keep a tight hold on the others who know.' He looked down at Martin. 'Is the delivery being made by one of Victor's men?'

'No. He doesn't trust them. The bank courier is bringing it.'

Davidson smiled coldly. 'Perhaps he thinks that some of them are dishonest. Why does he trust you?'

'A man named Gaffney recommended me. He is a kingpin in the business.' He squirmed uncomfortably.

Davidson walked to the balcony door, his brow creased in thought. The six men watched him. Martin moved his hands.

'What happens now? What are you going to do with me?'

There was a long silence. Outside, the world was dark. Crickets and beetles shrieked intermittently and they heard the roar of the homebound traffic on the freeway. Davidson turned abruptly.

'Cassim. Take this scum and stash him at the place we agreed upon. See that he's watched night and day until we need him again. Double payment if you keep him. Nothing if he gets away.'

Cassim smiled wolfishly. 'Can I cripple him if he tries?'

'Do whatever it takes.' He paused. 'Harry. How many of those fancy cellphones are available?'

'Four spare.'

'Pili can go with you and get one for Cassim. Bring two more and meet me at your flat.'

Cassim opened the door as Jack and Seddie ushered Martin to the red lift. They heard the lift descending.

'What about our own cellphones?'

'They're probably being monitored by the police.'

'That's illegal.'

'Yes, I know. If they monitor yours, report it

to the police.'

Harry walked over to the window and stared across the city to the Indian Ocean.

'Joe.' He turned. 'If Martin hadn't talked, would you have put a match to his mouth?'

Davidson smiled wryly. 'That's something I've never had to find out. A man's fear is the greatest motivation for confession.' He shrugged. 'Anyway, water won't burn. That's all we had in the bottle. The outside was wiped with meths so he could smell it.'

Harry laughed. 'You cunning bastard.' He was still shaking his head as he walked out. Pili followed him and paused at the door.

'Hey. Look after that money, friend.' He lifted a hand in salute and closed the door softly behind him.

Davidson sat down to wait for the courier.

*　　　*　　　*

Betty Rolands got the call just before she locked the safe and left for the day. Rupert's voice was placatory.

'I've been thinking about divorce. I think you're right. But we must sign the papers tonight. I'm leaving for Paris in the morning.'

She felt a surge of elation. Her pulse quickened as she thought about a future with Harry Collins. It was not too late. They still had a bright future.

'What do you want me to do?'

'Come out to Umhlali. I'll have an attorney and all the documents ready.'

Her joy was dampened slightly at the thought of the house Rupert owned in the country. She hated it. She hated the gloomy bedrooms and passages, depressingly unsuitable antique furniture and the loneliness. In spite of its quasi-opulence, the whole ambience was tasteless. She once described it to a friend. 'The trouble with it,' she told her friend, 'is that it's Rupert.' He had bought it before they were married. She refused to live in it, citing as an excuse the distance from her office in town. She had bought and furnished the house in Durban North herself.

She realized he was speaking. 'If you leave now you can be here in an hour.'

'I want a bath, and a change of clothes.'

'You can bath here. And you have a wardrobe full of clothes.'

She hesitated for only a moment. He was being agreeable, and she wanted to keep him that way.

'I'll be there in an hour.'

'I'll have everything ready.'

She replaced the receiver, her blood pounding with excitement. She paused. Thoughts of her house in Durban reminded her of the will she had made in his favour. She must remember to make a new one in the morning.

She stood for a moment, hesitant, debating

whether she should ring Harry. She picked up the phone and dialled. Harry answered.

'I'm glad I caught you.'

'You're lucky. I came in for a minute on an errand for Joe.'

'I have wonderful news. Rupert has agreed to a divorce. He wants to meet me at Umhlali tonight.'

'Umhlali? Why there?'

'Rupert has a mansion there.'

'I didn't know that.'

'He's had it for years, but we've never lived there. I hate the place. It's too isolated. It's way out beyond the Easterbrook sugar estate on Midlands Road. It would have been hell to commute.' She paused. 'And it's far too big.'

There was a long silence. 'Betty?'

'Sorry. This is the first time it has occurred to me to wonder why it must be done tonight, and why out there.'

'Is he going away anywhere?'

She pondered for a moment. 'Yes. That must be why. He said he was off to Paris in the morning.'

'That's it then.' He paused. 'It's great news.' His voice betrayed his happiness. 'We'll be married as soon as the divorce is through.'

'I love you, Harry.'

'I love you, Betts.'

She replaced the receiver, feeling the warm glow of pleasure steal over her.

She switched out the lights. The city was

already in darkness.

*   *   *

As the man called Asparagus watched the huge vehicles pull in one by one and park in the lay-by, he realized that, for the first time, all the girls were together. Behind them came a minibus and another car. If only he had a phone, they could close the whole operation in ten minutes. Grundling's cunning had prevented anyone in the group from having a phone. They were threatened with summary execution if anyone but the look-out car and one pantechnicon driver had a cellphone.

It was impossible to free them alone. All the men were armed, and the two guards had AK47s under their voluminous coats.

They had positioned themselves in front of and behind the convoy, and anything suspicious would bring them out.

He knew they were waiting for the money to arrive. He looked at the shadowed hills and the far rise of the Ongoye forest. The sun had warmed the still fields, deserted now by the labourers who had spent the hot day laying the sugar cane flat for the stacking. The air smelt of woodsmoke and burnt cane.

He wished he could convey some word of comfort to the frightened girls in the pantechnicons, but he knew that such foolishness would hasten disaster. He dropped

266

down from his seat and looked along the road towards the Forest Inn, a mile away. It was a small hotel whose circumstances were reduced by the construction of a new freeway two miles to the east. Grundling's cunning had placed the convoy enough distance from the hotel to prevent just such a communication as Asparagus had contemplated. He lay down on the thick grass and nursed his frustration.

CHAPTER TWENTY-ONE

The wrought-iron gates were closed when Roberts eased the Mercedes to a stop. Beyond the gates, a macadamized drive disappeared into the darkness, to reappear where the bright lights of the big house blazed from every window. Shrubs edged the drive and beds of cannas flourished across the lawns.

'I don't like it.' Roberts watched their escort car make a U-turn.

Janet shook her head impatiently. 'There's nothing we can do. We have to take risks for the sake of the girls.'

He stared stubbornly ahead. 'This is not a calculated risk. First, we are told to fly to Pietersburg. Then he decides we are to meet him at Virginia Airport to fly to some other unknown destination. Now this.'

This was a ten-bedroom mansion on a ten-

267

acre estate a short drive from the city.

'Uncle John said he would give us full cover.'

'Whatever that means,' Roberts said morosely. They watched the lights of the escort car disappear.

'You know what it means. It means he is doing everything possible to ensure our safety.' She glanced at his stony face.

'Damn you, Roberts. We knew the risks we were taking.' Her angry tone reflected their growing tension.

The months had placed an intolerable burden on their resolve. Their normal easy relationship had regressed into an uneasy tolerance. In the silence, they could hear the thump of a mindless pop-recording drifting faintly from some source in the big house. The air was still, and the humidity bore down on them, while from the trees all around them the chorus of insects was evidence of the summer's call to procreation. Hundreds of flying ants destroyed themselves against every light, while their wingless brethren crawled blindly over the macadam.

Roberts sighed impatiently. 'Well, I suppose we'd better get on with it.' He lifted his hand to the steering wheel, but before he could sound the horn, the gates moved silently inwards. 'We've been noticed.'

He drove slowly towards the house, coming to a stop before a magnificent mansion built of

268

stone, with trefoil-arched windows enclosing leaded lights, with here and there bronze medallions in the panes. The floor of the entrance hall was tiled, and the seventeenth-century monk's bench was indicative of the money spent on the house.

Grundling greeted them with a wide smile.

'Come through to the lounge and relax.'

Janet glanced at Roberts. He appeared to be more at ease, reassured perhaps by the effusive welcome, but she was not convinced of Victor's verity. Until he explained his vacillation and his indecision, she would continue to be wary.

Grundling seated them together upon a long sofa and walked behind them to the cocktail cabinet to mix the drinks. The lights were out in the chandelier, but the sconces gave out a soft glow that was dimly reflected in the high polish of the Steinway in the corner. A hand holding a whisky glass appeared over the back of the sofa. Roberts glanced at Janet and handed her the drink. He glanced back at Grundling. There was empathy between them that enabled her to interpret the look. He was uneasy about the drinks coming from behind them. As Roberts took his own drink, he stood up casually, and walked to the opposite wall to study an elaborately framed painting of a country scene. He turned after a moment to sip his drink and look at Grundling, who moved to the right of the sofa, sitting in the easy-chair that effectively blocked the way to the front door, had they wished to leave. Janet watched them both, aware of the significance of their positional relationships.

She felt the chill of dread, not for herself but for the children she was determined to find. She knew that if she failed tonight there would be no second chance. She watched surreptitiously as the big man sipped his drink. His attention appeared to be riveted on the main door to the living-room. He appeared to be expecting something to happen. There was a faint sheen of perspiration on his forehead, and she did not think it was from the warmth of the evening. She felt comfortably cool in the air-conditioned room.

Roberts glanced at her and drifted across the room to a position outside the periphery of Grundling's vision. She knew it was Roberts's way of testing Grundling's reaction. Uneasily she watched the big man rise and walk to the window.

At that moment, Victor bustled into the room.

'Sorry to keep you waiting.'

She was not too surprised at his bonhomie. It could be part of his masquerade if his intentions were malevolent. On the other hand, it could be his way of putting them at ease as a prelude to concluding an agreement. Her mind raced from one alternative to the other. If Victor's intentions were sinister, she hoped that Uncle John stayed within reach.

*   *   *

At that moment, Uncle John was sitting in the back of a small van that was crawling along the North Coast road. In front of him, resting on a miniature desk, were two small screens which were displaying the two signals received from two microchips, one of which was buried in the engine compartment of Roberts's car, and the other in the hem of Janet's slip.

He looked at the luminous dial of the clock above the screen.

'We're too far behind. Move a little closer.'

The driver, young Warrant Officer de Gaye, nodded and increased the speed of the van to a little more than sixty kilometres an hour.

'Take the next exit. The signals are coming from the north-west.' They were coming at a steady beat from some distance away.

The general looked over his shoulder through the small window in the rear door.

'We've still got our two escort cars. I hope we won't need them.' He turned his attention to the screen. The point of light crawled along the winding roads deep in the country. 'Turn right here.'

The young warrant officer drove carefully over a rail crossing.

'I wish we knew the exact location of the rendezvous.'

271

The general looked up impatiently. 'They weren't stupid enough to tell us.' He looked at the screens. 'Roberts was merely told to follow a car from the Royal Hotel.' He paused. 'That's funny.'

'What is, sir?'

'They're coming towards us.'

'Coming back here?' de Gaye stopped the car.

The general watched for a few seconds. 'No. They're heading for the North Coast road.'

'The N2? The toll road?'

'No. The old one. The North Coast road through Umhlali.' He studied a large-scale map on a table on his left. 'Follow them.'

A few minutes later, they were following signals that appeared to be moving steadily northwards. They passed signs pointing to Blythdale Beach and Darnall. Finally, they began crossing the John Ross bridge, which spanned the Tugela River. The signals were strong, but all at once, the general realized that the signals were coming from a point right below him, in the middle of the river. As he sat in the van, frustrated and angry, the signal stopped.

*   *   *

Victor went to the easy-chair that Grundling had vacated. He smiled at Janet.

'Well, at least you're not armed.' His smile

disappeared abruptly. 'You see, my dear, when you came through that door, you passed through a detector that would have screamed at you, had you violated my hospitality.' He smiled once more. Janet thought he had never been so repulsive as he was at this moment. Suddenly the subdued light from the sconces and the cool air from the air-conditioning gave the room a cold, sinister atmosphere.

He went on: 'Talking about violating, go along with Lizzie Wharton here, and she will inspect all your clothing to see that you're not hiding some nasty little device to lead your friends here.'

She realized that a woman had come silently into the room and was standing in a doorway that appeared to lead to the kitchen area.

'Oh, by the way. Her friends know her as Breakfinger.'

For a moment, Janet felt real fear. Deep fear, both for herself and the children. Then she dredged a semblance of courage from deep within herself. She took long breath.

'What the hell are you talking about?'

Roberts moved towards the seated man.

'To hell with this. We came here in good faith . . .'

Victor shook his head in mock sadness. 'Surely not in good faith, Mr Roberts. Or should I say PC Roberts. Or is your police rank a little higher than that?' He stood up. 'Before you consider anything rash, look behind you.'

Ford and Harrison had come through the doorway behind Roberts. Both were carrying Thompson sub-machine guns. Victor motioned to the Wharton woman who took two steps towards the girl. Roberts barred her way, but Grundling moved in with an ugly-looking cosh, and Roberts collapsed to the floor.

Janet stood up quickly. 'Leave him. I'll go with you.'

Sick with despair and anger, she followed the woman out of the rooms. Victor inclined his head, and Ford followed the women. They walked down a long passage at the end of which was a stout wooden door. Lizzie Wharton produced a key from her pocket and opened it. Beyond the door was a small room, bare of furniture. The window was covered with a net curtain, through which Janet could see thick iron bars. The woman went out, locking the door behind her.

She returned a few minutes later carrying a small grey box with a steel aerial attached to one side and a row of buttons and a rotary knob on the other. She stood just inside the room, pressed a button, and turned the knob. It took only a few seconds for the box to produce a high-pitched whine.

'Well, there you go,' she said jovially. 'Are you going to give me the bug, or must I call in Ford to take it from you?'

Janet shrugged helplessly, removed the chip

274

from the hem of her slip, and gave it to the woman.

Wharton nodded happily. 'Isn't science wonderful.' She sneered. 'And you thought you could outsmart Victor with one bug in the car and one in your slip. What a bunch of dorks.'

*   *   *

In the dark and dressed in black overalls, Spargel was almost invisible. He tucked himself between the mechanical horse and the trailer as he waited for the man he was to meet.

Stars blazed in a clear sky, but there was no moon and the darkness was almost absolute. To the east, he saw a faint glow from the lights of the village, while on the dark hills to the west, distant cooking fires glowed in front of numerous beehive huts. Occasionally cars passed him, each pair of headlights lifting his spirits, but each time leaving him more impatient and frustrated. Between passing cars, the silence was broken only by the singing of crickets. Finally, when he had ceased to expect the man to come, a pair of headlights stopped a hundred metres from the articulated vehicles. It was almost as though the driver was unsure of his bearings. Then the headlights crawled forward until a black van drew up on the grass alongside the articulated vehicle.

Spargel walked over to the driver. 'Martin?'

'That's me.'

Spargel peered into the van. The driver was alone. Spargel stared down at Davidson, his brow crinkled in a puzzled frown.

'Haven't I seen you before?'

Sensing trouble, Davidson got out of the cab and stretched languidly. 'I don't remember your face.'

Spargel dug a hand into his overall pocket and left it there. He walked slowly around the van, kicked the back tyres, looking into the rear window and watching Davidson every moment. The tension between the two men was palpable. Spargel returned to his original position at the front of the van. There was a long silence.

'I know who you are now. You're Joe Davidson. A long time ago, I saw you giving evidence in the Supreme Court.' His hand came out of his pocket holding a short barrelled revolver. 'Why are you pretending to be Martin?'

Davidson yawned. 'He was indisposed.'

'I'll bet. How did he get to be indisposed?' He lifted the barrel of the revolver.

'I'm afraid that gun isn't of much use to you.'

Spargel looked surprised. 'Oh? And why not?'

'At this moment there's a Uzi behind you.' Harry touched the back of his neck with the muzzle of the gun. 'I let this man off when I

276

stopped back there.'

Spargel sighed. He handed Davidson the gun.

'How the hell does a man like you get involved with this lot?'

Davidson was seething with anger. 'There was a minibus back there with several men aboard. Before they get here, you'll tell me where the girls are.' He took his Ghisoni from his holster. 'I'll find them if I have to destroy every bastard like you on the way. Now where are they?'

Spargel began to laugh softly. 'We both seem to be on the side of the angels, but what my boss is going to say when he hears about this, I don't know.'

'Who's your boss.'

'You don't want to know, but I can tell you, I'm a policeman.' He hesitated. 'Do you have a cellphone?' Davidson took his phone from his pocket. 'The girls are in those two furniture vans in front of this one.' He inclined his head towards Harry. 'If you and this character are on the level, we can sort this whole thing out tonight.'

'It all sounds too easy.'

'It isn't. There are eight armed men over there, and we need support. If I phone my boss, he'll have a whole squad here in an hour.'

'You were detailed to lead me and the money to Victor.'

'It's all come apart. None of the top brass is

here.' He waved an impatient hand. 'I was supporting two other agents, Roberts and La Barre. They're not here either. I need to speak to my boss.'

'What's his number?'

Spargel told him. Davidson dialled, and handed the phone to Spargel. He took it and sighed with visible relief.

There was a reply. Spargel said: 'This is Asparagus. I am at . . .' He stopped. The minibus rolled slowly towards them, lights ablaze. A voice hailed him. He spoke softly into the telephone. 'Wait. Trouble.' He slipped the phone into his pocket and called out. 'Is that you, Crowther?'

'Yeah. Are you coming?'

Davidson saw the packed minibus stop ten metres away. He stayed in the shadow of the big van.

'Where, for God's sake?'

'Victor wants us all back at the mansion.'

'That's crazy. What about the trucks?'

'We're leaving them here. Damn it. Are you coming?'

'I'll go back with Martin.' As the minibus bumped on to the road and disappeared, the three men ran to the nearest van. It was empty. So were the third and fourth.

Spargel banged the side of the van with his hand. 'The bastards switched vans on us with that tyre scam.' He remembered the general. 'Sorry, sir. It seems we have been had. The vans are empty.'

'We've lost our leading lady too.' The general's voice sounded desperate. 'They must have found the bugs. They sent us on a wild-goose chase.'

'Tell him the suitcase of money is all newspaper,' Davidson whispered.

Spargel relayed the message to the general, adding a word on the presence of Harry Collins. There was a long pause. Davidson looked across the hills to the flickering cooking fires. The trees above them whispered in the slight breeze. The three men waited in silence. Then the explosion came.

'What the hell are they doing there?' There was a pause. 'Oh, it doesn't matter. I'll deal with him later. I'm sending a chopper for you. I want you back at once.'

'There is a minibus with eight well-armed villains on its way to Durban. It might be wise to intercept it.'

'I'll put out an alert. Wait for the chopper. We'll have to find Victor the hard way.'

Davidson took the phone from Spargel. Harry pushed the Uzi on to the passenger seat of the black van.

'This Victor. What does he look like?'

Spargel was silent for a moment. 'He's a dead ringer for that movie actor Lee Van Kleef. He has a scar over his right eyebrow, and when he's angry, he goes berserk.' He walked towards the truck. 'I'll get my bag.'

Davidson put a hand on his arm. 'I take it you won't give us a lift in the chopper?'

'Are you nuts? It's a police chopper. No civilians permitted.'

Spargel strode off into the dark.

Harry opened the van door.

'Let's go, Joe.' Davidson heard the urgency in his voice. 'We have to hurry.'

'Any particular reason?'

'I'll explain on the way. Let's go.'

As Davidson drove, Harry explained his theory. He was clearly agitated.

'If you're right, Harry, there are a lot of people in danger, including the girls.' He glanced at the younger man. 'Are you sure?'

'It's no certainty, Joe, but it's our last hope.'

CHAPTER TWENTY-TWO

Victor looked with distaste at the policeman in the chair before him.

'Ford. Take this man's car and leave it in a cane field. Harrison can follow you in Grundling's car.' He looked at the bound and helpless policeman. Without looking at Ford, he waved him out of the room and looked at Roberts's bloodied face. 'You see what trouble you've caused your boss. Now he'll be chasing phantoms up the North Coast.'

Grundling waved an impatient hand. 'Let's

get on with it.'

Victor was enjoying himself. 'Don't rush me, Piet. I want Roberts to understand exactly what will happen to him.'

Grundling said angrily: 'This is unnecessary.'

Victor's voice was soft. 'You think so.' He walked to the Steinway. 'You see this, Piet. It's a beautiful piece, and I own it. Yet I can't play a note of music.' He paused. 'A note? Oh I can play a note.' He lifted the lid and pressed a bass note several times. The sound echoed through the room. He dropped the lid. 'You see, I just like to own things.' He walked back to Roberts and sneered. 'And I own this thing here.' He looked at Grundling. 'I own you, and the girls, and all the other people in this house to dispose of as I please.' He turned and smiled at Grundling.

'We're wasting time. We have to do a clean-up tonight. Not to mention disposing of Roberts and the women.'

Victor sighed impatiently. 'There now. You've given the whole thing away. I wanted to tell him myself.'

Grundling looked at Victor suspiciously. The man's over the edge, he thought. Stone bloody barmy.

Victor continued: 'But before we dispose of the women, we'll give them to the Graffiti twins.'

Grundling snorted impatiently. Like hell

281

you will, he thought. I'll be long gone before then.

Victor took a short-barrelled revolver from his pocket. 'But we can dispose of this one now.' He pointed the weapon at Roberts's head and pulled the trigger. As the hammer clicked on an empty chamber, he giggled inanely. 'Got you. One empty chamber and four full ones.' He giggled once more.

Grundling watched in disbelief. Stone bloody barmy, he thought; and I thought we were in it for the money.

Victor chuckled. 'With you three gone and the girls disposed of, no one can link us to their disappearance.'

Grundling grabbed his arm. 'Come on, Victor. We have to get on with it.'

Victor looked at him coldly. 'Don't touch me,' he shouted. 'How many times have I told you not to touch me.' Rage flecked his lips with spittle. He lifted the revolver 'I ought to send you to hell with the other three.' His left eye blinked rapidly.

Grundling backed away cautiously. 'OK, Victor. OK.' He smiled ingratiatingly. 'We'll do it your way.'

'Right. Let's get started.' He lifted the gun. 'We'll begin with this one.'

*   *   *

Davidson let the van coast to a stop outside

the tall gates. He peered at the sign. 'What does it say?'

Harry looked over his shoulder.

'This is it, Joe. We're on the right road. It must be the next entrance.'

Beyond the gates, dark buildings loomed against the starlit sky.

Ahead of them, thick bush lined both sides of the road. A soft breeze had blown up from the east, bringing with it some relief from the oppressive humidity. The intermittent chirping of the crickets was receding. Christmas beetles screamed in the trees. The air was redolent with the scent of magnolia and mown hay.

Davidson started the engine, touched the accelerator, and let the car run quietly down the hill until the road took a slight turn to the left. In the dark, the lights picked up the shape of two stone columns and a wrought-iron gate. Beyond the gates was a silhouette of a large building where lights threw tree shadows across the lawn. The wrought-iron gates were closed. Davidson let the van coast past until he saw a break in the trees that lined the road. He turned in, pulling carefully on the brake handle.

Davidson got out quietly.

'Stay there a moment, Harry.' He went to the back of the van, opened the door, and took out a small case. Inside were four black jerseys and two revolvers, the property of the unfortunate James Martin. He selected two jerseys and left the guns in the case. He went back to the cab. 'Here. You'll need this.'

Harry frowned and smelt the jersey. 'It smells clean.'

Davidson was busy fitting a silencer to the Browning.

'Don't be a pessimist.' He held up the gun. 'Are you ready?'

Harry indicated the silencer on his weapon.

The two men walked silently on the grass verge until they were standing before the pillars on which the gates were hinged. Davidson peered along the drive, his eyes searching the ground on either side. He was puzzled.

'No guards,' he whispered. 'It doesn't make sense. He must have some way of knowing when they have unwelcome visitors.'

'Could be electronic.' Both men spoke softly, their heads close together.

Suddenly a beam of light touched the stone pillar, and two headlights appeared at the bend of the road. Instinctively both men threw themselves into the shrubs on the verge. The car turned at the closed gate, the beams lighting up the drive. The horn sounded twice and the gates began to open. The car edged towards the gate until the gap was wide enough. Then it surged forward.

Davidson whispered: 'Follow it.'

As the car continued up the drive, the two men crouched inside the pillars. The car stopped at the front of the house. A woman got out and went inside.

'There's not a sign of a bloody guard. Are you sure this is the place?'

Tension was making Harry irritable.

'How the hell can I be sure of anything. You know bloody well that it's a wild guess from a wilder theory.'

Davidson sensed his uneasiness.

'We'll soon find out, and if it's not, we'll find the right place.'

'Yes. When it's too bloody late.'

'Then let's hurry things up.' Davidson led the way across the lawn, moving cautiously from shrub to shrub, until he was standing in the dark shadow of a tree six metres from the steps. At that moment, a man emerged from the front door carrying a Thompson sub-machine gun. He yawned, flicked a cigarette into a flower-bed, and strolled across the lawn. The two men remained still, watching the man closely as he patrolled the grounds.

Davidson whispered in Harry's ear. 'This is definitely the right place. He was one of the characters guarding you at the printing works.'

Harrison passed within metres of them. He was happy to be away from his employer's presence. Victor was behaving strangely. Here in the peaceful quiet of the night, he could relax. The last thing he expected was an arm around his neck, and an iron grip on the wrist that held the gun. He began to struggle, fighting for breath as the arm tightened on his throat.

'Take the gun.'

As Harry pulled at the gun, Harrison attempted to heave himself backwards. There was a crack and the man collapsed to the floor.

'Oh hell! His neck's broken.' Davidson carried Harrison into the shrubs.

'Tough.' Harry whispered. He was unmoved and impatient. 'You can grieve for the dirty little bastard kidnapper later. We have to find the women.'

Davidson grabbed his arm. 'Harry, wait,' he whispered. 'We can't rush in without a plan.' Davidson knew the signs. He had seen men with battle fever; men who rushed in, guns blazing, their impatience with caution making them reckless. It was a symptom of fear of fear itself, and the knowledge that the failure of the mission was an ever-present possibility.

'Take three deep breaths, Harry.'

'To hell with that, Joe,' Harry whispered hoarsely. 'It's a waste of time.'

'Three deep breaths, or I don't move.' Davidson was brusque. 'I won't let you get killed.'

Sobered as much by the tone as the words, Harry breathed deeply.

'Sorry Joe. It was stupid.'

'Good.' Davidson took the sub-machine gun, cocked it, and handed it to Harry. 'Be ready to use this. Remember, it has a tendency

286

for the barrel to lift up and to the left with the recoil.'

Harry nodded. 'Don't teach your grandmother to suck eggs,' he said. 'I've used them on the range.'

The men were speaking in whispers, both aware of the open door and the brightly lit rooms beyond. Suddenly they heard a voice raised in anger. Harry lifted his head.

'I know that voice.'

Davidson touched his shoulder. They went up the steps together, the width of the big double door between them, careless of the sounds of their entrance. The people in that room would have their attention fixed on the man called Victor, whose voice was raised to screaming pitch. As they entered the big living-room, they were greeted by the sight of Victor with his back to them, pointing a revolver at the head of a man tied to a chair. Grundling was staring at Victor in consternation, while a small dark man carrying a machine-gun, looked at the man in the chair.

Harry would never forget that tableau and its sequel. He had never seen Joe Davidson actually kill a man. He had always seen the aftermath. He did not realize how quickly the man reacted until he heard the light pop of the silenced pistol.

Victor was already taking up the slack on the trigger. His head snapped back, the gun fell from his hand and he fell across the man in the chair.

At the same moment, Grundling's revolver appeared in his hand, but Harry was quicker. He fired a short burst, swinging the muzzle towards the little man with the tommy-gun, but Ford had his hands in the air already.

'Don't shoot. For God's sake, don't shoot.' As the gun dropped from his hand, he fell to his knees, staring horrified at the body of Piet Grundling and the red blossoms on his chest.

The man in the chair spoke for the first time. 'This bastard's bleeding all over me. Get him off and untie me.'

Davidson hauled Victor to the floor.

'Who are you?'

'I'm a policeman.' As Davidson loosened his bonds, Roberts stared up at him. 'You're Joe Davidson.'

'Guilty. I hope you're not going to hold this against me,' he said sardonically.

'It's not my decision,' Roberts said drily. He chafed his wrists as Davidson untied his feet. He gestured to Ford. 'Watch him while I telephone.'

Davidson turned Victor's body over.

'Is this the man, Harry?'

Harry stared down at the aquiline features.

'That's him. That's Rupert Rolands. A ringer for Lee Van Kleef.' He looked at Ford. 'Who was the woman who came in just now?'

'Mrs Rolands.'

'Where is she now?'

The little man's voice trembled. 'Upstairs. First door on the right.'

Harry raced for the stairs. Davidson shouted at Ford.

'You. Sit down and don't move.' Ford sat abruptly.

Harry slowed for a moment, his caution overcoming his desperate eagerness to find Betty Rolands. He stopped at the top of the stairs, waiting for Davidson to join him. They looked down the long, carpeted passage, past a figurine in a niche. Lizzie, gun in hand, was opening the first door on the right. She lifted the gun, pointing it at the occupant of the room. Her voice was thick with rage.

'You brought them here. You brought the police here. If I have to go, you'll go with me.'

'Lizzie, no. It's all over.' Davidson saw her glance at him, turning the weapon in his direction. 'Victor and Grundling are dead. At least you're still alive. Think of yourself.'

The woman sobbed, dropped the gun, and fell to her knees.

Harry went past her into the room. Davidson heard a woman's voice.

'Harry. Thank God it's you.'

He took Lizzie downstairs, where he found Roberts and Janet La Barre. She looked at him and smiled.

'Hullo, Joe. It's been a long time.'

'Kay. Kay Kelsey. A long time, indeed. What have you been doing lately?'

She laughed. 'Still the same Uncle Joe.' She hugged him. 'For a while I've been calling myself Janet La Barre.'

CHAPTER TWENTY-THREE

Kay Kelsey thumbed the safety catch of Harry's Browning, pulled back the slide, and reached for the handle of the door to the yard.

Davidson stood at the left of the door.

'I'll go first,' she whispered. 'Cover me.'

'I'll cover you, but I'm not coming out.'

'Why not?'

'It's not a good idea. This is your show. When the floodlights go on, we don't want photographers with long-range lenses exposing me to the public gaze.'

'What photographers?'

'They'll be here.' He touched her shoulder. 'We both know that there're no villains out there now, but we also know it's wise to be cautious.'

She smiled up at him, her slightly dishevelled red hair falling over her left eye. She pushed it back. 'Scaredy cat.'

'I know.' He gave her a mock grimace. 'I can't help it. Now go.'

The smile left her face, and in one smooth movement she nudged open the door, stepped into the night and eased herself into the shadows. She stood against the wall, scanning the yard for any sign of life. From the left of the open doorway, Davidson looked across the yard towards the dark shape of the barn, where a solitary light burned over the doorway. The building, of ashlar and slate, had four barred windows in the wall facing the house, while the door under the light appeared to be constructed of heavy timber.

Davidson listened to the myriad insect sounds of the night, as an errant breeze rustled the trees. A horse stamped in the paddock behind the barn. There were no human sounds, and nothing to be seen in the yard, where pale moonlight threw ghostly shadows across the compound.

He glanced to the right of the doorway. The girl was no longer there and nowhere to be seen. Davidson smiled in admiration. She was a proficient pupil of her master, and although the heavy humid night would have muffled the sounds of her movements, he should still have heard the sound of her going.

He went to the main switch and waited.

The moon threw long shadows from the eastern boundary of the yard where thick shrubs hid the wall that enclosed the property. Kay moved quietly into the thicket, aware that if any of the gang were still about, it was likely that this was where they would wait. She stopped at the end of the building, breathing deeply to expel the tension that held her. Then she heard Roberts call out, and Davidson threw the switch that flooded the barn and the yard with light.

Kay saw Roberts emerge from the trees at the edge of the paddock. She ran to the door, where to her relief she saw a key in the lock. She unlocked the door, pushing it open to reveal a long passage with doors on either side. She sensed, rather than saw Roberts at her shoulder. She handed him the gun she carried, took a deep breath, and opened the first door on her left.

Her disappointment was like a physical blow.

Instead of the girls she expected to see, there were two women, a plump black and a sharp-faced white, both dressed in shoddy imitations of nurse's uniforms. They shrank away from her, the fear in their eyes an unmistakable confession of their guilt. In no sense could they plead ignorance of their involvement.

Kay looked at them with contempt, her apprehension at the fate of the girls dissolving into a raw anger that made her wish she had not given her gun to Roberts.

'Where are the girls?'

The black woman pointed at the next room.

'Both of you stay here and don't you dare move.'

As she began to ease open the door of the adjoining cell, Kay heard a brief shuffling sound, followed by a stillness that almost unnerved her. The door swung wide disclosing a dimly lit cell about four metres square, containing two bunk beds and a small table. Two young girls, the only occupants, sat huddled together, staring at her fearfully.

'I'm a policewoman,' Kay said simply. 'I've come to take you home.'

The girls stared at her in disbelief. Then the taller girl spoke.

'We thought you were one of them.'

'I've been trying to find you.' The younger girl sobbed and went towards her. Kay held her close. 'You're safe now.'

The girl looked up at her, her eyes brimming with tears.

'My father sent you, didn't he? I know he sent you to find me.'

'What's your name?' Her voice shook. She had anticipated this moment in her private thoughts. Tears coursed down her cheeks.

'Ramona Gomez. My father's here, isn't he?'

Kay paused. In a sense, he did send her; every parent had sent her.

'He sent me. He will be here soon.' Roberts entered the cell. 'Did you find the others?'

'Next door. They're all safe.'

*　　　*　　　*

The general arrived in a helicopter ten

293

minutes later. Within the hour, the place was swarming with doctors, nurses, ambulances, paramedics, and newsmen. General Anders insisted that the media remain outside the gates, and posted four men to see that his injunction was obeyed. Other policemen were collecting and tagging the weapons.

Davidson watched from a distance as the frightened girls were led out to the ambulances, accompanied by doctors and nurses.

He knew their ordeals of psychological evaluation would be difficult, and the next few weeks would be troubled ones for each one of them.

Davidson's own ordeal began a short while later, when he and Harry were summoned to the study on the first floor, where Anders had established a temporary headquarters. When they entered, they found Anders sitting behind a huge desk with Kay Kelsey to the left of him and Roberts with his back to them, staring out of the window. Below them, police technicians worked around the barn under the bright lights.

The atmosphere in the study crackled with tension, and it was obvious to Davidson that a serious difference of opinion had arisen amongst the three policemen. Although there were chairs in front of the desk, Anders did not ask them to sit.

Davidson sat anyway. Harry glanced at Joe,

at Anders, and remained standing.

When General Anders spoke, his voice was soft, but the two men could see he was containing his anger. He went straight to the point.

'You two knew that the girls were here, yet you did not reveal that to anyone.'

'Collins and I—'

'Quiet. I haven't finished.' Kay realized that he was no longer the benign Uncle John.

Davidson stood up. 'You can stay if you wish, Harry. I'm going where I can speak my mind.'

Kay took a pace towards him. 'Joe, please . . .'

Harry held out a hand. 'Joe, I think—'

Anders silenced them. 'Quiet! All of you.' Davidson stood where he was as the silence lengthened. Anders was clearly endeavouring to regain control of himself.

'You listen to me, Davidson. I have half a dozen charges I can throw at you, so don't give me any smart-alec remarks. I want a statement from you later, but for the moment I want to make my position clear.' He paused. 'You withheld important information from the police. You killed two men that we know of, and I don't know how many more. I can charge you with possession of unlicensed firearms, and that is just a start.'

There was a long silence. Davidson sat down.

'Are you going to allow me to speak?'

'When I've finished.' The general stood up and paced the floor behind the desk. 'Both Roberts and Kelsey said you saved both their lives. That may be true, but if we had had the information in your possession, it is possible that their lives would not have been in danger.'

Davidson inclined his head. 'May I speak?'

'Go ahead. But I don't want to hear any rubbish about stumbling on this place.'

Davidson regarded him coldly. 'General, I never lie unless it is to save my life, or the lives of others.' Roberts turned from the widow and watched him closely. 'It is true that Spargel's description of Victor gave Collins to suspect that Betty Rolands was in mortal danger from her husband. Since he had told her to go to Umhlali, it seemed a possibility that this is where he would dispose of her. We had no reason to believe that the kidnapped girls were here—'

The general waved an impatient hand.

'Nonsense. It's obvious that if Rolands were here, everyone else would be here.'

'Why was it obvious? Two hours ago, no one had connected Rolands with Victor, and Mrs Rolands was a completely separate issue.' He sat back comfortably, apparently unimpressed by the general's threats. 'As for the two men I killed, you have conceded that I had adequate reason.' He shrugged. 'I would be interested to hear of others.' Davidson knew he was walking a fine line on that issue. 'As for the unlicensed firearms, they were the property of the people in this house.'

Harry looked at all three policemen in turn. He realized how adroitly Davidson had sidestepped the issues. He had not lied about a single accusation. He merely asserted that he would be interested to hear of them.

Davidson concluded: 'That is all I have to say at present. If I am to be charged with any crimes, I want my attorney present.'

There was a long silence. Anders went to the window and stared down at the activity in the floodlit compound. At last he turned.

'At the moment there are no charges, but I will want you in my office tomorrow for statements. I have too much on my hands to deal with you at present.'

Davidson inclined his head and stood up. He knew he had been lucky. He saw Kay's mouth twitch in a suspicion of a smile, and he thought Roberts's left eye closed for a moment. He and Harry left the study, and Davidson made a mental note to have Martin picked up.

*　　　*　　　*

The two men went to Harry's flat, Joe to fetch Margaret and Grace, and Harry to wait an agonizing day before Betty had completed endless questioning and made two statements before she was released.

297

Grace insisted on going back to Rydal Avenue. She declared it was the only place where she would be comfortable. Davidson took Margaret home. As soon as they arrived, Margaret sat Joe in his favourite chair and bustled about preparing bacon, eggs, and coffee. When he had eaten, she sat opposite him, watching him quizzically.

'Something on your mind, Joe?'

He stood up, lifted her until he was holding her close, and then kissed her.

'I couldn't bear it if I lost you.'

Her eyes widened. 'Why would you lose me?'

'When those men kidnapped you, I swore I would kill them. I did. If that ever happened again, I couldn't live with myself. I would have to give up this life.'

She freed herself and went to the sofa.

'That's what I was afraid of, Joe; that I would be the reason for your decision.' She stood up and went to him. 'One day there may be other reasons why you have to stop, but never because of me. I love you too much for that.' She held up her hand as he was about to speak. 'No, let me finish. I know of at least four people who lead happier lives because of what you have done for them. There will be others, Joe. You may never help another person, but you must be free to try.' She smiled. 'Besides, I've seen you in action. You're a hell of a lot better at what you do

298

than anyone the ungodly can throw at you.'

He smiled, took her in his arms, and asked himself what he had done to deserve a woman like this.

*   *   *

It was autumn before he saw Kay Kelsey again. She called one night when Harry and Betty were visiting Joe and Margaret. She and Roberts, who was with her, were due to return to Pretoria the next day. The trials were over and the criminals had received long sentences.

Kay sat in Joe's favourite chair and looked at him over the drink that Margaret had poured for her.

'There was a kind of insane logic to this whole affair. Rupert Rolands wasn't killed because he was Victor. Victor was killed because he was Rupert Rolands.' She paused. 'If Victor had been anyone else, Betty would not have cared that he was lunching with me. She would not have involved Harry and consequently you, and Victor would have got away with murder.'

Roberts shifted uneasily. 'I wish I knew what alerted him to the fact that Kay and I were policemen. We thought we had a cast-iron cover.'

Kay nodded. 'It was a shock when Victor confronted us. I was so confident of our cover.'

Betty spoke softly. 'I think I may have been

299

responsible for that.'

Kay was incredulous. 'How could it have been your fault? You didn't even know I was involved.'

Betty's voice remained soft. 'You talked about insane logic.' She nodded slowly. 'I agree. On the face of it, coincidence played a big part, but there was no coincidence at all really. It was a question of cause and effect.' She took a deep breath. 'You see, I phoned Rupert to tell him that I was seeing a lawyer about a divorce. When he fobbed me off once more, I tackled him about his women.' She looked at Kay with slight embarrassment. 'I accused him of having an affair with you. When he denied knowing you . . .'

Kay laughed. 'Good heavens. You told him about the Blue Bonnet and he put the pieces together. He knew then that I was Kay Kelsey and not Janet La Barre.'

Betty nodded mutely. 'I am so sorry.'

'Why be sorry? It's all over, Betts, and now we know we didn't have a leak in the department. It caused a great flurry for a while.'

Roberts smiled. 'It was eventually decided that Victor just got lucky.'

'I caused so many problems for you.'

Davidson growled. 'You couldn't know what would happen. Stop whining, girl.'

Betty said with mock contrition. 'Yes, Uncle Joe.'

Davidson laughed. He turned to Kay. 'What were you up to at Rydal Avenue and Durban North? None of it made sense.'

'For a while there, it got a bit hairy. I thought Victor had got on to me then.' She paused for a moment, staring unseeing at the glass in her hand. In the dim light of the chandelier, flecks of light touched her red hair with tiny tongues of flame. Her perfect features were marred by the frown that gathered on her forehead, reflecting the sombre memories so recently endured. The silence of the room was broken by the soft sound of a rising east wind.

Kay continued: 'When Rolands took the bait, I said I would agree only if I could review his security personally. The general thought that if I could get into his organization, we could clean it up in a week. But it didn't go as easily as that.' She placed her glass on the side table and shook her head when Davidson held up the bottle.

She continued: 'First, he insisted that one of his men remain with me constantly, even to the extent of living in the same house. Secondly he would let me know where the girls had been kept after he had moved them. I didn't dream that there was a cellar at Durban North, and that they were there.' Her hands fluttered restlessly as she spoke. She shook her head as though she were discarding unpleasant memories.

'That was when Carl Lindquist came to chaperon me. The first time I saw him, I knew we were in for trouble. He was vaguely familiar, but it wasn't for a week that I remembered where I had seen him before. I had been on holiday in the Drakensburg. It was my misfortune that we both went to the same place.' She rubbed her temples. 'I told Uncle John, but he decided that unless Lindquist made any suspicious moves, he would continue to wait and watch.'

Davidson poured himself a soda water. 'Wasn't that reckless?'

Kay glanced at him. 'It was a risk that had to be taken.' She paused for a moment to gather her thoughts. 'Eventually he made the connection and remembered where he had seen me. He taxed me with it.' She smiled. 'I told him I had been on the run and that Kay Kelsey was an alias. I told the general at once.'

Margaret said drily: 'It was a good try, but not convincing.'

Kay nodded. 'The general decided that we would take action.' She rubbed her temples once more. 'Excuse me. That drink wasn't a wise choice.' She continued: 'I put knockout drops in his drink, and later that night, put him in the trailer and drove him to the general, who put him away. I told Rolands that I killed Lindquist when he tried to rape me. He wasn't happy, but had to accept it when Lindquist never turned up.'

Davidson looked puzzled. 'But why the fedora and raincoat?'

She shrugged. 'In case I was being watched. I wanted as much confusion as possible. Rolands appeared to be getting suspicious. I think he regretted letting me get close to his organization, because he arranged for me to stay at Rydal Avenue with Brett Lindquist, Carl's brother.'

Harry said: 'It *was* getting hairy.'

Kay nodded. 'It got worse. Carl had told him my real name, and he decided to check, and went to my father.'

Davidson smiled. 'Was the general having him watched?'

'He was. So the general arranged the murder, chicken blood and all.' She grimaced. 'Rolands sent Li to check it out.'

Davidson frowned. 'What reason did you give for killing him?'

'I told Li that I had discovered that he was a police informer, and that I was compelled to act quickly.' She smiled 'We had planted enough evidence in his effects to convince the Chinaman.' She smiled. 'They bought it.' She wrinkled her nose in contempt. 'Then the stupid sods had to try and kill Mrs Eripides because they thought she knew too much.' She glanced at Betty and then at Davidson. 'You realize he was quite mad, and getting worse by the week.'

Betty nodded and took Harry's hand. 'I was

lucky everything happened when it did.'

Roberts placed his empty glass on the coffee table and stood up. When he spoke, his tone was neutral.

'Did you know that two of Rolands's men were found in the boot of their car in the Star Garage? They were both shot.'

Davidson looked at him, his expression blank. 'The Star. Now that's a strange place for bodies to be found.'

'I was sure you would think so. Fortunately, the murders have no connection with our case.'

Kay looked at Joe with a bland expression. 'I'm sure Joe has no interest in our unsolved crimes.' She stood up and smiled at Margaret. 'Thank you for a lovely evening.'

*   *   *

Harry Collins and Betty Rolands were married in September, just as summer was coming around again. Joe and Margaret went to the wedding, and both agreed that weddings were not for them.

As Margaret put it: 'Who needs it when we've got each other?'

In early December, Joe received a Christmas card with a one-word message. 'Thanks.' It was signed *Uncle John*.

Margaret had it framed for him.

Dodge City Public Library
Dodge City, Kansas